Her smile seemed especially potent today.

Her cheeks were glowing with color, and her eyes were sparkling. Her laughter put the sunshine to shame.

Gabriella Monroe made Luke feel young and alive. Like he could run and jump and take on the world. Like he could hold her in his arms and love her until the stars came out.

The intensity of his sudden hunger startled him. He felt he had been lost in the desert and had just found water. Had been starving and had just seen food. Had been asleep deep under the earth for years and had just been given the sun.

He wished he could hold on to this moment forever.

But he knew he had to let Gabbi go.

Dear Reader,

Welcome to Silhouette Special Edition . . . welcome to romance. We've got six wonderful books for you this month—a true bouquet of spring flowers!

Just Hold On Tight! by Andrea Edwards is our THAT SPECIAL WOMAN! selection for this month. This warm, poignant story features a heroine who longs for love—and the wonderful man who convinces her to take what she needs!

And that's not all! *Dangerous Alliance,* the next installment in Lindsay McKenna's thrilling new series MEN OF COURAGE, is available this month, as well as Christine Rimmer's *Man of the Mountain,* the first story in the family-oriented series THE JONES GANG. Sherryl Woods keeps us up-to-date on the Halloran clan in *A Vow To Love,* and *Wild Is the Wind,* by Laurie Paige, brings us back to "Wild River" territory for an exciting new tale of love.

May also welcomes Noreen Brownlie to Silhouette Special Edition with her book, *That Outlaw Attitude.*

I hope that you enjoy this book and all of the stories to come.

Happy Spring!

Sincerely,

Tara Gavin
Senior Editor

ANDREA EDWARDS

JUST HOLD ON TIGHT!

Published by Silhouette Books
America's Publisher of Contemporary Romance

To Kari, who's tougher than she thinks

ISBN 0-373-09883-9

JUST HOLD ON TIGHT!

This edition published by arrangement with Harlequin Enterprises B. V.

Printed in U.S.A.

Books by Andrea Edwards

Silhouette Special Edition

Rose in Bloom #363
Say It With Flowers #428
Ghost of a Chance #490
Violets Are Blue #550
Places in the Heart #591
Make Room for Daddy #618
Home Court Advantage #706
Sweet Knight Times #740
Father: Unknown #770
Man of the Family #809
The Magic of Christmas #856
Just Hold On Tight! #883

Silhouette Intimate Moments

Above Suspicion #291

Silhouette Desire

Starting Over #645

ANDREA EDWARDS

is the pseudonym of Anne and Ed Kolaczyk, a husband-and-wife writing team that concentrates on women's fiction. "Andrea" is a former elementary school teacher, while "Edwards" is a refugee from corporate America, having spent almost twenty-five years selling computers before becoming a full-time writer. They have four children, two dogs and four cats, and live in Indiana.

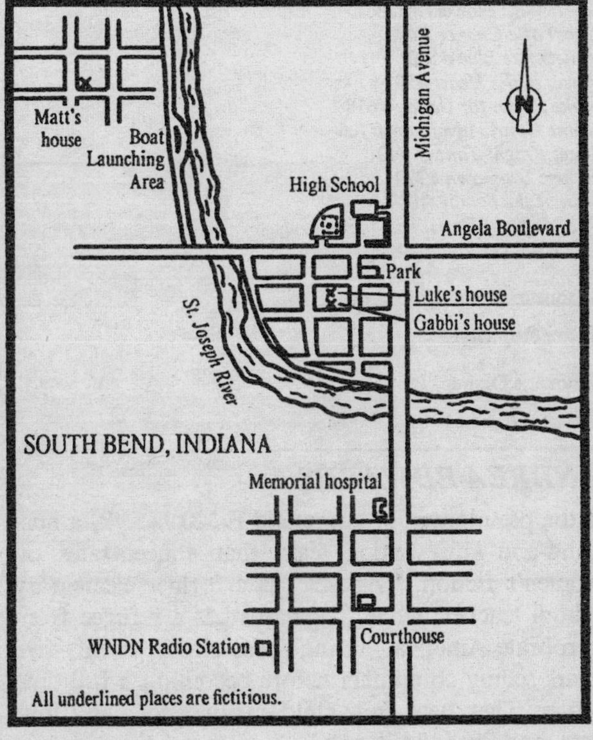
Matt's house
Boat Launching Area
Michigan Avenue
N
High School
Angela Boulevard
Park
Luke's house
Gabbi's house
St. Joseph River
SOUTH BEND, INDIANA
Memorial hospital
Courthouse
WNDN Radio Station
All underlined places are fictitious.

Chapter One

"Ball two!" the umpire called out.

"Hey, pitch to him!" Trisha yelled. "The bum can't hit a watermelon."

Gabriella Monroe bit back a sigh before she touched her daughter's arm. "Isn't it poor sportsmanship to yell negative comments?"

Trisha just gave her a look that literally shouted "get real" and turned back to the high school baseball game. Gabbi let loose her sigh. Once again, she'd come up lacking in this mother-daughter companionship thing.

Would she ever get the knack of motherhood? It had seemed so simple six months ago. Gabbi was thirty and single. Trisha was thirteen and a ward of the state. Gabbi wanted a child. Trisha needed a mother. They were made for each other—or so she thought.

Now that the adoption would be finalized in a few weeks, it seemed that Gabbi could do nothing right.

"Strike one!" the umpire called out.

"Now you got him," Trisha shouted. "Two more and the bum's out."

Gabbi took a deep breath and made herself relax. It was the middle of April but it felt like late May, a real treat here in northern Indiana where South Bend's winters usually paid fleeting visits well into spring. But today the sun was warm, the breeze tickled and the air held that wonderful promise of spring about to erupt.

Trisha was afraid, that was all. She'd been through a lot in her thirteen years—her father's death when she was three, her mother's four years ago and then a succession of foster homes since. But fear was the one area Gabbi was an expert in, and she could handle anything Trisha threw her way.

"Strike two."

A mixture of groans and cheers surrounded them. Trisha jumped up and hollered "Yahoo!"

Gabbi smiled at her. The girl was all gangly points and rough edges, but in a few years, she'd blossom into a beautiful young woman. It would be a challenge for someone as short as Gabbi to teach Trisha to carry her long length with pride, but Gabbi could do it. She could do all of it because, in spite of what Doug had said that day he left, love was enough. Love could conquer any obstacle.

"Swing, batter," Trisha shouted. "Swing, you bum!"

As if following the girl's instructions, the batter did swing. But instead of flying straight across the field, the ball went up in the air and arced over the fence toward them.

Nimble as a squirrel, Trisha jumped to her feet and scrambled over to the edge of the next row of the bleachers. She reached over and snatched the ball out of the air. The small crowd cheered. She bowed and held the ball high over her head.

One of the baseball players rushed over to the stands. "Hey, kid," the tall, thin boy called. "Give me the ball."

"In your dreams, Stretch," Trisha snapped.

"I said, give me the ball." It was meant to be a fierce command, but unfortunately the boy's voice broke and it came out more like a screech.

"I caught it, I keep it," Trisha insisted.

The boy climbed up along the edge of the first few rows of the stands. "You do not." He looked ready for a fight.

A wave of worry washed over Gabbi. A tussle here in the stands was the last thing they needed. It would be a sure bet that someone would get hurt. She stood and put herself between the two kids.

"Trisha, give him the ball, please."

"No. I caught it, so I get to keep it. That's the way it works."

Play had stopped and all the players, officials and spectators were staring at them. Great. What had seemed like a pleasant little diversion was turning into a disaster.

Gabbi wanted to tell the boy that she'd buy them a box or a bag or a truckload of balls. Whatever the darn things came in. But their adoption counselor had said Gabbi had to be firm with Trisha. She had to show who was in charge.

"Trisha—"

"You don't know nothin' about sports," Trisha told her.

One of the coaches had joined the crowd and called up to the boy. "Adam, what's going on?"

"She won't give me the ball."

"We've got others."

The man's voice was easy, tinged with laughter, the way the spring day was tinged with warmth. Gabbi could feel Trisha relax, and in that moment the boy reached around and snatched the ball from Trisha's hand.

"Hey!" she shouted and tried to grab it back.

It was too late—Adam had already thrown the ball to one of the players on the field and had jumped from the stands—and in her sudden grab, Trisha bumped into Gabbi's shoulder. The jolt caught Gabbi by surprise and knocked her off balance. She tottered on her low pumps for a long moment until Trisha grabbed her one arm and the coach grabbed the other.

"Look what you did, you pea-brained jerk!" Trisha shouted out toward the distant Adam.

"You okay?" the coach asked.

"I'm fine," Gabbi said. His touch was too nice—gentle, but strong and protective. The way one would hold a wounded bird.

And she was definitely not wounded. She pulled away from him slightly.

"She could've been killed," Trisha pointed out hotly.

Gabbi just gave her daughter a look that she hoped said "I don't think so" and turned back to the coach. "My own fault for wearing heels to a baseball game."

"Well, if you're sure...." The coach took a step back. His eyes were the warmest shade of brown.

"Play ball!" the umpire shouted.

Gabbi stepped back down to the row where they'd been sitting. "Yes, I'm fine. Thanks, anyway."

"No thanks to the pea-brain," Trisha muttered.

"Honey." Gabbi put her hand on Trisha's arm. "Maybe we should be going."

The coach glanced toward the field, then glanced over at Gabbi. "I'll catch you guys after the game."

Before she could reply, he was trotting back to the field. Yes, get back to your game, Gabbi thought as she patted her pocket for her car keys, and let us get out of here. She had more than enough on her plate right now and definitely did not have time for daydreaming about Mr. Brown Eyes.

"Trisha, let's—"

But Trisha had flopped down onto the hard bench. "Don't worry," she said. "I ain't going to embarrass you."

Clenching her jaw for a moment, Gabbi took a deep breath. "That's not what I—"

"Besides, that coach dude said he wanted to see us after the game."

The longer she'd had Trisha, the fewer sentences she'd been allowed to finish. "Coach Dude?"

"That ain't his name," Trisha said, rolling her eyes. "That's what you call a guy if you don't know his name."

"Dude?"

"Yeah, like when you're walking down the street and you catch this hunk strolling on down."

Gabbi stared. Obviously, she had been rather naive about Trisha's interest in boys.

"You yell, 'Hey, Dude. What's up?'"

"I see. Then what happens?"

Trisha didn't bother to reply, choosing, instead, to send her eyes on another roll toward the heavens. Gabbi sank back onto the bench. She guessed they were staying.

"He was giving you the eye," Trisha pointed out after a moment.

"He was not," Gabbi argued. "He was probably concerned I'd fall and sue the school."

"Sure." Trisha's voice was annoyingly know-it-all.

"Besides, he's probably married."

"He wasn't wearing a ring."

"How'd you notice that?"

"Somebody's got to be on the lookout."

"For what?"

Trisha just turned back to the game. Gabbi wanted to pursue the issue, wanted to assure Trisha that there was no need for her to be on the "lookout." But she wimped out. Maybe in the privacy of the ride home, she could bring it up. Maybe not.

Gabbi's gaze wandered from the batter over to Coach Dude, where he stood near a far base. He looked easy, relaxed. Like someone who wasn't easily thrown. From the sprinkle of gray in his hair, she'd guess he was in his early forties. Not that any of that mattered. She wasn't on the "lookout."

She'd had her try at "happily ever after" right after college. It hadn't worked out, though. A number of rough years later, she was ready to build a life on possibilities, not improbabilities. Gabbi wasn't waiting around for a Prince Charming, who would run at the first cloud that came over the horizon. She'd come to accept that the steady, rock-solid man she needed just didn't exist. So she'd built a life that didn't need towels labeled His in her bathroom. She had a great job—her own radio talk show each weekday. And now that she had Trisha, she had a family of her own.

Not that she didn't have any worries that sneaked up in the middle of the night. Lord, even after seven years of perfect checkups, the fear of finding another lump was enough to bring out all the monsters from under the bed. And then once she'd started proceedings to obtain Trisha, she had the monsters in the closet laughing at her, too. But, hell, problems were just challenges to be conquered.

"Brush him," Trisha suddenly shouted. "Brush the chicken!"

Gabbi had no idea what that meant, but didn't need to. "That doesn't sound very sportsmanlike, either."

Trisha didn't even bother to reply or roll her eyes, choosing instead to glare intently at the batter. Gabbi kept quiet and watched the game. Suddenly the colors of the batter's uniform intruded on her mind.

"Isn't he from Cathy's school?" she asked Trisha. "Why are you rooting against them?"

"Because Cathy is a snot."

What happened to the budding friendship that had given Gabbi such hope that Trisha was settling in? "I thought she was your best friend."

Gabbi got the "get real" look in response again. "She thinks she's so cool," Trisha said. "She thinks her mother's better than everyone else's because she drives a Mercedes."

Suddenly Gabbi understood and was proud of Trisha's stubborn nature. "Your mother did the best she could," she said gently. "I'm glad you see that."

Trisha gave her a strange look before turning back to the game. "Cathy was talking about you. She thinks your Taurus is a nerdy car."

"Oh."

Gabbi didn't know what to say, so she shut her mouth.

All her life Gabbi had lived in the suburbs—in Atlanta, where she was born, in Minneapolis, Chicago and San Diego as her father climbed the corporate ladder, and in St. Louis, where she and Doug has lived during their brief fling at marriage. When Gabbi decided to adopt a child, it seemed only natural to rent the perfect house in the suburbs—big lawns, lots of fresh air and space, and a clubhouse offering tennis, golf and swimming.

Except, Trisha fit in there as well as a cactus in a wheat field.

"All right!" Trisha was suddenly standing up and cheering.

Gabbi looked out over the field. The players had formed lines and were walking past each other, shaking hands. "I take it the game is over," she said. "Who won?"

"The St. Joe Indians."

"Why are you cheering?" Gabbi asked. "Do you know anyone who goes to St. Joe?"

Trisha frowned at her. "It's Coach Dude's team." She spoke slowly and carefully, as if talking to a particularly dense child.

"I see." Gabbi got to her feet. She definitely did not want to pursue that line of discussion. "So, do you want to eat at home, or do you want to grab something on the way?"

Trisha shrugged.

"Well, think about it," Gabbi said. "But you have to decide by the time we reach the car." She stepped off the bleachers.

"We gotta wait here," Trisha said. "Remember Mr. Coach Dude?"

Gabbi did but was more than willing to try to forget him. Her life was exactly as she wanted it. There was no room for any brown-eyed dudes to wander through her dreams. "That's okay, honey. I'm sure he just wanted to explain the rules to you."

"I already know the rules."

Gabbi sighed to herself.

"Hey, ladies."

Coach Dude was walking slowly toward them along with the tall, thin boy. The boy seemed uncertain, but the man looked like Gary Cooper strolling into town at high noon. He was tall, lean and muscular. In control.

Gabbi sighed again. They should have left ages ago.

"Yes?" Gabbi asked.

"I wanted to explain about the baseball," he said, his smile with enough wattage in it to melt the ice caps. "We're working on a tight budget, so we can't afford to let people keep foul balls. Even once the balls get beat up, we use them in practice."

"It's okay." Trisha's smile seemed to come from nowhere, dispelling the usual storm clouds that hung around her brow. "Gabbi'll get me a baseball of my own."

What a little con artist, Gabbi thought. But when she was being so agreeable, what else could Gabbi do?

The brown-eyed dude held his hand out to Gabbi. "I'm Luke Bennett," he said. "I help coach the team. And this is Adam."

She took Luke's hand, though she would rather not have. It was just as she'd feared—his touch was as warm as the look in his eyes. "Pleased to meet you, gentlemen," Gabbi said, letting go of his hand as quickly as was politely possible. "I'm Gabbi Monroe, and this is my daughter Trisha," Gabbi said, as she started toward the parking lot.

Luke nodded, then followed her glance. "I'm parked over there, too," he said. "Why don't we walk you over?"

"Sure."

Adam and Trisha moved up ahead, walking side by side but not too close and not speaking to each other. Trisha kept gazing around the park as if it were the most fascinating place she'd ever seen.

Gabbi fell in beside Luke. He towered over her, and unnerved her. Being just over five feet, she was used to feeling small. But this was different, unsettling, and she fought to regain some measure of control.

"Thank you for explaining about the ball," she said. "Trisha was rather upset when Adam took it away."

"No problem."

"She's been rather touchy lately," Gabbi said. "Flies off the handle real easy."

"What is she—a freshman?"

Gabbi shook her head. "Eighth grade."

"She's normal," Luke assured her. "Things are scary for them at that age, so they put on this big, fierce mask."

He seemed so understanding. "You have teenagers of your own?"

"No," Luke replied. "Adam just lives with me right now. But I teach here at the high school and I coach. Football in the fall. Basketball in the winter. And baseball in the spring."

"Must keep you busy."

Luke shrugged. "Keeps me out of the bars and from chasing wild women."

Gabbi took in his easy smile and athletic grace. It was doubtful he'd have to chase any kind of woman too far. He stopped at a pickup truck, the body perched high on a four-wheel-drive bed.

"Awesome," Trisha said.

Adam tried to look nonchalant while Luke dug around in his pocket. "Here's our schedule for the rest of the year," he said, handing Gabbi a card. "Come anytime. We can always use the spectators."

"Thank you." She slipped the card into her pocket. "We'll try and work some games in."

As they started toward their car, Gabbi wondered whether Trisha would consider her statement a promise and insist on them going to more games.

Suddenly Trisha stopped walking and turned around. "Hey," she called out as Luke was climbing into the truck. "You married?"

"Trisha!" Gabbi cried.

Luke just grinned. "Nope. Neither is Adam."

They could hear a fierce protest from inside the truck. Obviously Trisha wasn't the only one who was going to be killed in a moment.

"Gabbi's single, too," Trisha told him. Told the world, actually, since she was shouting at the top of her lungs.

"Good to know," Luke said.

With a wave, he closed the truck door. Gabbi waved back feebly, then hurried over to her car. The schedule seemed to be a weight in her pocket, daring her to take him up on the invitation.

"That really wasn't necessary," Gabbi said as the pickup drove past them. Both Luke and Adam waved, so Gabbi had to join Trisha in waving back. "I'm really doing fine looking out for myself."

"Right. Four dates in six months is great," Trisha said as they settled in their seats.

Gabbi started the car. "Six in six months."

Trisha rolled her eyes but was silent until they left the parking lot. "So is it 'cause of me?" she asked.

Gabbi frowned as she pulled around a slow-moving car. "Is what because of you?"

"Why you aren't dating. Do you think I'll act like a jerk and embarrass you? I do know how to behave, you know, and I only call a guy a nerd-face if he really is."

"That certainly sets my mind at ease," Gabbi said with a laugh. "But, no, it's not because of you. I don't date much because I don't meet too many men I want to date."

She stiffened as she felt Trisha's eyes on her.

"You can't tell, you know," Trisha said. "Just from looking at you, you can't tell one breast is different."

"It isn't really," Gabbi said. "They just took out the lump and a little tissue."

"So it shouldn't stop you from dating."

"It doesn't."

"Oh, no?"

"No." She didn't date much because she didn't want to. It was as simple as that. Maybe not all men would react to the cancer the way Doug had, but she just wasn't interested in finding out. If she didn't grow dependent on a man, then she wouldn't get hurt when his heart wasn't strong enough to stand by her.

"So where are we going to eat?" Gabbi asked.

"You had a good game today," Luke said. "Four hits and two RBIs."

"I was hoping for a homer." Adam's voice reflected his disappointment.

"It'll come. Don't forget, you're only a freshman."

"How can I forget?" Adam said with a touch of bitterness in his laugh. "Everyone on the team keeps reminding me."

Luke gave the boy a quick smile. "Hey, you're the only freshman on varsity."

The boy fell silent and a gentle melancholy filled his face as he stared out the window. Luke was sure he knew what was bothering the boy.

"Your dad would be proud of you," he said.

"Do you believe in heaven?" Adam asked.

Luke stopped at an intersection and carefully checked both ways. This parenting bit was tricky. Not only did you have to watch where you stepped every minute, but you had to keep opening up new doors in yourself. Sometimes doors that even you weren't sure what lay behind.

"I think that as long as you remember your parents, they'll keep on existing," Luke said quietly.

Adam went back to looking out the window, and Luke fell back into silence. Now what? Were his words any comfort, or were they a source of more pain? Damn. Kids should come with an instruction manual. This parenting business was a hell of a lot harder than teaching. He turned onto their street.

"Oh, good!" Adam exclaimed. "Matt's here. We're gonna have something good for dinner tonight."

"You can cook anytime you want," Luke told the boy.

"You're okay," Adam insisted. "Matt's just better."

That was true. Luke's father was one of the best cooks around. He was a widower who lived alone, and he spent a lot of time at Luke's house. Luke would have welcomed him even without his culinary skills.

"How come Matt doesn't live with us?" Adam asked as they pulled up behind Matt's panel truck. "He's here most of the time."

"He likes his privacy." They stepped out of the pickup. "Kind of like yourself. You don't spend all that much time in your room, but you like knowing it's there when you want it."

Adam nodded as they walked toward the house. After Ron and Laura died last year, Luke had been terrified at the thought of raising their kid. It was everything he'd avoided for years rolled into one huge responsibility. But what could he do? Ron had been his best friend since second grade. They'd gone to the same camp each summer and learned how to talk to girls together. He'd been there through term papers and algebra, football and sprained ankles. They'd been best man at each other's weddings. And Ron had handled Luke's divorce and fought with him until he dried out and joined AA. Luke owed him more than he could ever repay.

"Hey, Matt," Adam shouted as he walked through the house to the kitchen. "We won."

"Good job." Luke's father turned away from the stove. He was a short, stocky guy with a mop of white hair and a dark handlebar mustache. "How did you do?"

"Okay," Adam replied, going over to sniff at the food.

"Two ribbies," Luke said.

"No home runs."

"They'll come," Matt said.

"That's what I told him," Luke added.

"I gotta work on the weights," Adam said.

Luke hung his jacket on the hook by the back door. "You'll have time in the summer."

"Speaking of time in the summer," Matt said. "I got the job wiring those homes on Washington. You gonna have time to work with me?"

"Don't I always work with you in the summer?" Luke asked. "Why else would I keep paying my union dues?"

"Just checking," Matt said with a wink at Adam. "Never know when you might take up with some wild women and spend your summer running around naked in the woods."

"Fat chance of that," Luke snorted.

"Aw, come on, boy," his father protested. "Don't tell me you don't like wild women."

"Wild women are fine," Luke replied. "I just don't want to get bitten to death by mosquitoes."

"No pain, no gain," Matt muttered, while Adam snickered.

"Hey, talking about wild women," Adam said, his face lighting up. "We met this really foxy chick at the game."

"Oh, yeah?"

"Yeah," Adam said. "About so high, black hair, brown eyes. And built." He dropped his hands down in a slow, wavy pattern.

"Sounds good," Matt said.

Adam nodded. "Luke likes her."

"I don't even know her."

"He gave her a card," Adam said.

"It was a schedule of our games. I just thought since her daughter was interested in baseball, they might want to come."

"How come she smiled at you like she did?"

How did she smile at him? Politely, was all he could remember. "What was she supposed to do?" Luke snapped. "Snarl at me like some junkyard dog?"

Adam turned to Matt. "He's getting testy again."

"Old age," Matt muttered. "And the lack of regular female companionship."

This conversation was dumb. Why did everyone feel the need to reorder his life?

"Go get washed up," Luke ordered Adam.

Adam rolled his eyes slightly, but he left quietly. Luke began to clear the table. He tossed the mail onto the counter along with the newspaper, then picked up a grocery bag Matt must have left there. It was heavier than he expected.

"Oh, hey, that's mine," Matt said quickly as he took it from him. "I meant to take it back out to the truck."

Luke had recognized the feel of a six-pack of beer. "It's okay, Dad. Just having beer in the house isn't going to start anything. Everything's under control."

"Hey, did I say it wasn't?" He folded the top of the bag down several times, as if locking the beer in. "You keep an eye on the noodles, will ya? I'll just take this outside."

"I'm lousy at noodles." Luke took the bag from his father's hand and put it on the counter. His father's transparent worry was disheartening. Did he think Luke was that weak? "It really is all right."

Luke got silverware out from the drawer, the noises loud in the strained silence in the kitchen. Matt cleared his throat.

"So, this woman, you gave her your telephone number?" he asked, his voice a bit forced.

"I just gave her a schedule of Adam's baseball games."

His father nodded. "That's good. Sort of like an IQ test."

"What?" The old man had a rather Byzantine mind that was hard to follow at times.

"She knows you're a coach?"

"Yes." Luke put the simple answer out slowly and cautiously.

"And the schedule has the telephone number for the school, right?"

"Correct."

"So if she wants to get in touch with you, she can call the school and track you down that way, right?"

"I guess."

"Good. Real good." Matt nodded as he lifted a cover and released some heavenly smells into the kitchen. "If the woman can't do that much, she's so dumb you wouldn't want to date her. I should work out a little qualification test of my own."

"You and Irma have been going together for five years now. Isn't that test enough?"

"You never know what life's going to give you tomorrow." Matt poured the water off the noodles. "Salad's in the fridge."

Luke took it out, along with a bottle of Italian dressing.

"You know," Matt said, "you really should get yourself a lady."

"Yeah, I know. But I just haven't had a chance to get down to the lady store."

"I'm not joking."

Luke sighed. "I have lady friends, Pop. A lot of them."

"You have too many," Matt said. "I'm talking about a single, special one."

"That's not for me."

Matt shook his head. "It would be good for Adam."

"Adam is doing just fine. I'm doing fine. Everything is great."

"Nothing is ever great. If it is, that means something bad is coming your way."

They'd had this conversation many times before. The best way to handle it was to let it pass. Luke turned away and took the milk out of the refrigerator.

"I saw in the paper that St. Joe is advertising for a head football coach," Matt said.

Oh, hell, Luke thought. His father's obsession number two.

"Are you going to apply?" Matt asked.

"Dad," Luke said tiredly. "You know I'm not the head coach type."

"Don't see why not. You know more about the game than any six people put together."

"I like being an assistant."

"Nobody likes being an assistant."

Luke concentrated on filling the glasses with milk. "I do. I can enjoy the kids and not feel the pressure of winning and losing or deal with all the administrative nonsense."

"Not dealing with responsibility, you mean." Matt brought a basket of bread to the table. "One of these days, you're going to have to stop running. Forget the past."

"The past has nothing to do with anything," Luke said sharply. "I just happen to like things as they are."

"And they're great."

"That's right," Luke snapped. "Just great."

Adam came back into the room and looked from Luke to Matt. "What're you two arguing about?"

"Nothing," Luke snapped.

Matt grinned at the boy. "Just about how happy Luke is."

"Look," Trisha said. "They got sidewalks here."

Gabbi glanced around as she drove the car down the narrow street. They were in a little neighborhood south of the school where they had watched the baseball game yesterday.

She'd thought about it all night. If Trisha was going to have any chance of growing up reasonably civilized, she needed to live in a place that felt like home. And obviously that wasn't a country club suburb.

"They got a place for kids to walk around. Where we live, you gotta walk in the street."

"You can walk on the yards down by the street," Gabbi said.

"Right," Trisha snorted. "And then some old geezer will come out and yell at you."

To the best of Gabbi's knowledge no one had come out and yelled at Trisha for walking on their lawn or anything, but she wasn't feeling accepted. That was obvious.

And Gabbi could no longer tell herself Trisha just needed time. She'd had plenty of time and it was only getting worse. Gabbi had been called to the school today; Trisha was being suspended for fighting. She said that the other girls started it, and they may have. The problem was that Trisha went from verbal to physical in the flick of an eyelash.

The bigger problem was that Gabbi was feeling more than a little inadequate. The kid refused to talk about her studies, classmates or teachers. All she wanted to talk about was sports—at the moment, baseball, soccer or professional basketball. All areas in which Gabbi was totally illiterate.

"Hey—" Trisha sat up in her seat "—there's that coach dude."

They were driving past a small park, and two people were playing basketball on a cement court. One of them was indeed Coach Dude. The other was Adam.

"Don't he just give you the shivers?" Trisha asked.

"Which one?"

Trisha made a face. "Adam's just a kid."

"You remembered his name."

"It ain't like I'm some kind of dummy, you know." A sly little grin spread across the girl's face. "What's the coach's name? Huh?"

"Luke Bennett." Gabbi blurted out the name before she had a chance to think.

"Aha."

"I meet a lot of people in my job," Gabbi said. "I make it a point to remember names."

"Sure." Trisha unfastened her seat belt. "Let's go play ball with them."

"I don't think—"

Trisha already had the door open, so Gabbi had no choice but to stop the car.

"I'm not dressed for playing," Gabbi said.

"Maybe you should stop wearing those stupid dresses," Trisha said as she climbed out of the car. She stopped and looked at Gabbi. "Your shoes are okay."

Gabbi stared after Trisha in horror. She knew almost nothing about basketball, remembering from some distant gym class that she could never make a basket. She'd go out there and totally humiliate herself and Trisha. She'd set back their relationship about ten years.

But Trisha was already gone, running across the grass toward the court. Gabbi slowly got out of the car.

"Trisha," she called. But it was like calling back the wind. Gabbi went after her.

"Hey, guys." Trisha had already reached Luke and his son. "How about a game? Two on two. Guys against the gals."

Gabbi was close enough to hear Trisha's ridiculous challenge. And to see the sneer on the boy's face.

"Sure," Adam said.

Luke turned around to smile at Gabbi. His eyes seemed to take in the panic in hers, and probably the fact that she looked totally incompetent, basketball-wise. He took pity on her.

"I'm a little tired today," Luke said. "Let's save the game for another time."

Perversely, Gabbi was annoyed. Pity was not the emotion a woman wanted to inspire in a man. Not that she was looking for anything else from Luke. Just not pity.

"How about you and I go one-on-one, Stretch?" Trisha said.

"Why don't you two play Horse?" Luke suggested. "Adam's got a baseball game tomorrow, and I don't want anything to happen."

The two kids made equally disgusted faces at each other, then began to shoot baskets in some sort of competition.

"What kind of game is Horse?" Gabbi asked.

"A game where they stand around and shoot baskets."

"Sounds on the quiet side."

"Exactly." Luke smiled at her, as if sharing a secret. "I didn't want them to play one-on-one. Before we'd know it, they'd be tripping and elbowing each other and someone would get hurt."

They sat and watched the kids shoot for a few moments, though Gabbi found her eyes straying to the tall man at her side. He seemed to be able to control the situation so easily, any situation. Whereas, lately with Trisha, Gabbi felt as if she was never in control.

Luke turned back to her. "You two live around here?"

"No. We live up north of the city. But we're thinking of moving in the summer. We were just driving around, looking at areas."

He waved his hand to take in the quiet neighborhood. His smile invited her to relax. "There are some nice homes here. Want to take a walk?"

Gabbi paused for a minute. Which was worse—being alone with that smile or losing the chance to hear about a potential neighborhood? Her own comfort versus Trisha's well-being? No contest, even for a beginning mother like herself.

"Sure."

After telling the kids they'd be back soon and ignoring sly remarks from Trisha, they headed west of the park. The houses were older, maybe built in the thirties and forties, and looked sturdy. No trendy circular windows or roof lines, and the yards were fairly small, but there was a variety of styles from compact brick bungalows to two-story frame farmhouse types. And the trees were full grown.

"That house over there is nice," Luke said, pointing to a stone cottage across the street. "Two bedrooms, but only one bath. Probably too small for you two."

"Are you saying two women can't share a bathroom?"

He just laughed. "Two anybodies getting ready at the same time in the morning couldn't share a bathroom." He nodded down a side street. "There's a bigger house for sale down that way. Three bedrooms, a bath and a half, and an unfinished area on the second floor that could be made into another bedroom. Plus the owners have moved out already, so you could move right in."

They turned down the street. "You sell real estate on the side?"

"Nah, strictly a humanitarian gesture. We need more ball players in the park in the evening so I can get some rest."

"Rest or more time to sit around and drink beer and watch baseball on TV?"

"You found me out," Luke said with a glimmer of a smile. "So why are you waiting until the summer to move?"

"You know, when school is out." Gabbi paused, then sighed. "Although I don't know why that should matter. Trisha just got suspended for fighting and informed me that she's not going back there ever again."

Luke just laughed. "She always been that stubborn?"

"Probably." She looked up at him, half embarrassed and half eager to talk to someone who seemed to understand so easily. "I'm in the process of adopting her. We've only been together for six months, and so far she's broken all my stereotypical ideas of how girls behave. She fights at the drop of a hat. Can swear a blue streak and couldn't care less about permanents and pierced ears."

"You're a brave woman."

Gabbi shrugged, though his words brought her warmth. "Or a very foolish one."

"Nah. I don't think doing something good is ever foolish. You're just picking things up at a tough time."

"That's what I'm finding out." The problems seemed less formidable when telling him about them.

"The junior high and early high school years are tough for kids and their parents," Luke said. "But most parents have the advantage of having grown up with their children, so they have a feeling for things. Someone in your position has no idea where her kid is coming from."

"They told me a little of her background," Gabbi said. "But it doesn't begin to cover things."

"I was luckier than you in that regard."

Gabbi frowned at him, not following his train of thought.

"Adam's not really mine," he said. "His dad and I were best friends. When Ron and his wife Laura died in a traffic accident last year, Adam moved in with me. It was what Ron had wanted."

"That was generous of you."

Luke just shrugged and looked away in obvious embarrassment. "Howdy, Mr. Beamer," he called out to an elderly man in a yard up ahead. "How are you?"

The man stopped his raking and walked to the sidewalk to meet them. "Tolerable, Luke. Tolerable. You got company?"

"This is Gabbi Monroe. She's looking for a house, and I'm showing her the neighborhood."

"None better, Mrs. Monroe. None better."

"It looks very nice," Gabbi agreed.

"You tell her there's none better, Luke? You tell her?"

"Yes, sir. I surely have."

Mr. Beamer gazed at him a moment before turning toward Gabbi. “Where is your husband, ma'am? Or are you a widow?”

Gabbi laughed at the twinkle in the old man's eye. “I'm divorced.”

“Your former husband from around here?”

Luke shifted from one foot to the other. The interrogation didn't bother Gabbi, but Luke seemed to be uneasy. She bit back a laugh as she answered. “No, he lives in California.”

“Oh.” Mr. Beamer nodded for a moment. “Luke here is one fine fellow. One of the best.”

“We have to be going,” Luke said, taking hold of Gabbi's arm as if to speed her along. “We have to get back to the park in a few minutes.”

His touch was gentle, yet her feet obeyed as if he had her heart on a string. A thoroughly foolish idea.

“Pleasure meeting you,” Mr. Beamer called after them.

“Nice meeting you, too,” Gabbi called back, then turned to Luke. He looked so chagrined that the urge to tease him was overpowering. “Apparently, a number of things in this neighborhood are the best.”

He just grunted.

“I'm surprised there are any houses available here at all,” she went on.

“There's the one I was talking about,” he said, pointing up ahead.

It was a two-story frame house with a wide front porch. Shaped pretty much like a big brown box, it still gave off a sense of cozy security. Somehow it seemed more like Trisha than the cedar-shingled Dutch colonial they presently lived in.

“It's nice,” Gabbi said. “I should call a real-estate agent and take a look at the insides of some of these.”

“Most of them have been treated with loving care,” Luke said. “We have a lot of folks just starting out here and a lot of retirees. Either way, they tend to keep the places up well.”

Another For Sale sign down the block caught Gabbi's eye. “Can we walk that way?” she asked.

“Sure, but you don't want that house.”

"I don't?" She couldn't even see the house from here, and wasn't sure she appreciated his making decisions for her.

"Nope. Basement floods every time it rains."

"Oh." He was right. She didn't want that house. "How do you know so much about the houses here? And how can I get your inside knowledge before I buy?" she added with a laugh.

"My dad's an electrician, and I help him. You get to know a lot about a neighborhood that way." He stopped walking. "If you want, I'd be glad to look at some of these with you and your agent."

It was such a tempting offer, but Gabbi wanted to refuse in spite of her joking question. She appreciated his counsel about Trisha and the stages she was going through, but she really didn't want to grow dependent on anyone. She and Trisha would do just fine on their own.

Still, a house was a huge investment. Could she afford to make a mistake and buy one that needed major repairs?

Gabbi loved the feel of the neighborhood, and that love should be enough to steer her right, but a little expert advice wouldn't go amiss.

"Thank you," she said slowly, as if she were stepping into a pit of snakes. "We'd appreciate your help."

Chapter Two

"Hey, Luke." Adam came into the kitchen, grabbed an apple off the counter and dropped into a chair at the table. "I was thinking, you know. I got a lot of algebra homework. I should really stay home this afternoon and work on it."

Luke turned to face the boy. A few days after they'd met Gabbi and Trisha at the park, Gabbi had called him about his offer to look at houses with them. They settled on Saturday afternoon as a good time. Except, Adam obviously wasn't keen on accompanying them.

"You'd rather stay inside and work on algebra than go out on a beautiful April afternoon?" Luke asked. He'd been looking forward to the outing personally.

Adam kept a straight face. "We've really got to start concentrating on education in this country," the boy said. "If we don't, all the other countries of the world are going to beat us in the global economic competition."

Luke tried not to laugh. "We'll only be out a couple of hours, and the fresh air will do you good. Then once we come home, you can stay in the rest of the day and do your homework. I promise."

The pain in Adam's face was just too much, and Luke was glad the doorbell rang at that moment. He hurried into the living room to open the front door for Gabbi, Trisha and a middle-aged woman.

He couldn't take his eyes off Gabbi. She was small, but there was something about her that was so riveting. Her dark, tight curls seemed to echo the intensity that burned in her brown eyes. She seemed to radiate life and energy, drawing him into her spell.

"Hi," he said.

She smiled at him, and the warmth of it could put Mount Etna to shame. All the oxygen was pulled from the air, and he couldn't breathe.

"This is Beth O'Neal," she said. "Our real-estate agent."

Luke forced his eyes away from Gabbi's. It was a battle, but once his gaze was free, he was able to breathe again. He nodded at the older woman.

"Sure, Beth and I go way back," he said. "How's Judy? She's down at Purdue, right?"

"Yep. She just loves it there." The woman turned to Gabbi. "He taught my youngest. Was one of her softball coaches for a season, too."

"Oh." Gabbi looked beyond Luke. "Hi, Adam."

Luke turned to pull the boy into an easy embrace, resting his arm on Adam's shoulders. Luke had been stunned at his reaction to Gabbi, but all he needed was a little breathing room to gain his equilibrium. "Guess we're all here."

"Hey, Stretch," Trisha greeted Adam with exuberance.

"Hi," Adam muttered.

"Try to control your excitement, Adam," Luke said.

As Beth shepherded them all out to her van, Luke was happy to see Adam and Trisha trade glances of disgust. If he could keep both of them irritated with him, there'd be less chance of him getting hypnotized by Gabbi's eyes again.

Luke and Adam took the back seat. Gabbi and Trisha sat in the middle one. Luke tried to keep his gaze moving, but the curve of Gabbi's cheek caught him. There was such strength there, such confidence. She was a woman who was not afraid to rely on herself.

"This is such a nice area for a family," Beth was saying. "There are houses of all different sizes."

"They got sidewalks, Gabbi."

"I see that, dear," Gabbi replied.

"We live in a real chintzy place," Trisha told them all. "They ain't got no sidewalks."

Gabbi turned to glance Luke's way, sharing a small smile with him, and it caught him off guard. His heart felt seared by her nearness.

"I mean, that's like really dangerous, you know," Trisha went on. "A kid is walking in the street, only because he's gotta. And bam! He gets hit by a big car."

"This is a nice little house," Beth interrupted as she pulled up in front of a white one-story cottage. "Needs a new kitchen, but otherwise it's in good shape."

Luke opened the side door and let Trisha and Gabbi get out before him. The scent of her perfume wafted around him, teasing.

"You know what happens when a little kid gets hit by a car?" Trisha asked. "Splat! That's what happens. Splat and you got kid guts all over the street."

Luke felt, rather than saw, Gabbi's sigh as the girl went on. He put his hand lightly on Gabbi's shoulder as he leaned closer to her ear. "Don't worry," he said. "She's not bothering anybody."

Gabbi looked up at him. "Adam is such a nice, quiet boy."

"Yeah, I suppose." Up close, her eyes weren't as dark as they appeared. Tiny flecks of fire danced in them. He pulled back slightly so as not to get burned. "My father thinks he's too quiet."

Gabbi shrugged. "Still, I wouldn't protest if some of Adam's quiet slipped over on Trisha."

Beth unlocked the door, and they all went inside. It was a nice-enough house, but it seemed small to Luke. To Gabbi, too, apparently, for they didn't stay long.

Next, Beth drove them past the historical district along the river. The big old houses were impressive, with most of them close to a hundred years old, but they were also pretty expensive. Somehow, he thought Gabbi was more practical.

"These houses are really big," Trisha said.

"My friend Ric lives in that brown one on the corner," Adam said.

"Oh, yeah?"

"There's only one house along here that's for sale right now," Beth said as she slowed down in front of a huge white house with two-story pillars. "I didn't make an appointment, but I could probably arrange for us to see it, if you're interested."

"That's okay," Gabbi said with a laugh. "We don't need all that room for just the two of us."

"Yeah," Trisha said. "Besides, we don't like to clean house."

"Trisha."

"We don't ever dust," Trisha said with a snicker. "We just open the windows and let the wind blow it out."

Adam laughed out loud.

Beth took them next to the house Luke had walked Gabbi by last week. It was the one he thought would really suit them. Also the one that was across the alley from his house. A fact that had no bearing on anything, except that he perhaps knew the house's history a bit better.

"This looks more my size," Gabbi said as they walked through the house. A touch of irritation sprinkled her smile. "I might even be able to keep it clean."

"You know they don't let a kid become a teenager until they swear to work on their parent's humility," Luke said. "I think it's some kind of universal law."

"That's what I like about Trisha," she said. "She takes her duties so seriously."

Trisha burst in through the kitchen door. "You see the fence?" she asked.

"Yes, dear."

"We don't have any fences where we live now. They don't allow them," Trisha told everyone. "So even if we had a dog, it would just run away and get hit by a car."

"You must have some dangerous cars in your neighborhood," Beth pointed out.

"Apparently," Gabbi agreed.

"They don't like kids or dogs out where we live," Trisha said. "It's a really weird place."

"Hey, Trish. Look at the basement," Adam called, and Trisha went flying down the stairs after him.

"You can see my challenge," Gabbi said with a laugh as she looked into the pantry. "The girl has a mind of her own, and I don't seem to be able to reach her. Our counselor said I should find something she's interested in and cultivate an interest in it myself, but..."

"You're not too interested in the lack of sidewalks?" Luke asked.

Her eyes lit up with laughter. "I think the subject's been covered."

Beth took them to three more houses—the one with the flooding basement, a three-bedroom one with a finished basement, and a four-bedroom one by the railroad tracks. Between stops, the seating arrangements in the van somehow got rotated so that Luke was sitting with Gabbi and Adam was with Trisha. The kids were chatting away like old friends, and Luke felt as tongue-tied as Adam had been earlier.

This was stupid. He wasn't fifteen and trying to figure out girls. He was forty-two and divorced. He might not understand women very well, but he sure ought to be able to make some small talk. He did it all the time with female teachers at school, the checkout clerks at the grocery store, his female friends. What was wrong with him now?

What was wrong was that part of him was so drawn to Gabbi that the rest of him couldn't think coherently. Maybe he was still fifteen years old someplace deep inside.

"I like this neighborhood," Trisha announced after Beth had dropped them back at Luke's house. "Let's buy one here."

"Well, we've got lots to think about," Gabbi said, flipping through the stack of listings Beth had given her.

She seemed to take a mental step to her car, and Luke suddenly didn't want her to leave. "Want to come in for something to drink?" he asked. "Lemonade. Iced tea. Orange juice. Milk."

"Pepto-Bismol," Adam snickered.

"Olive oil," Trisha suggested.

"Mouthwash." Adam and Trisha went off into hysterics.

Gabbi just shook her head and started toward her car. "I think I'll pass, but I really appreciate your help."

"Catsup." Another round of hysterics.

Luke glared briefly at Adam, then fell in step beside Gabbi. "You know, I was thinking about how you want to share an interest with Trisha, and I thought maybe a little tutoring in sports would help."

"Tutoring?" She turned toward him.

"Hey, I'm a coach. I have a good grasp of almost all sports. Everything from tennis to lacrosse. It wouldn't take that long to teach you some of the basics of the more popular sports."

"I guess." She seemed to be giving the idea more thought than it should need.

"Why don't you two come to dinner tonight?" he suggested. "We can have our first lesson afterward."

That seemed to push her into decisiveness. "No, we've imposed enough on you. How about you come to our place? It won't be anything fancy, just pizza."

"I'll finish my algebra before dinner," Adam said.

Luke looked at the boy. Was he enjoying Trisha's company or did he just want to have a meal where it wasn't all men?

"Sure," Luke said. "Sounds like fun."

Trisha made a face.

"Great," Gabbi said. "Seven o'clock okay?"

"Sure."

Luke watched the scowl grow on Trisha's face. Didn't she want them to come?

"Well," Adam said. "Looks like I'd better hit those old algebra books."

"Looks like we're going to be cleaning house," Trisha grumbled.

Gabbi shared a smile with Luke, sending shivers all down his spine. A little voice wondered if it was wise for him to get more involved, but the force of her smile made all decisions impossible.

"See you tonight," he said.

"Hey, you bums. Get your butts off the grass."

What was that girl up to now? Gabbi rushed out of the kitchen and into the living room. "Trisha, what are you doing?"

But Trisha, doubled up with laughter, didn't answer. Gabbi looked out to see Luke and Adam walking toward the door, but staying on the little walkway.

She opened the front door and stepped aside. "Come on in."

Luke was dressed casually in jeans and a cotton shirt. Nothing out of the ordinary, but her stomach tightened with a sweet tension.

"Scared you guys, didn't I?" Trisha laughed.

"Did not," Adam snapped.

For once, Gabbi was glad of Trisha's need to needle. It gave her a moment to recoup. Her reaction to Luke was nonsense. He was here to teach her about sports, give her a way to be closer to Trisha.

"Boy, did you two jump. It was really funny."

"Stuff it, punk," Adam said.

"Adam." Luke just put his hand on Adam's shoulder, and the boy subsided into silence. A slightly surly silence, but silence nonetheless. Luke smiled over at Gabbi. "Something smells good."

"It's a pizza from Little Naples," Gabbi said.

"We could've picked it up for you on our way here," Adam said.

Gabbi shook her head. "I doubt that Miss Manners would approve of having your guests pick up the food on their way over."

"We wouldn't have to tell her," Luke pointed out.

The promise of a secret between them made her heart dance for some silly reason, and her cheeks flush. She shooed them ahead of her toward the kitchen.

"We're going to eat at Little Naples all the time when we move," Trisha said.

"Did you pick out a house already?" Luke asked.

"No." Gabbi felt her cheeks warm again as he looked down at her. "We do like the area, but I'm just not sure."

"It's a big decision," Luke said.

"And quite a change from what I was originally planning." She turned to Luke, trying to maintain a business-like attitude. "Could you open the wine for me? I always mangle the corks and get pieces in the wine."

Luke's face seemed to tighten. "I really shouldn't have any," he said. "I just took some allergy medication, but I'll open the bottle for you if you like."

"Oh, no," Gabbi replied. "I don't want to drink alone. I'll put it away for another time and have lemonade."

"Super," Luke replied. "That goes great with pizza."

"I thought wine went better with pizza," Trisha said.

"Trisha," Gabbi said, her voice a warning not to push. "Would you get the salads, please?"

"Okay."

Gabbi watched her back for a moment before turning to Luke with a short smile. "Why don't you two sit down?"

When Trisha was back with the salads, Gabbi poured lemonade for all, and they dug in. The food was good, but conversation was a little sparse. Adam and Trisha ate with the dedication of active teenagers, and Luke seemed to tend toward the quiet. Gabbi didn't know whether to talk or to keep her mouth shut. She didn't want to be like her mother, poking at everyone, asking whether they liked the food, but the silence was unnerving.

"We'll clean up," Luke said once they were done.

"That's all right," Gabbi said, springing up from her chair. "Trisha and I can do it."

Trisha frowned at her. "Yeah, we can," she said. "But why should we? Guys can clean up stuff, too."

"We'll do it because they're our guests," Gabbi explained.

"They offered," Trisha said.

"But we can't let them do everything they want, dear," Gabbi pointed out. "Then they'll expect to get their own way all the time."

Luke laughed aloud while Trisha looked argumentative.

"Now, bring those dishes over to the sink," Gabbi said.

Luke brought his own load of dishes after her. "So we'll expect our own way, will we?" he teased.

The laughter in his eyes tickled her, warming her heart and leaving a strange yearning in her soul. She tried to turn off her feelings. "Hey, I haven't grown to this ripe old age without learning some truths." She grabbed a washcloth to wipe off the table.

By the time she came back to the sink, Adam had rinsed off the dishes and Luke was stacking them in the dishwasher. Trisha had put the leftover salad away and was taking the pizza carton out to the garbage can. Adam trailed along after her.

Being alone with Luke in the kitchen made Gabbi suddenly nervous. It was just too homey and comfortable for her. Luke carefully folded the dish towel Adam had left on the counter and hung it up.

"Boy," she said. "Your mommy trained you well."

"Actually, it was my father," Luke replied. "My mother died when I was eight."

"Your father never remarried?"

"No." Luke shook his head. "He dated a lot, but I guess nothing ever really clicked."

The silence swallowed them up again. It was overpowering, a living entity all its own. Suddenly Trisha's and Adam's voices could be heard.

"Guess we'd better get them busy before they start stuffing each other into the trash."

"I thought it was younger kids who got into that kind of trouble," Gabbi said.

"If they'd grown up together, they'd be ignoring each other by now," Luke said. "But those two are caught up in this boy-girl thing and aren't quite sure what to do about it."

Gabbi followed his broad back outside, letting her eyes take in his trim build from top to bottom. Teenagers weren't the only ones who had problems dealing with this boy-girl thing.

"Okay, guys," Adam said. "Let's give Gabbi her baseball lesson."

"Oh, boy," Trisha said.

Gabbi didn't like Trisha's evil grin at all. Given a choice between being alone with Luke or giving Trisha all sorts of ammunition, Gabbi would choose Luke. Actually, even if Trisha was soft-spoken and sweet, being alone with Luke was a tempting idea.

Gabbi tried to look tough. "It's going to be a private lesson. Why don't you and Adam play a few games of tennis? The courts should be pretty empty."

"That's a wimpy sport," Trisha said, pouting.

"Would you prefer golf?"

"That's for old geezers who can hardly walk."

Gabbi gave the kid a hard stare.

"All right," Trisha said, looking over at Adam. "I'll get some rackets. Then I'll take you over and beat your pants off."

"In your dreams," Adam replied.

The two were soon racing off, leaving Gabbi there to stare up at Luke. Did he seem taller now that they were alone? And weren't his shoulders suddenly broader? Lucky she hadn't had any wine, if just being with him had this effect on her.

"I have some equipment out in the truck," Luke said, and she followed him out front.

"Sometimes I wonder how that girl made it to age thirteen."

"Rough sailing?" he asked gently.

"She has a mouth that just won't quit."

"She's just testing you. I bet a lot of her attitude will go away once things are finalized." They walked side by side toward the truck. "I have the opposite problem with Adam. I could pay him by the word and he still wouldn't talk to me."

"Do you talk much to him?" Gabbi asked.

He shrugged. "If he seems to want to."

"I don't think you can leave it up to him. You should just keep talking. Even if he doesn't answer, he's listening. And when he's ready to talk, he will."

Luke reached in his truck and pulled out a bat, two gloves and a ball. "I'll give that a try."

Once they were around back, Luke laid the bat on a patio chair and gave her a glove. "We'll do a little catching first. I thought we'd go into the basic skills today, then next time we'll discuss the game itself."

Next time. Gabbi liked those words, though she told herself she was being silly.

"Okay, put your glove on."

"It's for the left hand," she said, staring at it. "I'm right-handed."

"You throw with your dominant hand. You use the off hand for catching."

Gabbi made a face. "I'm a real dummy, aren't I?"

"Stop your whining. I came to give you lessons, not sympathy."

"Boy, aren't you a sweetie pie?"

"I'll start out throwing underhand." He lightly flipped the ball toward her. "Catch the ball with your glove."

Gabbi held her hand way out in front of her. The ball hit the glove and bounced off.

"Close your hand over it," he ordered her.

They worked for several minutes until she started getting the hang of it, until the ball spent more time in her glove than on the ground. As she got better, Luke began moving farther and farther away from her. Finally, she was so far, she couldn't throw the ball back to him anymore.

"Throw it overhand," he said.

She tried. And failed. "I'm sorry. I throw like a girl, don't I?"

"You're not throwing it properly," he said. "You should bring your arm across your body." He lofted the ball to her. "Like that."

Gabbi concentrated on catching the ball before she spoke. She wondered why she felt as if she had to apologize. "I am a girl, you know."

"That's rather obvious."

His grin did wicked things to her peace of mind, but she concentrated on bringing her arm across her body. The arm went where it was supposed to, but the ball didn't.

"It stands to reason that I should throw like a girl."

Luke retrieved the ball. "Trisha's a girl," he said. "But I bet she doesn't throw like you."

Gabbi caught the ball and shrugged. "All girls don't have to be the same."

"True," he agreed. "And how much nicer the variety is."

Her cheeks warmed not at his words, but at something in his eyes, some teasing notion in his voice. It had been years since she'd felt this giddiness around a man. She'd dated and had male friends, but hadn't felt this light-headed silliness since she and Doug had first met.

Doug. Thoughts of him and his betrayal were enough to sour any sweet thoughts trying to take root.

Gabbi threw the ball, this time to Luke's other side. Her mouth was about to pour out apologies again when voices from the front of the house distracted her. Trisha came stomping around the corner with Adam following, a crooked grin on his face.

"Were the courts crowded?" Gabbi asked, her stomach tightening.

Adam's grin grew bigger, and Gabbi's stomach sunk. The answer wasn't going to be yes.

"There were courts open," Adam replied as Trisha threw herself into a patio chair. "But we had some other problems."

"Other problems?" Gabbi looked at Trisha. "What kind of problems?"

Adam answered again. "According to the dude in charge, we didn't exactly meet the dress code."

Gabbi looked at Adam's neat shirt and jeans and then Trisha's ripped jeans and over-sized sweatshirt. Genteel attire was something they hadn't tackled yet.

"So you left?" Gabbi asked.

"Sure," Trisha replied.

"That's all," Gabbi said slowly. "You just left."

Trisha shrugged. "I might've said a few things."

A few things. That would mean a lot of things. Did Trisha tell the manager that he should have a nice day? Or did she discuss a possible profession for his mother?

"A few words were exchanged," Adam said.

And they weren't "hello" or "how are you." Even Gabbi wasn't that naive anymore. Her heart sank. Was she doing Trisha *any* good? Just because Gabbi had decided the only way she'd ever have a family was to adopt, didn't mean that there were actually kids out there who would benefit from the arrangement. Maybe she was just being selfish.

Luke gave her a piercing look, as if reading the despair dancing at the edge of her thoughts. "What were you doing during this conversation?" he asked Adam.

"Spreading a little peace and trying to get everyone to chill out," Adam replied.

"Uh-huh."

Adam shrugged. "He says something. Trisha says something. Things go back and forth. He loses his cool. Waves his finger in the girl's face. And the next thing I know, the dude is making like Chester on 'Gunsmoke.'"

Chester? Confused, Gabbi looked at Trisha.

"You told me you didn't want me punching anybody no more."

"So you broke his leg?"

"Nah, she just kicked him in the shins pretty good," Adam said. "He was kind of a jerk. I mean, it wasn't like there was anybody there to get upset about us."

Gabbi felt her heart deflate. All her energy and hope and excitement just seemed to fade away. Every time she turned around there was another problem. Another problem she had no idea how to tackle.

Luke put his arm around her shoulders and gently took the glove off her left hand. "We've probably had enough baseball for today."

The strength of his touch was too inviting. It took all her willpower not to lean into those arms and forget everything for a moment, an hour, a lifetime. She shook herself free.

She did not need someone to lean on. She had herself, and that was more than enough. She'd find a way through this mess with Trisha; she always found a way.

Gabbi put a smile on her face. "I think you're right. We'd best wait for another lesson."

"Did she get a hit?" Trisha asked.

Gabbi just gave the girl a look, a long, hard look.

Trisha shrugged. "Just thought it would be nice if we could share some common interests."

Why not an interest in civilized behavior or polite conversation?

Gabbi just turned to Luke. "Thanks for everything," she said. "I'll call you about the rest of our sports lessons."

"Okay."

"I have a lot to do in the next few weeks." She needed time to figure out where the chink in her armor was and mend it.

"Gabbi, I'm sorry," Trisha called to Gabbi through the bathroom door.

Gabbi stared at the mirror as she dried herself off from her shower. Would Trisha ever call her Mom? Maybe it was a foolish thing to hope for, since Trisha had had a mother and remembered her quite well.

"It's okay, honey," she called back.

"No, it's not," Trisha insisted loudly. "I just can't go around losing my temper all the time. I'm gonna try really, really hard to be nice from now on."

Gabbi couldn't help sighing and was glad Trisha couldn't hear her. Trying really, really, really hard might mean ten percent of the fights would be avoided, but Gabbi guessed that was better than nothing.

"Just as long as you try," she said. "That's what's important, honey."

Gabbi put her towel down and checked out her breasts in the mirror. If she turned just so, the scar and slight puckered indentation wasn't visible and she could pretend she was like everyone else.

But she wasn't and never would be again. She would always have that threat hanging over her. Not exactly like a sword, but maybe like a persistent cloud on her horizon.

She shook her head, her chin held high. Clouds weren't a bad thing. The threat of rain made her appreciate the sun all the more. And the chance of her cancer returning someday made her appreciate each and every day she had. It had taught her not to sit back and wait for her dreams to come true, but to work for them. Like not waiting for a man to come around to build a family with, but to start one herself.

She turned to face the mirror once again, raising her arms over her head, and ran a critical eye down the line of her breasts. No strange shadows, no dimples where there should be none, no visible differences from last month. So far, so good. She slipped her nightgown on and went into the bedroom.

Trisha was sprawled on the bed, staring at the ceiling, but she sat up when Gabbi came back into the room. "How come people are always so worried about how you look? Why should people care what you wear to play some dumb game?"

Gabbi sat down on the bed, putting the pillows up against the headboard as she leaned back. "The tennis thing is just their rules. If you want to play, you follow the rules. But why people care so much about how you look, I don't know. But it's been that way for ages."

Gabbi'd never figured it out herself, but it had always been there—from her father calling her his "pretty little princess" to Doug assuming she was washed up in TV journalism after her surgery. Why was it that her father never complimented her for being smart or clever or persistent? The only way she'd been able to win his approval was through her looks. And Doug, he'd been so obsessed with his own appearance that she shouldn't have been surprised when a "flaw" made her undesirable.

"And then those kids in school," Trisha went on. "Always getting on my case because I don't wear makeup."

"You're at an age when everybody is afraid," Gabbi said. "All those other girls think it's safe being just like everybody else. They think it guarantees that everyone will like them. But when someone comes along and doesn't follow their rules, it scares them. Maybe you're the way everybody should be, not the way they are. Just be true to yourself and everything will work out."

Trisha looked at her for a long moment, then lay back to stare at the ceiling again. "You should get a house wherever you want," Trisha finally said. "I mean, the houses are nice here. They have big yards and stuff."

"And killer cars."

Trisha refused to be baited. "I know you like it here."

Gabbi stretched her legs out and stared at her feet. "I didn't even think about it when I moved in here. It was just like a lot of places I'd lived in before. But now that I want to buy, I am thinking about it. The houses in town are nice and convenient. We don't need a lot of space, and I don't want to spend all my money on a house. It would be nice to have money for trips, eating out, getting nice clothes, stuff like that."

Trisha nodded. "You like the houses we saw today?"

"Some of them, yeah."

"That coach dude is a cool guy. I mean, he's like so smooth, so mellow."

"Are you talking about a guy or about a bourbon?" Gabbi asked.

"Huh?"

"It's getting late, honey. You should get to sleep."

"You should go after him," Trisha said.

"He's not a deer, and I'm not Diana the Huntress."

Trisha got to her feet. "You can't just sit around and wait for him to make the first move. I mean, this is the nineties."

"I have a lot of things going on right now, kid. Talk to me about this stuff when things settle down."

Gabbi got to her feet and walked with Trisha down to her room. "Good night, sugar," she said, and kissed the girl on her cheek. "Sleep tight."

Trisha gave her a hug in return. "Good night, Gabbi. And I really am gonna be nice from now on." With that, she fled into her room and closed the door.

Gabbi went back to her own room with a sigh. She turned out the lights and climbed into the bed. In the darkness, she did the rest of her monthly breast self-exam. Right hand behind her head, as her left hand checked out her right breast in a tight spiraling pattern. Then she did the same with her left breast. She could still remember the feel of her lump—like a tiny BB buried under layers of tissue, a bomb waiting to detonate—but she felt nothing tonight and relaxed, staring into the night.

Diana the Huntress. The idea was almost tempting.

Chapter Three

Gabbi pulled her car up in the alley behind the two-story brown house and looked around a moment before stepping out. It was silly, but she was afraid that Luke would be here someplace. He was a nice guy and everything, but he was dwelling in her thoughts far too much. She had to stop mooning about like some teenager and start remembering her priorities.

And that's precisely what she had done this past week since Luke and Adam had looked at houses with them. She'd reviewed the house specs, talked to various people about what high school would be best for Trisha and tried to instill some sense of decorum in the young lady.

They'd actually reached some compromises. Trisha promised to stop fighting at school, and Gabbi promised to consider moving soon, rather than waiting for the summer. All in all, it had been a pleasant week.

Except that she'd dreamed of Luke every night.

Gabbi took a deep breath and looked around the alley. She'd never actually been in one before, and the ones on TV were always filled with muggers and rapists. This one was a pleasant little gravel lane lined with fences, garages and basketball nets.

"Hey, you. Get out of there before I call the police."

Startled, Gabbi looked around, but she could see no one.

"This is the supreme commander of the galaxy speaking. Leave immediately, earthling, and you will not be harmed."

The voice, coming from across the alley, sounded too familiar. The way it had been in her dreams this past week.

"Maybe I'll just shoot you myself."

Gabbi's heart should have shouted out warnings. Instead, it jumped for joy. "Luke?" She stood on her tiptoes and looked over the top of the wooden fence across the alley from her.

"Up here."

She trained her gaze up higher and found him on a ladder by the side of his garage. "What are you doing?" she asked.

"Some spring cleaning," he replied. "I was just clearing the dead leaves from the gutters."

"I meant, what were you doing harassing me?"

"I didn't recognize you from way up here. For all I knew, you might have been some burglar."

She watched him come down the ladder and was alarmed at the way her lips broke into a smile. He was a nice guy, a helpful guy, but just a friend. The gate across from her opened, and Luke stepped out into the alley. A damn good-looking friend.

"You taking another look at the Koch house?" he asked.

"Koch house?" Gabbi's brows furrowed. Was she more befuddled by his presence than she thought? "I thought the Petersons own it."

"The Petersons lived here," Luke said. "But only for five years. The Koch family lived here for forty years. I think they were the ones who built the house."

She glanced at the solid old place. So whatever time she spent here was transitory; it would never really be hers. Just as her marriage had been fleeting, leaving no visible proof of its brief existence. It was a disheartening thought. If her cancer came back tomorrow, would anyone know she had been here?

"You okay?" Luke asked. His eyes were shadowed, as if he'd read into her heart.

She forced her blues away. "Sure, just fine." She turned to look at the house. "It's a nice place. Has a lot of possibilities."

"It's actually bigger than mine. You can easily add another bedroom in that unfinished half upstairs."

"It's big enough for Trisha and me the way it is now."

"Well, you never know how things might change in the future."

Gabbi shook her head. "I'm a stable person. There aren't many changes coming in my future."

"Goodness, a psychic."

"No, just someone in control of her life." And she would show that control now.

Luke came by her side and leaned his elbows on the roof of her car. She refused to notice the hard line of muscles on his upper arm or the way his hands looked so strong yet gentle. She stared at the yard, studying the brown lawn coming back to life.

"Got a nice fenced-in yard," he said.

"We noticed," Gabbi said. "Trisha will be safe if any of those killer cars come in from the suburbs."

Luke laughed. "And your dog won't run away."

"Please, Trisha is already bugging me about that."

"Where is she?"

"She's up at your high school taking a placement test."

Gabbi kept her eyes ahead. The bushes were starting to leaf out. Braving the still chilly nights to bask in the joy of the sun. A little voice asked her if the bushes were braver than she was, if she was still hiding away in the winter of her cancer and failed marriage.

What a crazy notion. It was spring for her, too. Hadn't her adoption of Trisha proven that she was moving ahead?

"This is a good location," Luke said. "Trisha can walk to school next year. Although that won't last more than a few weeks. By then, she'll have wheedled a ride out of someone."

"I'm not sure Trisha would do that. Threaten, yes, but not wheedle."

"She's a nice kid."

"Yes, she is."

So what if she had pretty much discounted marriage in her future? There were a lot of reasons for that. Being strongly advised not to get pregnant was one. Not wanting to trust her happiness to someone else was another. Neither was a sign of weakness. She wasn't so sure about this moping about she was doing at the moment, though.

"Well," Gabbi said, pushing herself away from the car. "Time to get to work."

"You want to finish up our baseball lesson?"

He had the warmest brown eyes she'd ever seen. They were so open and honest. Trust me, they shouted, I won't let you down. She turned away.

"No, no. I don't have any time. I have a lot to do today."

"Like what?"

"The house." She swallowed hard. "I'm going to measure rooms, check out the kitchen, that kind of thing."

Doug had had great eyes that promised trustworthiness, too. And he was dependable as the day was long. Until she found the lump.

"Want any help?"

"With what?" Her voice had come out rather brusquely and she felt guilty. He was just being nice. "I'm not going to do anything heavy."

"Measuring is a two-person job."

"Two person?" Like kissing? Hugging? Loving?

"If you want accuracy."

"I just want an estimate. A general idea." Where were these crazy thoughts coming from?

"If you aim for accuracy, you'll get an estimate. Aim for general and you'll get nothing worthwhile."

"Who said that, some famous philosopher?" she asked.

"Yeah." He nodded. "My father. He's a tradesman. He has an electrician's card, but he can do anything. He's the best."

"Is he here?"

"Nope."

"Then I'll just have to struggle along on my own."

"Did I tell you who's second best in the world?"

"At what?" She shouldn't have asked, but couldn't help herself.

"Anything. But in this case providing accurate measurements."

Gabbi tried desperately not to smile. What were all her silly worries about trust and honesty? He would be her neighbor and was offering to help her with a mundane chore. It must be the spring breezes that were stirring up long buried dreams.

"All right." She gave up and smiled. "Come on."

Luke opened the gate, and they walked through the yard. "You put a new net on that backboard and it'll be as good as new."

"Trisha's already pointed that out."

"Sharp kid."

"It would be nice if she applied some of that intensity to her studies."

"She will."

Luke stopped her when they reached the back steps. "Why don't you let me open the door?"

"The big man is going to protect the little woman," Gabbi said.

"You never can tell what you might find." He took the key and opened the door.

But her bogeymen weren't waiting inside a kitchen door. Gloom descended over Gabbi once again, as if a cloud had passed over the sun. It was the little things like this that misled a person into believing they could rely on someone.

Doug has always been so concerned about her safety. *Don't drive home alone at night. Lock your doors. Stay on busy roads.* But the monster that destroyed her had been living in his heart all along.

Luke opened the door to the enclosed back porch, and from there they went into the kitchen. Gabbi stopped and surveyed the scene before her, anxious to derail her thoughts and needing action to do so.

"I'm going to have the kitchen completely redone," she said. "The cabinets look really faded, and I'm not crazy about the layout."

"Did you buy the place?"

She caught herself. Silly, talking as if it were hers. She should know better than to count her chickens before they hatched. Sometimes she wondered if she'd ever learn.

"Not yet, but I'm considering it."

"Kitchens can be expensive."

"I can manage," she said and moved into the dining room.

Luke followed her. "Let's start measuring. Do you have the tools?"

"Tape measure. Pencil. Notebook." She held each up in turn.

"Okay." He took the tape measure from her.

They went from room to room, taking measurements. Luke pointed out that the fireplace in the living room worked and he thought there was one in the rec room in the basement. Gabbi suddenly saw a wintry day, snow falling outside, while she was cuddling up with—

Cuddling up with Trisha. Gabbi in one chair and Trisha in the other. Reading books. Maybe watching TV while the toasty fire warmed the room.

"You want to check the upstairs?" Luke asked.

"Huh?"

"Do you want to measure anything upstairs?"

"Oh, yeah. Right."

She followed Luke upstairs. She really should send him home. Even if it was just spring fever, her thoughts were becoming wilder and wilder. Things that should be confined to nighttime dreams were invading her daytime thoughts.

"You can put in a good-sized bedroom in this space," Luke was saying as he stood at the door to the unfinished area.

Gabbi's vision blurred as she looked at the attic's bare rafter. That would make two big bedrooms. One for the girls. The other for the boys. They wouldn't be needed right away, though. Not until they had that snowy day in winter and that blazing fire in the fireplace.

One for the girls and one for the boys? Lordy! Where was her sanity?

Here she was spouting off about not being able to trust a man, when it was her own mind that was turning traitor! There would be no boys or girls. Not ever.

She turned and practically fled down the stairs. "I have to go pick up Trisha."

Luke stared at her.

"I do." Gabbi knew there was a note of panic in her voice, but didn't care. "She'll be done with her placement test soon."

He was following her. "Trisha can wait in front of the school. There'll be a lot of kids there."

"She gets upset if she has to wait."

She grabbed her purse from the kitchen counter and hurried out to the porch. Luke closed the back door. Gabbi snatched the key from his hand.

"I'm sorry. I really have to go."

She didn't look to see if there was puzzlement or hurt in his eyes, but hurried out to her car. She didn't breathe a sigh of relief until she was on the street, blocks from the house. Then she allowed herself to pull over and wipe at the tears that were leaking from her eyes.

What an idiot she was! The first sign of spring and she gets spring fever worse than any teenager, sighing and mooning and dreaming of all sorts of impossible things. She knew what her life could contain and couldn't. And it was about time she faced up to them.

She was damn lucky to have caught the cancer when she did. If it meant her life wouldn't contain everything another woman's would, then so be it. She would still be happy and content, even if she had to force herself to be.

"Hey, Luke, look. There's your girlfriend."

"I don't have—" Luke looked across the grassy open field to where Adam was pointing. Gabbi was standing near a picnic table talking to the youth minister. Trisha was with her. "I don't have a girlfriend. She's just a casual friend."

"I bet she's following you."

Gabbi was dressed like most of the people at this picnic, in jeans and a T-shirt. Nothing fancy, but even from this distance he could feel her energy. He pulled his eyes from her with difficulty.

"Better let me check that stuff you're drinking," he said to Adam. "You must have something stronger than lemonade in there."

"Let us check the facts, my man." Adam flexed his shoulders and then raised his hand in front of his face. "Number one, she came to our baseball game, right?"

"Yeah, so what? A lot of people did."

"Number two, she came and found us in the park."

"They were driving around looking at the neighborhoods."

"Number three, we get invited to her house for a little pizza that we could have gotten ourselves."

"She wants to learn about sports. She's trying to relate to Trisha better."

"Number four, she's gonna buy the house that's just across the alley from us."

Luke didn't say anything. The dippy kid wasn't listening, anyway. A woman with all the brightness and vitality of Gabbi wouldn't look at someone like him. Somebody ordinary with an ordinary job and an ordinary life.

"And finally, number five," Adam said with a flourish. "She's at the same picnic we are. A place she ain't never been before."

The thought of being so ordinary irked Luke, though it was what he'd been striving for for years. He didn't want the glamour positions, if being a high school varsity head coach could be considered glamorous. He just wanted to be able to do his job unobtrusively.

Sometimes, though, unobtrusive was lonely.

"I'm going to have to talk to your teachers," Luke said. "You obviously don't have enough to occupy you. If you did, you wouldn't be coming up with all this wild stuff about me and a woman I barely know."

"I tell you. The lady's after you."

He didn't want to look at Gabbi. It would just fuel the kid's already bizarre imagination, but Luke's eyes went in that direction, anyway. Sure she was a nice woman. A gorgeous woman. But he wasn't looking to get involved. Luke forced his gaze away, watching some kids playing touch football and some others tossing a Frisbee around.

"Man," Adam said. "You just have to look at her eyes. She thinks you're hot stuff."

It suddenly dawned on Luke that Adam had talked more in the past few minutes than he had in the past few weeks. Maybe Adam was the one with a romantic interest. Gabbi was a little old for him, but Trisha wasn't.

"Trisha is a nice-looking girl." He smiled at Adam.

"Oh, no." Adam backed away, shaking his head, hands out before him. "No way, man. I'm not into pain. And that's all that girl puts out. Heaping chunks of pain."

"Yo, Stretch." Trisha was waving at them.

"You were talking about girls chasing after boys. It looks like you're the one who has a girlfriend."

Adam made a sour face. "I'm too young to die."

Trisha and Gabbi came toward them, with Trisha in the lead. Luke found himself frowning. Didn't Gabbi want to see him? It wasn't as though he wanted or needed a girlfriend, but he sure didn't want to be rejected, either.

"Hi, guys," Trisha said. She was all bright-eyed and enthusiastic.

"Hello," Gabbi said.

Up close she looked even more beautiful. Her eyes were sparkling, though not—Luke told himself—with passion for him. She was just a lady who seemed to enjoy life.

"Did you make an offer on the house?" Luke asked.

"Yes, I talked to the real-estate agent last night. She was going to call the owners today sometime. I should know by tomorrow what they decide."

"That's good," Luke said.

"What do you think of that, Stretch?" Trisha punched Adam on his shoulder. "Looks like I'm going to be your new neighbor."

"Wow." Adam's reaction was hard to read. "What are you doing at our picnic?"

"I'm going to join the youth group," Trisha answered. "Our adoption counselor said it would be fun."

"It's a good group," Luke said. "Adam's been in it a couple of years."

"Cool," Trisha replied.

"Want some ice cream?" Adam asked.

"Yeah, sure."

"Me, too."

"Cool," Trisha said yet again.

The two kids walked off, and Gabbi took a step closer to Luke. Her perfume was gentle, a faint flowery fragrance that teased him with the promise of spring.

"We came to the picnic so Trisha could get acquainted with some of the kids," Gabbi said. "I guess a lot of them will be going to high school with her."

"Probably most of them," Luke said.

"That'll be good for her."

They stood a moment. He was watching Gabbi, she was watching Trisha. Sounds of children's laughter and adults talking swirled around them. Luke was more than conscious of Gabbi next to him, of her soft, feminine curves that enticed him. He knew she wasn't chasing him as Adam insisted, but he did wonder what type of guy she would go after. And how was it that she was unattached with no boyfriend to help her choose a house or measure the rooms?

"I don't know when we'll move," Gabbi said. "If I do get the house, I want to do a lot of fixing up."

"My dad knows just about all the contractors in the area. Let me know if we can help."

"Okay."

He glanced around them. All the things he'd like to ask her seemed too personal, too much a violation of her privacy. He watched as some adults grilled hot dogs on a couple of barbecues, while others monitored food tables. Adam and Trisha were over by the ice-cream stand. He could offer her ice cream. But that would seem as though he was copying Adam.

"Do you think it'll rain?" Gabbi asked.

He looked her way. She was staring at some storm clouds to the west. Luke sniffed the air the way his father always did.

"It might. Those look like lake-effect clouds. The wind picks up a little and we could have a storm before you know it."

"Weather is really changeable around here," Gabbi said.

"Yep. We always say if you don't like the weather, just wait a minute."

"I like it like that," she said. "It's impulsive."

Did that mean she liked impulsive behavior? Boy, she must really be disappointed in him.

"You want something to drink?" Luke asked.

"No, thank you. I'm fine."

So much for his impulsive nature taking over. Luke looked around, clenching his jaw. If the lady were chasing him, which he didn't believe for one cotton-picking minute, it certainly wasn't for his conversational skills.

"We're going to need to get back to your lessons," Luke said. "Otherwise you'll forget everything you learned."

"I suppose." She looked toward Trisha. "But if Trisha starts making new friends, she won't really care what I know or don't know about sports."

He supposed that was true, but he hated to be fired as a teacher after only one session. It left him no excuse to see her.

"Team sports could be fun for you, too," he said.

"I suppose."

"You can get exercise as well as enjoying the company of friends."

"Yeah, but I'm not a spring chicken anymore."

He looked down over her trim little body, all the curves just right and all the firm places perfect. He never saw a chicken, spring or otherwise, that looked so good.

"Most sports have a geriatric division," he noted.

"Oh, really?" Gabbi punched him.

"Ouch." He rubbed his shoulder. "Trisha giving you lessons again?"

"I just needed lessons in kicking," Gabbi replied. "I've always had a strong punch."

"That's good to know."

The sparkle in her eyes had increased, along with a little flame deep in his soul. It teased at him, pushing him closer, even as habit kept his feet still.

"Hey, Luke," Ted Kramer called over to him. "Want to see if you can get a softball game together?"

"Sure." Luke breathed a sigh of relief. A task he could handle.

He wasn't good at this man-woman stuff. Jackie would testify to that. Their stormy three-year marriage was a testament to how much one person could disappoint another. He'd been consumed by the nightmares, the dreams of that day in an Asian jungle, and had somehow thought he could bury it all in a life with Jackie. Sweet, gentle, helpless Jackie. The best thing he ever did for her was to set her free.

"I'd better let you get to your game," Gabbi said. "I really should see what Trisha wants to do."

"Not so fast," Luke said, taking her arm lightly in his. It seemed as if he was trying to hold fire, judging from the searing charge that raced up his arm. "You've got to play."

"Me?"

He had to look away, but kept his light hold on her arm. "Hey, Adam, Trisha. Bring some of the kids over. We're going to play some softball."

"Great," Adam replied as he led a crowd over.

"Cool," Trisha said.

"Who're captains?" another kid asked.

"I'll pick one team," Adam said. "And Luke can pick the other."

That wouldn't have been Luke's suggestion, but he was too stunned by Adam's taking charge to contradict him. Was this Trisha's influence?

"Okay," Luke said. "But you can't have all kids."

Adam frowned. "You want us to have old people?"

"Yep," Luke replied. "You alternate young and old in picking."

"What a bummer," Trisha exclaimed.

Luke just smiled and slid his arm around Gabbi's shoulders. "I pick Gabbi for my team."

"Oh, no," Gabbi said. "I'm not—"

Adam let out a whoop. "I pick Trisha."

"You guys are dead meat," Trisha said with a snicker.

"Oh, yeah?" Gabbi was frowning; her jaw was set firmly as she turned to Luke. "Pick us a good team. I'm in the mood for stomping some kid butt."

It took some arguing and some pauses to drag people away from the food tables, but they eventually got their teams ready. Another set of discussions followed before they all had their positions assigned. Gabbi walked along with Luke as they carried the equipment to the playing field.

"I think it's going to rain," she said.

Luke looked up to the sky. It was dark, but it couldn't rain. Not now when he and Gabbi were going to beat their kids. "Nah, I think it's going to hold up."

"How do you know?" Gabbi asked.

"If it was going to rain soon, there would be lightning by now."

"Are you sure?" she asked.

"Absolutely."

"The other team is at bat first, aren't they?" Gabbi asked. "And since I'm an outfielder, I have to go way out there by the railroad tracks, right?"

Luke nodded.

"Well, I don't want to get out there and then have it start pouring."

He wanted to tell her to trust him, but the words wouldn't come out, not even in a joking way.

She made a face at him, apparently not expecting an answer. "If I get wet, you're in trouble." Then she trudged out with the rest of the outfielders.

Luke watched for a moment, emotions warring within him. There were some things he just couldn't joke about. Some things that were sacred that others wouldn't understand. Concentrate on the game, he told himself, do what you do well and leave the rest alone.

With that philosophy in mind, he walked onto the pitcher's mound. "Okay," he bellowed. "Let's play ball!"

The first batter on Adam's team was a girl of about fifteen, with a long blond ponytail and bare feet. Luke lofted her an easy ball, which she whacked solidly between first and second base.

It was enough to get on first base, but his outfielders got in an argument over who was going to get the ball. By the time the discussion was resolved, the kid was on third base.

"Let's have a little teamwork back there," Luke shouted.

The other team jeered, and he could hear Adam's voice over all. Luke had hoped the boy would be coming out of his shell soon, but he would rather have had a more gradual exit.

The next batter was a young woman about seven months pregnant. Luke gave her a hard look and wound up to pitch. Then, just as the ball left his hand, an enormous bolt of lightning raced across the sky. Everybody paused to stare open-mouthed, and then the deluge came.

There were a few minutes of pandemonium as people raced around in the pouring rain, gathering up picnic gear and kids. Luke picked up some bats and looked around. In the midst of everybody scrambling, he couldn't see Gabbi or Trisha.

They can take care of themselves, he told himself and followed Adam in a dash for the truck. Once inside, he looked around the parking lot.

"Where are Gabbi and Trisha?"

"In their car."

Luke spotted it across from them. "Wait here," he said, but Adam came racing with him toward Gabbi's car.

"It won't rain," she shouted through the open window as he reached the car. "Hah!"

"I said there would be lightning before it rained."

The rain continued to beat down on him, but he barely noticed. Gabbi was soaked to the skin, her hair hanging straight down on her face, and her clothes seemed to cling closer than her own skin. He was caught between wanting to laugh and other emotions that he didn't want to admit to. Her glare told him to play it cool.

"You guys are soaked," he said.

"No fooling," Trisha snapped.

"Why don't you come to our house? You can change into some dry clothes."

"That's okay," Gabbi said. "We'll just—"

It was time to take charge a little. "Adam, ride with them so they don't get lost."

Gabbi wasn't sure she should be going to Luke's, but he was probably right. They were soaked through and through. And there was a bit of a chill in the air. Better to get into something dry before they caught cold. Besides, she had to take Adam home, anyway.

"I think I know the way from here," Gabbi said as she pulled from the parking lot.

"Cool," Adam replied.

"Don't worry," Trisha said. "I know how to get there."

Getting lost on the way to Luke's wasn't what Gabbi was worrying about. She was more concerned with her heart getting lost once they got there. They went south on the street, past the little shopping center, left at the light and across the bridge, which brought them on the northern edge of Luke's neighborhood. She turned down his street and saw his truck already in the drive. A panel truck was in front.

"Oh, boy!" Adam said. "Matt's here."

"Who's Matt?" Trisha asked.

"He's Luke's father," Adam replied. "He's the coolest dude."

"Neat," Trisha said.

Gabbi parked behind the panel truck, and they went to the door. A short, white-haired man waited for them there.

"Hi. Matt Bennett," he said as he stepped aside to let them in.

"Gabbi Monroe, and this is my daughter Trisha."

"And I'm Adam."

Matt gave Adam a playful punch. "Luke's upstairs changing. Adam, take the ladies upstairs and show them to the bathroom. We put some dry stuff in there. If you bring your wet clothes down, we can toss them in the dryer."

Adam took them through a tiny foyer with an empty coatrack and up some carpeted stairs to a large bath. Gabbi closed the door behind her and Trisha. The room had a faint smell of Luke's after-shave—a spicy scent that made her think warm thoughts.

Trisha was looking at the sweatshirts and sweatpants on top of the hamper. She held up a red one with a grin. "I get the Bulls' sweatshirt."

"Be my guest." Gabbi picked up a towel and dried off her hair.

"Jeez, I'm soaked," Trisha said as she stripped off her jeans and T-shirt, then her socks. "What about my underwear?"

Gabbi put down the towel and slowly stripped off her jeans. She hated wet jeans. They clung like plaster. "Is it so wet that you can't stand it?"

"It'll make the dry stuff all wet," Trisha said, as she stripped her bra and panties off. She grabbed up a towel and dried herself before slipping into a sweatshirt and sweatpants.

"Want me to take my stuff down?" Trisha asked.

"No, leave it. I'll bring it down."

Trisha slipped out the door as Gabbi pulled off her T-shirt, then hesitated before taking off her bra. It was soaked, there was no denying it. But not wearing it would put her scarred breast against Luke's shirt.

It was stupid, she told herself. Absolutely, positively idiotic. But it almost seemed as though he would know about her cancer if she wore his shirt without a bra.

Talk about stupid, Gabbi thought as she pulled off her bra. That took the prize. As if shirts could talk!

In a few minutes, she was retracing her steps back to the foyer downstairs. Following the sound of voices, she went through the dining room and into the kitchen. Trisha was there with Luke, Adam and Matt.

"I made some hot chocolate," Matt said. "Grab a cup and have some."

"We can't really stay long," Gabbi said, clutching the wet clothes.

"Then drink fast," Matt said.

Trisha giggled and looked at Adam, probably sharing his high assessment of Matt's cool index.

"The dryer's down here," Luke said as he led Gabbi into the basement. It was painted in bright yellows and reds. A thoroughly wild-looking place that took her by surprise.

Luke seemed so quiet and laid-back. She put the clothes into the dryer.

"I like your basement," Gabbi said. "It's really colorful."

"Thanks."

He seemed quiet. More so than usual. Did he invite them because he felt he had to?

"We won't stay long," she told him. "The clothes should dry soon."

"Stay as long as you like," he said.

Ah, that was the wrong thing to say. The way her foolish heart was acting, she might choose weeks or years. They met Adam, Trisha and Matt coming down the stairs as they were going back up.

"We're going to play pool," Trisha said.

"Okay," Gabbi replied.

"Make sure she gets some hot chocolate," Matt ordered.

"Yes, sir." Luke obeyed, pouring her a cup once they got back to the kitchen.

Gabbi wasn't sure she wanted it, but it gave her something to do with her hands and hopefully something to occupy her mind. She leaned against the counter, partially crossing her arms over her chest as she held the cup. Luke's shirt smelled faintly of his after-shave.

She glanced around the kitchen. It was set up for efficiency rather than style. There were no plants, no pictures on the walls. A revolving rack was on the counter next to the stove, holding spices. Oregano, paprika, garlic salt, chili powder as well as the usual salt and pepper. The refrigerator door held a large calendar with notes in almost all the squares. Between his schedule and Adam's, Luke was a busy man. She turned back and found him watching her.

"I guess since I wasn't invited, I don't look like a pool player," she said.

"Matt and Adam play cutthroat games," Luke said. "I'll take you down some other time and give you lessons."

"You're rather pushy on this lesson thing."

Luke shrugged. "Teaching is my life."

She sipped her chocolate. It must be nice to do something so meaningful. She wondered what kind of a legacy she would leave. Not that she was figuring on leaving soon, but it was something she was conscious of. Maybe Trisha would be her legacy.

"I didn't realize when we met that you were a celebrity," Luke said.

She looked up, startled. "I am?"

"Gabbin' with Gabbi. Noon on WNDN."

She shrugged. "I'm not sure that makes me a celebrity. It's just a job."

"A high-profile one."

"Trisha's not impressed."

Luke laughed. "I'm not surprised. She looks like a tough audience. Want to do a little book review?"

Gabbi was lost. "Book review?"

"I mean of sports," he replied. "I have a lot of books on all kinds of sports."

"Okay."

She followed him into the living room. There was no set style of decor here, either, but there were a few paintings on the walls. Newspapers, magazines and books covered the end tables, and the wide picture window that she would have had filled with plants was empty. The room felt friendly, but slightly distant. Luke went to a nook filled with bookshelves, and she followed. While he was perusing the titles, she saw a picture album.

"What's this?" Gabbi asked. "Family pictures?"

"Nah. Just pictures of me playing stuff. Matt's into photography."

"Let's see." She pulled the album down. "Were you cute as a kid?"

"Not very."

Gabbi walked over to the sofa, and Luke followed. She wanted to know this man who had been haunting her thoughts. Maybe she'd find out he was obsessed with appearance, like Doug had been. She opened the album.

The pictures started with Luke as a boy, playing Little League baseball in a uniform that looked about three sizes too big. He hadn't been concerned with appearances back then. The pictures continued with shots of Luke on grade-school football, basketball and track teams, and on a YMCA swimming team.

"Looks like you were into everything," Gabbi said.

He shrugged and sat back. In order to see the pictures with her, he had to be close, which she didn't mind at all. He put his arm around her shoulders. She didn't mind that, either.

"I enjoyed sports, and Dad seemed to enjoy going along. Especially after Mom died."

"Did your mother like sports?"

"Yeah, but by the time I was into them, Mom was getting sicker. She had cancer, and her last years were pretty hard." His voice turned grim, a raw pain lay beneath the surface.

Gabbi felt a hollowness in the pit of her stomach. There was a bond linking them, but it was a horrible, dark shadow, not one to treasure.

"Hard on her," Luke went on. "Hard on us. There's nothing quite so painful as watching someone you love suffer and knowing you can't do a thing about it."

Gabbi touched his hand, wanting to reach out to him. "It must have been doubly hard being so young."

"I remember feeling angry and resentful, but most of all I felt helpless."

She remembered that feeling from her own battle. That her body could be doing traitorous things to her and she couldn't stop it. "I think—"

She looked up as she spoke, and their eyes met. Her words were forgotten as some deep and treacherous current raced between them. She tried to look away, but the pull was too strong. She didn't want to read his eyes, didn't want to be drawn by the emotions in the air.

But then they moved together, their lips touching gently. It was an overture, a question, a slow dance of exquisite softness. Their hearts beat in the same rhythm, their breaths came in the same pause. Then they pulled apart.

Luke didn't say anything, but his eyes suddenly changed. The slow dance shifted as urgency crept into their song. His arms slipped around her and he pulled her to him. Their lips met again, but this time the touch was not as gentle. There was a hunger to their caress, a need that was echoed in her own heart.

"Gabbi. Gabbi, where are you?"

Reality intruded and Gabbi pushed away from Luke. "I'm in the living room." Her voice came out all quavery. Shape up, Gabbi, she told herself.

She stood up from the sofa just as Trisha walked in. She could feel her cheeks blaze with color, but the girl didn't seem to notice. Trisha was carrying their clothes, apparently all dry now.

"I forgot these were in my pocket," Trisha said, holding two red strips of paper. "Tickets to that fifties dance Mr. Kramer was talking about."

"Oh?" Gabbi replied. Her mind was all fuzzy, as if she'd just woken up from a deep sleep.

"They got all wet, so I can't give them back." Trisha handed Gabbi the tickets. "You and Luke can go."

"Trisha, I don't—"

"You doing anything Friday night?" Trisha asked Luke.

"No, I'm not."

Trisha turned back to Gabbi. "Take him."

What she needed to take was control here. "Honey—"

"Hey," Trisha said in a scolding tone. "He's done a lot for us. We should do something for him."

"Maybe he doesn't like dancing."

"But I do."

Chapter Four

"Hey, looking good," Trisha announced as Gabbi stepped in front of her mirror.

Trisha was sitting on Gabbi's bed, critiquing everything Gabbi put on. She almost wished the kid was an MTV fan so that she'd go off and stare at the TV and leave Gabbi alone. She needed some time by herself about now. She wanted to be alone so she could relax and let the dread in her heart show in her face.

This whole stupid dance thing was just totally dumb. It was bad enough that she had to waste a Friday evening listening to Buddy Holly and Elvis Presley tunes, but she'd also wasted the whole afternoon looking for bobby sox and saddle shoes. And what for? To spend an evening with a guy she was going to have to start avoiding, unless she wanted to court disaster.

"You feeling okay?" Trisha asked.

"Of course I am," Gabbi said. "I'm feeling just great."

She could feel Trisha's eyes on her, but fortunately the kid, for one of the few times in her young life, kept her mouth shut. Gabbi fiddled with her sweater set, borrowed from the wife of the station's manager, and her poodle skirt, on loan from one of the noontime newswomen.

The fashions of the fifties were definitely not Gabbi's style—the sweater fit just a bit too snugly. Put a bit too much emphasis on her breasts for Gabbi to feel comfortable. But then, when *didn't* society place too much emphasis on a woman's looks?

"Are you sure you're all right?"

"Sure, kid," Gabbi replied. "I'm just ginger peachy dandy."

"You looked funny."

"Thanks a lot. I'm trying to look nice for my date and you tell me I look funny."

"I'm sorry, I didn't—"

She looked so pained that Gabbi was stricken with pangs of conscience. She reached out and hugged Trisha. "I'm fine," Gabbi said. "Honest, I am."

"You do look nice," Trisha said softly.

Appearance. Their whole society was fixated on appearance. Even a thirteen-year-old girl who professed she didn't care what she wore or what she looked like.

Gabbi had been through all that—the need to look like a Barbie doll and then the depression when you realized you never would—but she would never give society that kind of power over her again. And she would do her damnedest to see that Trisha wasn't imprisoned by society's beauty standards.

"You going to be okay here all alone?" Gabbi asked.

Trisha laughed. "I know how to take care of myself." The girl's dark eyes suddenly turned old.

"You have the telephone number for the hall," Gabbi said. "Don't hesitate if you have to get ahold of me."

"If I have a real problem, you won't be able to get out here in time, anyway," Trisha said, laughing again.

"I know, but—"

"Besides, why isn't Luke picking you up? I thought that's what guys were supposed to do."

"The dance is near his house. It would be dumb for him to come out here, then drive right back to almost where he started from."

"At least you wouldn't be driving around alone late at night. Kids worry, too, you know."

"I'll remember next time." Not that there'd be a next time, but Gabbi didn't want to get into another discussion about it with Trisha. The girl had been a pain all week with her jabbering about how Gabbi needed to get out more.

"We should be in our new house by then, shouldn't we?"

"I think we should be finished with buying the house in the next few days, but I don't know when we'll move in. I want to do some remodeling first."

"We can live there during remodeling, can't we?"

Gabbi sighed. The kid wanted to get out of this neighborhood so bad.

"We'll see," she said.

After a few more last-minute instructions, Gabbi left. She really didn't mind driving alone. In fact, she rather liked it. It gave her time to think. Actually, it gave her time when she didn't have to make any small talk. Luke was a nice guy, but she knew she wasn't up to a half hour or more of being alone in a car with him.

She'd thought this whole thing out all week, as she lay in bed at night trying to sleep. She'd go to the dance, then ease back into just being friends with him. That kiss at his house last Sunday was enough of a warning. She didn't need lightning literally to strike before she took precautions. Luke was nice, but she was feeling too attracted to him. Friends, that was what they would be.

She pulled up in front of Luke's house and found him waiting outside. He came down the walk as she stopped. He was wearing blue jeans and a white T-shirt with its sleeves rolled up, having gone for the hoodlum look while she'd tried for wholesome.

"Wouldn't Adam let you wait inside?" Gabbi asked as he got into the car.

"I didn't want to." Luke shut his door and put a small box on the floor by him. "Darn kid was doing nothing but making smart-ass comments, and Matt was criticizing my choice of clothes. I went outside for the peace and quiet."

"It's nice that Adam has someone to stay with him."

"Yeah," Luke agreed. "You can never tell. A few friends might come over and they might bring some more friends, and then before anyone knows it there'll be some serious problems with fighting or alcohol or whatever."

"Thanks," Gabbi said.

"Sorry, I forgot. Trisha's alone, isn't she?"

Gabbi didn't reply. She didn't think Trisha would get into any trouble. She hoped she wouldn't.

"Besides," Luke said. "You told me that Trisha didn't have any friends at school. So no one will come visit her, anyway."

Gabbi laughed shortly. "And I used to think that her lack of friends was a problem."

Luke laughed with her, reaching over to pat her hand. His touch was electric, causing her body to respond with a sudden warmth that raced up to her face. Luckily, it was dark in the car and the drive to the church hall was short.

She definitely had to get her wayward heart under control. It wasn't as if she hadn't been out on a date since her divorce. She'd actually dated some very nice men, but hadn't felt the sort of sparks she felt when close to Luke. So what was the difference? Was there some invisible magnetism that pulled her to Luke? Maybe they couldn't even be friends.

She pulled into a parking spot and Luke got out of the car, hurrying around to open her door. She took his arm with only the slightest of misgivings, and they went into the hall. After depositing their coats in a side room, Luke handed her a small white box.

"It's a corsage," he said as she opened the box to find a white flower. "A gardenia. I was told that was the flower to give in the fifties."

The sweet scent wafted up to surround her. It had been forever since someone had brought her flowers. "It's beautiful." She felt a wetness in her eyes and quickly blinked it away.

Maybe she was being silly to think they could only be friends. Maybe Luke was the one guy whom she could trust. Maybe she should take a chance.

Luke took the flower out. "It's got a wrist strap, but the florist also gave me pins if you want to pin it on." He began fiddling with some pins.

"I'll put it on," Gabbi said quickly and took the pins from him. "I get a little nervous when someone waves pins around my chest."

"Okay." He handed her the flower.

Gabbi pinned it on her sweater and was ready to go into the dance, but Luke was watching her, a slight smile on his lips.

"You are one beautiful lady," he said. "I'm going to be the envy of every guy here."

Her delicate beginnings of a dream were suddenly crushed. She was ten again, and her father was telling her how cute she'd looked in the spelling bee. She was twenty-two and Doug was telling her she'd worn the wrong color coat to a fire she'd been reporting on. She was thirty and had been weaving silly dreams about a man she didn't really know. She shouldn't be surprised that Luke valued good looks. Didn't everybody?

What would he say if she told him her left breast was imperfect? Would he still think all the guys would envy him or would he pull back?

As if she'd ever tell him. She threw a blanket over her scattered thoughts and composed herself. They were at a dance for the evening and she would play her part.

"Thanks," she said stiffly. "Maybe we should go in."

Luke looked a little puzzled at her abruptness, but led her into the hall. She looked at the balloons and crepe-paper decorations and felt like one balloon that was way up at the ceiling. It had popped and was hanging limply from the rafter.

"There's Ken and Myrna," Luke said. "Remember them from the picnic?"

"Sure," Gabbi said, though she hadn't the faintest idea who he was talking about.

"Want to sit with them?"

"Why not?" She tried to keep her voice bright and cheerful.

Luke led her over to a table where two people who looked vaguely familiar were sitting. "Ken. Myrna. You remember Gabbi?"

"Hi. Great to see you again."

"How'd you rope this guy into coming? We haven't seen him near a dance floor for ages."

Gabbi just laughed, hoping that was answer enough.

"Hey, what red-blooded male would pass up a chance to hold such a lovely lady in his arms?" Luke asked as he pulled out a chair for Gabbi. "Can I get you something to drink?"

"A glass of wine would be nice," she said, trying not to cringe even more at his words.

He looked over at Ken and Myrna. After they shook their heads, he went off to the bar in the corner.

"It really is great to see you again," Myrna said. "And with Luke. He's such a nice guy."

"He seems like it," Gabbi said, holding firmly onto her smile.

"He's dated some since his divorce, but not all that much," Myrna went on. "And you two seem to have so much in common."

"Myrna," Ken said with a laugh. "For all you know, this is their first date."

"It is," Gabbi admitted.

"But not their last, right?"

Gabbi just smiled some more, feeling like the Cheshire cat. Thankfully, Luke returned at that moment with her wine and a glass of soda for himself. He must still be on his allergy medicine, she thought.

"Want to dance?" he asked.

"Sure." Though she wasn't certain that this slow number was the place to start. Resting in his arms for four or five minutes at a time might not be the wisest thing in her present fragile-feeling state.

Luke led her over to the dance floor and took her into his arms. It was a bittersweet time as they swayed in a slow echo of the music. She realized how much she missed being loved. Not just the actual act of love, but all the little things that went into it. The caring, the whispers, the looks and the touches.

She didn't want to be alone for the rest of her life. She wanted someone to share her hopes and her fears with. She wanted someone she could laugh with and someone who would hold her through the long, scary nights that sometimes came. But that someone would have to be so very special. And maybe he didn't even exist.

"You okay?" Luke looked down at her, his eyes serious and worried. "You seem distant."

"I'm fine," she lied. "Well, maybe a little worried about leaving Trisha alone."

He pulled her closer to him, closer to his strength and security. How she wanted to rest there, to lie close and believe that everything could be perfect. But she wouldn't. She couldn't.

Why couldn't Luke have been different? Why couldn't she have been?

The night went on endlessly. The balloons all sagged slightly as the evening wore on, as if they felt the same strain of holding a smile that had no meaning.

The note on the kitchen table read simply, "Your father called."

Gabbi sighed and kicked off her saddle shoes as she reached for the phone. It was almost midnight here in Indiana, but it wasn't that late in Arizona.

"Hi, Dad," she said when the phone was answered.

"Hey, beautiful. What's up? Hear you were on a date."

Of all the times he would call, he had to pick tonight. "It wasn't a big deal," she said. "How's Mom?"

"Just tickled pink to hear you've got a beau."

Gabbi sighed and sank onto a chair at the kitchen table. "Dad, he's just a friend."

"Sure, sure. That's why you guys are buying a house."

What did Trisha tell him? "Luke and I aren't buying a house. I'm buying one."

"You are? By yourself?" His disapproval came over the lines loud and clear. "What are you going to do with a house when Prince Charming comes along?"

"Invite him in." She knew it was futile, but she had to make the attempt. "Dad, I'm not delaying life until Prince Charming comes around. I could get to be eighty and still be waiting."

He sighed. "Princess, you're a beautiful girl. You've got to give those men out there a chance. Maybe you should slow down a bit."

She knew what that meant. She shouldn't have adopted Trisha since "most men don't want the burden of someone else's child." And now she shouldn't be buying a house because most men would want to choose their own castle.

"Dad, I've had a long week. Let's not argue."

"I wasn't—" He cut himself off. "I just wanted to let you know that we're leaving for Hawaii on Sunday. I've got the hotel number if you need to reach us."

"Okay." She copied down the number, then chatted for a few more minutes before hanging up.

As usual, talking with her father left her depressed. She knew he loved her, but he sure didn't understand her. What would putting her life on hold get her, except regrets?

Gabbi walked upstairs slowly and looked in on Trisha. The girl was sound asleep. She was going to an amusement park north of Chicago tomorrow with the youth group and her clothes were all laid out on her chair. A paper lay on top of them, and Gabbi walked over to see what it was. It was a brochure about the park, listing the major rides and attractions. Trisha had circled ones that she obviously wanted to go on, adding stars to a few of those.

She put the brochure down with a smile. Trisha had her day all planned out, determined not to miss out on anything.

Gabbi walked slowly down to her own room. In spite of her brave words to her father, she wasn't really going all out for her goals as Trisha was. Sure, she had found herself a family and was buying a house. But what about companionship? Wasn't she shying away from relationships for fear of finding Doug's clone?

Rather than be so paranoid about men who valued appearances, she should just relax and enjoy herself. She didn't have to look for "forever," but an occasional night out wouldn't be a problem.

Starting tomorrow, she would circle all the things she wanted from life to make sure she wouldn't miss any of them.

"Is that how I taught you to fold towels?" Matt asked.

Luke was doing some Saturday chores. The kind he'd been doing since he was a kid. The kind he was an expert at by now—cleaning, dusting, folding towels and all the other dippy little chores involved in keeping a home reasonably neat.

"Luke?"

"No," Luke snapped. "This isn't the way you taught me to fold towels. And, although you may find it hard to believe, I don't care."

"The corners aren't straight."

Luke closed his eyes a moment and sighed. "I'm making a statement."

"What kind of a statement?" his father asked.

Luke placed the poorly folded towel on the pile before him. "Something along the line of 'Why the hell don't you go and bug someone else?' "

"Little on the grumpy side, aren't we?"

"I don't know about you," Luke said. "But I was fine until a few minutes ago."

"How was your little outing with Gabbi last night? I fell asleep before you got in."

"Fine," Luke said. "Great. Super."

"You guys have an argument?"

"No, we didn't have an argument." Luke threw a folded towel down. "What the hell would we argue about?"

His father shrugged.

"We danced. We talked with people. We danced some more. And then she brought me home."

"She brought you home?"

"I didn't have anything but soda all night, Dad. Gabbi didn't want me to drive all the way up to her house, then back here again twice in one night. So she drove down, picked me up and then brought me back home."

"Considerate lady."

"Very."

It should have been a fine evening, but something had gone wrong. She'd seemed fine when she'd picked him up, but then she got quiet. Maybe she'd just gotten tired. Or maybe he'd just been a lousy date.

"Did you invite the lady in?" his father asked.

Luke shook his head. "She wanted to get back. Trisha was all alone at home."

Luke finished folding the towels. They just hadn't hit it off, that was all. No big deal. Hell, it wouldn't be the first time he didn't really hit it off with a lady. And it wouldn't be the last time. Still, he had more than enough lady friends. There was no need to add Gabbi to his little black book. Actually he hadn't added to it in a while, but what the hell. That was life in the big city. Or even a medium-sized city, for that matter.

"You want me to fold those towels for you?"

"Leave them alone," Luke snapped.

"You ought to work on that attitude," Matt said as he slid off his chair. "Keep up with the grumpies and you'll have to go to Borneo to get a date." He started toward the front door.

"Thank you for your advice."

"You have company," Matt said.

"Great? What are they selling?"

"I doubt if she's selling anything," Matt said. "Looks like she just wants to bring a little sunshine into your drab life."

Now what was he talking about? Luke hurried to the front door just as Matt was stepping out onto the porch.

"Hello, young lady." Matt was letting his fake Irish brogue slip into his voice. "You're looking in tip-top shape this afternoon."

Luke stepped to the door. Gabbi was there, and she had a big smile on her face, obviously swallowing the old goat's words. Hook, line and sinker.

Luke watched as his old man took Gabbi by the arm and kissed her on the cheek before he turned back to Luke.

"Keep those corners neat," he said with a wink and made his way to his panel truck.

"Your father is a very nice man," Gabbi said.

"Oh, he's super." He ignored Gabbi's quizzical look. "Trisha go on the Great America trip?"

Gabbi nodded. "She was all excited about it. She even has a couple of friends in the group."

"Sounds like things are going well."

"Really well."

He took a long look down the street. Another Saturday, another active day in the neighborhood. Luke wished his tongue could be half as active.

"So how are you?" he asked. That was rather a stupid question, since he'd just seen Gabbi last night.

"Great," Gabbi said. "The real-estate agent called this morning. Everything's finally straightened out. The owners accepted my counteroffer and we should close next week, assuming the title search goes through quickly."

"Hey, super."

"Looks like we're going to be neighbors."

"Welcome, neighbor."

She smiled at him, grinned really, and seemed her normal self. What had gone wrong last night? Maybe she'd had a hard day at work, or maybe she hated Elvis. His heart lightened, and he found himself smiling back, really smiling. He no longer cared what had been wrong last night, just as long as everything was fine now.

"Actually, I was hoping you'd be in," Gabbi said.

"You were?" He found the sunshine had grown a little brighter.

"Yeah. I bought a net for our backboard, and I was hoping someone could help me put it on."

"Sure," Luke said. "Let's go around back. I have a ladder in the toolshed."

"I can come back later if you're busy right now."

"Nah, I'm just cleaning house. Besides, Adam would be disappointed if I did it all."

"I bet."

The laughter in her eyes made him feel young and alive. As if he could run and jump and take on the world. As if he could take her in his arms and love her until the stars came out. The intensity of his sudden hunger startled him and he tried to push it back.

"I'll get the net out of my car," she said.

"Drive your car around back," he said, needing time to breathe. "I'll get the ladder."

"Okay."

Luke went back into the house. Away from her, away from those dancing eyes, he could think. Trouble was, all he could think of was her. Maybe thinking wasn't the answer. He picked up a basketball, then went to get the ladder. Gabbi was waiting by the time he stepped out into the alley.

"We'll need to test the net once it's installed," he said, indicating the ball under his arm.

"Good idea."

Her smile seemed especially potent today. Maybe he should rip the net down after she left. Then she could come back and smile some more when they put up a new one. In fact, he could keep putting them up and ripping them down. That way, he could insure that he wouldn't ever be too far from her smile.

"What do you want me to do?" Gabbi asked.

An interesting question, but he chose the safe route. "Hold the ladder." He set it on the concrete apron in front of her garage.

"Okay," she replied. "But be careful. I don't want you falling."

"Don't you like men falling for you?"

"Not quite that dramatically, thank you."

What way would she like it, then? He tried not to speculate and climbed up. It was a beautiful day, with the whole magic of spring spilling forth. The birds sang chorus after chorus, while the breeze carried the applause of nature. He hooked up the net.

"Thank you," he said as he climbed down. "You did an outstanding job of holding the ladder."

"Just my latent athletic talent coming out," she said.

"Okay." Luke folded up the ladder and put it down by the garage door. "Let's test the equipment now." He bounced the ball a few times and then shot a basket.

"Very good." Then Gabbi paused. "I presume that's what you wanted to do."

"Put the ball through the hoop. That's the name of the game." He made a jump shot and retrieved the ball. "Your turn."

Gabbi shook her head. "Uh-uh. Sports aren't my thing."

"Come on," Luke said. "Anybody who can dance as well as you has to have athletic ability."

"Maybe it's my eye-hand coordination that's off."

"Try a few," Luke said. "You know Trisha is going to badger you until you do."

"Maybe she'll give up when she sees how bad I am."

"She doesn't look like that type."

Gabbi made a face. Luke knew it was supposed to be a sour look, but it made his arms ache even more to hold her. He quickly shot another basket. "That's all there is to it." He handed her the ball.

She shot it awkwardly and it bounced high off the backboard. Luke retrieved it and demonstrated again, slowly. Gabbi tried again.

By the time several minutes had passed, they were both perspiring slightly and Gabbi looked even more beautiful. Her cheeks were glowing with color and her eyes were sparkling. Her laughter put the sunshine to shame. She even made a basket.

He wished he could hold on to this moment forever.

"How about a game of one-on-one?" he suggested.

"Jeez, I didn't know you were into humiliation," she said, making a face.

"Okay, I'll give myself a handicap. How about if I have to shoot with my eyes closed?"

She gave him a look remarkably similar to those the kids at school gave him. "Right. And I believe in the Easter Bunny, too."

Putting his hands on Gabbi's shoulders, he looked into her eyes. It was suddenly so very important that she understand just who he was.

"You can trust me," he said. "I won't break my word."

He might not be able to keep the rain from spoiling a softball game, but he could give her a chance in this basketball game.

Gabbi just wrinkled her nose at him and twisted away with the ball. Before he could react, she had taken a shot and made it.

"Hah!"

He made a face at her and retrieved the ball. "Even in the face of that blatant cheating, I will play fair."

They went back and forth for a while. She only made about one out of every four shots she took, but he didn't let his aim be too good, so the score stayed close. In fact, Gabbi was ahead.

"Are you letting me win?" she asked with sudden suspicion.

"Me?" he asked and missed his shot.

"That's not being a gentleman," she warned him. "A gentleman would respect me enough to try."

"I am." But he also wanted the game to last, to go on forever.

"Sure."

They both darted after the ball. To prove her suspicions wrong, he grabbed it, holding it over his head. She jumped, but didn't come close to the ball, so she grabbed his shirt and tugged.

"Hey, that's not fair," he cried.

"Oh, yeah?"

But as she turned slightly, their eyes met and the basketball game was forgotten. That spark in her eyes lit a flame in his heart and all he knew was a hunger for her. He dropped the ball and let his arms slip around her. She felt so good close to him.

Their lips touched, then paused and touched again. He had been lost in the desert and had just found water. He'd been starving and had just seen food. He'd been asleep deep under the earth for years and had just been given the sun. His arms tightened around her, his lips devoured hers.

There was nothing in the world but them. The birds were singing the joy in his heart. The breeze carried his happiness. The sun was taking warmth from him. His mouth moved against hers as his hands spread over her back, pressing her softness into him.

She moved away slightly and he had to let her go. It was like letting the sun go behind a cloud. She looked confused, uncertain. He was afraid she would leave.

"Want to go out for dinner?" he asked.

"Is it that late already?" She looked up and must have seen that the sun had slipped down toward the horizon.

"Getting there."

"I can't," she said as she moved away even more. "I have some stuff I have to look over for work. And I have to start planning for the move. Trisha's convinced me to move in first, then remodel."

He wanted to keep her, but, barring that, he wanted to make sure she'd come back. "Want me to get some contractors lined up?"

"If you can get the names from Matt, that would be great."

The day was winding down. A slight breeze blew in from the west and Luke knew that he had to let her go before she got chilled. She'd turned him down for dinner, but should he ask her out for some other day?

He took a deep breath. As every coach in the world said—no pain, no gain. "I have some tickets to a Silver Hawks game tomorrow night at Covelski," he said. "Would you and Trisha like to go with us?"

"If we can pick you up," she said, her smile peeking through and promising him the sun would return.

He felt hope grow in his heart. "Make it around six. We'll go to Little Naples for pizza." He wanted to take her hands in his, but shoved them into the pockets of his jeans instead. "We'll have lesson number three at the game."

A worried look flashed through her eyes. "I'm not going on the field," Gabbi protested.

"It'll be all lecture."

"Great." She looked at the ladder. "Need any help putting your stuff away?"

"Nah."

She was stepping away from him, leaving him lonely, but it wouldn't be for very long. She got into her car. After starting the motor, she opened her window. "Thanks for the help."

"Glad to do it."

And he was. Very glad. Hell, why wouldn't he be? Spending time with a good-looking woman beat folding towels any day.

"Boy," Trisha exclaimed as she flopped back in her seat. "I'm stuffed."

"That's why they call them stuffed pizzas," Adam said. "You know, on account they stuff you when you eat them."

"Hardy-har-har," Trisha said.

"Trisha," Gabbi said. "Be nice."

"I would if he didn't tell such dumb jokes."

Gabbi stared down at the dark head in front of her. She and Luke were sitting together in the municipal baseball stadium with Trisha and Adam in the row in front of them. The game had started a few minutes ago.

Adam turned to look up at Luke. "Can I go down by the railing to watch?"

"Sure," Luke replied. "Just don't start any riots."

"Funny." Adam rose from his seat. "Wanna come with?" he asked Trisha. "It's more fun down there."

Trisha looked up at Gabbi. "Yeah," she replied. "Sure."

They watched as both kids went down. Gabbi wasn't averse to being alone with Luke, if you could call it being alone when they were amid several thousand other baseball fans. She turned to smile at him. He reached over to put his arm around her shoulder.

"I noticed you didn't tell Trisha not to start any riots," he said.

Gabbi laughed. "I didn't want to give her any ideas."

"Sounds wise."

She leaned closer to him, resting her head against his shoulder. It was a perfect evening for an outing. The air was warmer than normal for early May, or maybe it was just the peace in her heart that made everything seem so right.

Ever since the night of the dance, when she'd been so upset, she'd forced herself to chill out. Why had Luke's remark so upset her? Because her heart had been hoping for more from him.

But just because he hadn't reacted perfectly, it didn't mean they couldn't have fun. Her expectations had to be realistic, that was all.

"How's your title search going?" Luke asked.

"Great. Looks like we'll close in the middle of the week."

"So when are you moving in?" he asked.

Gabbi just rolled her eyes. "We'll probably start next weekend with some stuff, though it's liable to take a couple of weeks because we still have a lot of packing to do. Trisha's offered to get suspended again so she'll have more time, but I put my foot down."

"I can round up some kids to help if you want," he suggested. "And I've got the truck. We should be able to get you in pretty quick."

Was he anxious to have her as a neighbor? The thought made her smile deep inside. "Sounds good."

There was a sharp crack of wood striking ball. The ball went high into the air, and a man, wearing a whole bunch of protective equipment, dashed out and caught it. White-suited players left the field to be replaced by blue-suited ones.

"Want to tell me what happened?" Luke asked, his arm tightening around her shoulders.

"What is this? A test?"

"Yep," Luke replied. His eyes laughed with her, pulling her into their own private little world of warmth.

"What will I get if I answer correctly?" Gabbi asked.

"You'll be allowed to proceed to the next lesson." His gaze seemed to caress her.

"Wow." She felt cared for, secure, and let the rest of the world vanish.

"Plus, the teacher might be persuaded to buy you a goody of your choice." His eyes made promises to her heart.

"Now you're talking."

"Well?"

"Okay." Gabbi took a deep breath and looked down at the field. It was easier to think once their gazes weren't locked. "The batter hit the ball. It was a foul. That means it went outside that line there. But the catcher caught it before it hit the ground so the batter is out. And, since that was the blue team's third out, the white team gets a turn at bat."

"Very good," Luke said. "And what would we have if the catcher had not caught the ball?"

"It would be a plain old foul ball."

"So?"

She looked at him, a question in her eyes. "Foul balls are strikes?"

"I'm the teacher," Luke said. "I ask the questions."

She stuck out her tongue. "Foul balls are strikes."

"So would the batter have been out then?"

"Ah." Gabbi batted her eyes at Luke, but he maintained his stern teacher look. "If he had three strikes, he would."

"How many strikes did the last batter have?"

"A few?"

Luke continued looking sternly at her.

"I sort of lost track," she admitted.

"Your treat's getting smaller," he said.

"I don't need the calories, anyway."

"That would have been the batter's third strike," Luke said. "But the batter's last strike can't come off a foul ball. So he would have remained at bat."

Gabbi shrugged. "Next time I'll bring a paper and pencil so I can take notes."

"You should, the tests are going to get tougher."

She gave him a teasing look as she leaned closer into him and yawned.

"I take it you don't want to review anything else?"

"No." Gabbi shook her head. "I've got this game down pat. The pitcher and the catcher play Keep Away with the guy in the middle, while the rest of the guys spit and scratch, unless the ball comes out their way. If the guy hits a ball he runs round the bases. The team scores every time one of their guys crosses home plate."

He nodded. "A reasonable summary."

"Reasonable." Gabbi sat up and gave him a small shove. "Hey, with all I know now, I could become a sportswriter."

"I'm more concerned with your expertise as a fan."

She was more concerned with other things—like the way his eyes could make her tremble inside, or the way his touch set her heart afire. The way he made her feel all woman and all alive.

Her eyes drifted down toward the rail where the kids had congregated. Trisha was laughing and talking. This move into the city was going to be good for both of them. Trisha would make new friends and feel at home. As for Gabbi herself, she was making new friends, too. Like Luke.

"Oh-oh," Luke murmured. "Looks like the start of a riot."

A foul ball was soaring overhead, its arc bringing it down near the railing below them, and a bunch of kids were racing there to try to catch it. Laughter and shouting muted the sounds of the game as the ball disappeared into the group. Adam popped out, holding a ball high in his hand. The kids and the crowd cheered him.

"Hey, he caught it," Gabbi said. "Is he going to have to give the ball back?"

"No," Luke replied. "Not at a pro game."

"I see," Gabbi said slowly. "So some rules change depending on who's playing."

"Yeah."

She stared thoughtfully down toward the field, though not really seeing it. Rules should change depending on the situation, she agreed, but not just in sports. Her rules for a husband dictated that he be supportive and not appearance-fixated, but to apply those rules to a boyfriend was dumb. A little relaxing of the rules was allowable because the relationship was more relaxed.

Trisha came running up the steps, interrupting Gabbi's thoughts. Adam was close behind her.

"Adam gave me the ball," Trisha said, holding it up for them to see.

"Wow!" Gabbi was impressed.

Adam just shrugged. "She said she'd stomp me if I didn't give it to her."

"I want you to have it," Trisha said, handing Gabbi the ball.

Gabbi didn't know what to say. Trisha would drive her up the wall, then turn around and do something like this that left her speechless. "Thank you." She took the ball. "That's very nice of both of you."

"I just didn't want to get stomped," Adam repeated, then the two of them ran back to the group at the railing. Gabbi looked at the ball and chuckled, feeling warm all over.

"That was very nice of Adam," she said.

"Yeah," Luke said. "But he didn't want anyone to know it."

Trisha stared at the ball for a moment, then leaned back into Luke's arm. It was indeed a perfect evening.

Chapter Five

"You don't have to come around and make dinner for us," Luke said. "Adam and I are quite capable of taking care of ourselves."

"You guys had practice today," Matt replied, "you have a big game tomorrow, and Adam said he had three tests to study for tonight."

Luke shrugged. "Yeah, this is one of those tight days. But we could have ordered in a pizza."

"The way you guys eat, you're both going to turn into a ball of mozzarella," Matt grumbled.

"We eat good, balanced meals," Luke insisted. "Just like you taught me."

"Fine."

Luke opened the oven door to check the chicken. His father was making oven-baked fried chicken, one of Adam's favorite meals. Luke knew exactly how the kid's plate would look. Two chicken legs, a big pile of potatoes with gravy flowing like lava out of a volcano and a sprinkle of vegetables.

"You really ought to get yourself a lady," his father said as he let the oven door close. "You and Adam are missing out on a lot just batching it."

"Live-in maids are hard to come by."

"You know what I mean," Matt snapped.

"You and I did fine," Luke said. "And I learned how to take care of myself. Batching ain't all bad."

"We didn't do all that fine," Matt said wearily.

Luke turned to look at him, hoping to read something from his expression, but Matt had his back turned and was busy setting the table.

"Maybe if your mother had lived, things would have been different for you," Matt said. "Maybe you would have done better in school and gone straight to college, instead of into the marines."

"I don't see how," Luke said. "It wasn't like you ignored me."

"No, but having a woman around makes a difference." Matt sank down onto one of the chairs, as if exhausted. "I don't know. They bring a softness, a love into your life, that men just don't. Your mother would have talked you out of joining the marines. I just blew up, called you a damned fool and made you more determined to do what you wanted."

The words came out soft, but they sure seemed full of hurt. Luke didn't know what to say. Obviously his father was carrying a load of guilt about the mess Luke had made of his life.

"Hey, I knew what I was doing," he said.

"You were eighteen," Matt said with a snort. "You didn't know anything."

Unfortunately, Matt was right. What eighteen-year-old knows what the consequences of his actions are?

"I think I'll go over to Gabbi's house," Luke said. "Told her I'd keep an eye on it since it's vacant."

"That's one nice lady there."

Luke wanted to agree, wanted to tell him that she'd been haunting his thoughts for the last few weeks, not how he'd tried to stay detached. But he knew enough not to give his old man ammunition.

"When are we eating?" Luke asked.

"In about thirty minutes." Matt was up again, working back at the stove.

"I'm going to shoot a few baskets as long as I'm there. Keep that new net in shape for her kid."

His father's words danced in his head as he walked across the yard, and out the back gate. Flitting in and out of his conscience, blending with memories from his past.

Luke put the ball down by the backboard and walked into Gabbi's backyard. He occupied his hands and thoughts as he checked the doors, looked into the windows and gave the front of the house a once-over. Everything appeared in order, so he retraced his steps back to the alley.

Putting his body on automatic pilot, he reached for habits that years of practice had built into him—dribbling and shooting as his mind wandered far from the little court in the alley.

There was never any question that Matt had loved Luke's mother. And Matt certainly must have missed her after she'd died, but his father had never indicated there was a problem. In fact, as the years went on, everything seemed just fine. Matt had a number of lady friends and never seemed to lack dates. Otherwise, he was free as a bird.

And what was wrong with that? The man could do what he wanted, when he wanted. Why was his father in such an uproar about Luke being alone? He talked about Adam needing a mother, but, hellfire, the kid was fifteen. Another three or so years and he would be pretty much gone, away at college and starting his own life.

Luke took the ball in and tried to slam dunk, but the ball bounced off the side of the rim. Damn! The years had taken some of the spring out of his legs. He couldn't jump as high anymore. Maybe that was what his father was concerned about. He didn't want to see Luke growing old alone.

He took a jump shot and it caromed off the side of the rim. Damn it! Everything was off today. He hustled to retrieve the ball.

But what was wrong with being alone? You didn't have a bunch of people clawing at you for their piece of you. You took care of things and you didn't bother anybody. If people were leaning on you, you were bound to let them down some time or other in your life.

If other people wanted to be rooted to the earth like a tree, then let them. He was happy to be like a bird, floating through life, free and easy.

And it wasn't as if he spent his life alone. In fact, between Adam and Matt, and his teaching and coaching duties, he was lucky to get a few minutes to himself. He didn't need any more people to support and take care of.

And there were any number of people around when he wanted just some companionship. People like Gabbi.

The thought of her laughing eyes and teasing ways made him smile. They'd had some fun together in the last week. Playing basketball, going to the baseball game. Of course, there were other ways that two adults could have fun. Ways he wouldn't mind exploring with her.

"Yo, Luke."

Startled, Luke looked toward his house. Adam was standing in the open gate.

"I was yelling my lungs out," Adam said. "Didn't you hear me?"

"Maybe you should learn to speak up."

"Matt says dinner will be ready in a few minutes."

"Thanks." Luke took one last shot. It bounced off the backboard, never coming near the rim. Clenching his jaw, he picked up the ball and came to the gate.

"Oh, well," Adam said as he stepped into the yard. "You didn't want to play in the pros, anyway."

"Shut up, kid."

Adam ignored his grumpy attitude. "It'll be nice to have that backboard in the alley. There's more room out there than on our drive."

"Yeah," Luke said, nodding.

"How come you bought a house with such a small B-ball area?"

Luke shrugged. "My wife of that time liked the house."

"She didn't play, did she?"

Luke smiled as an image of Jackie playing basketball danced before his eyes. She was a timid little flower who had hated any pushing and shoving and sweating. "No, team sports weren't her thing."

"What about your kids?"

"We didn't have any," Luke replied.

"Yeah, I know," Adam said. "But you were thinking of some, weren't you? I mean, where were they supposed to play?"

"Well, they would have been pretty small when they first came. And when they got larger, we would have moved to a bigger house."

"She live around here anymore? Your first wife, I mean."

"Nah, she lives up in Grand Rapids. Her husband is a dentist."

A dentist and four kids, the last he'd heard. He hoped she was happy now. He knew he was.

"I really appreciate your helping me," Gabbi said.

Luke looked up from the book of kitchen layouts and flashed that easy grin at her, the one that brought an aura of peace and contentment into her heart. Well, not total contentment. More like contentment mixed with longing.

"No problem."

He was back to looking through the book. Gabbi thought she should go over and look with him. After all, she had lots of ideas for her kitchen. She should just walk over to his side where she'd...put her arm around his waist and lay her head on his shoulder.

She spun away from him and forced herself to look at her kitchen area. Trying to make herself imagine a stove, refrigerator and all kinds of kitchen stuff. But all she saw was a tired old kitchen, one that had once been somebody's dream but now was forgotten. Someone had once stood here and dreamed of baking cookies at this counter. Of making a steamy soup for their family on a cold winter's night.

Gabbi turned away. "Trisha had to work on some group project for science," she said brightly. "And her group was meeting at a kid's house over on Marquette. Rather than go back home, it seemed easier to zip over here and get some ideas for my new kitchen. I wanted to get my ideas set before the big move this weekend."

"Uh-huh."

Gabbi took a peek at Luke, trying to will him to look at her. Apparently her mental telepathy wasn't all that great or he had his receiver off the hook.

Her hands slipped into the pockets of her jumper and discovered some candy kisses that Trisha had given her the other day. She took one out and threw it at Luke, hitting him on the shoulder.

"Hey." He looked down at the small candy nugget lying on the floor, then at her. "That wasn't nice."

"So?"

"Sugar and spice and everything nice," he said. "I thought that's what little girls were made of?"

"Boy." Gabbi took a candy out of her pocket, unwrapped it and popped the chocolate in her mouth. "Old as you are and you still believe in those fairy tales?"

"You're getting rather vicious." He bent and picked up the candy she'd thrown. "You get some mean pills mixed in with your vitamins this morning?"

"I don't need any pills," she replied. She just had to remember what day it was.

"That's good to know," he said, munching on his sweet.

Gabbi forced her eyes to take in the kitchen again. She'd been all excited about planning her new kitchen an hour ago, but once she and Luke had come over here, all those thoughts had just fled. She really didn't want to look at pictures or decide where she wanted her stove.

She walked over and opened the pantry door, staring sightlessly at the shelves lining the walls. She wished he'd come over and slip his arms around her. They'd already had lessons in baseball and basketball. Those were all team sports. Maybe they should move on to a type of sport played in pairs—like wrestling.

"You're not going to be able to fit an island stove in here."

She turned around. "Huh?" What was he babbling about? Why would she want an island in her house?

"A stove. Set in an island of cabinets in the center of the kitchen." He pointed to a picture in the kitchen book. "Just like you told me you wanted."

Gabbi stared vacantly at the picture. There weren't any real islands in it. No white sandy beaches. No palm trees. No blue, cloud-free skies. Nothing. "Oh, well," she said.

"You don't want an island stove anymore?"

She shrugged.

"You seem to be fading," Luke said. "Got some kind of allergic reaction to that chocolate?"

She didn't say anything.

"Anyway, you need more space."

She didn't need space. She needed less space. She wanted to be close to him. She didn't want any space at all.

"It's seven years today since my divorce," she said suddenly.

He looked up, his eyes softening. "It still hurts?"

She shrugged and felt silly for mentioning it. "No, not really. I mean, it's not like I still love Doug or anything. It's just..." She let her words drift off.

He nodded. "It's just that you sometimes have trouble with the 'what ifs.'"

"Yeah." She rubbed at a stain on the floor with her foot. "We were too young when we got married. Maybe not in years, but in maturity."

"Marriage isn't the best place to grow up," he said softly.

"No." She looked up, her eyes suddenly getting teary for no reason at all. "This is crazy," she said with a shaky laugh as she wiped at her eyes. "It's just that being here, and planning to redo this kitchen, made me think how this old room was like an abandoned marriage. Once surrounded by all sorts of hopes and dreams, and now it's somebody else's junk to clean up."

"Hey." Suddenly he was at her side, pulling her into his arms.

His embrace was just as safe a haven as she thought it would be. She closed her eyes for a moment and leaned against his chest, taking refuge from her runaway emotions. She refused to let herself feel silly or weak or anything but his strength. His heart beat right next to hers, and she forced her breathing to match its steady rhythm.

"I guess the death of dreams is the worst part of divorce," he said, his voice quiet. "You can adjust to seeing the other person move on, and even stop loving them, but it hurts to think of how far you fell from your expectations."

"We used to talk about the house we wanted, and here I am buying one alone. And I'm a single parent."

"Jackie and I bought the house together, but I never put up the picket fence."

"It's not that I even want the same things anymore."

"It wasn't until last year that I finally put sod over her garden."

"I've grown up. I like making my own decisions and not worrying what his reaction would be."

"I guess we were never really honest with each other," he said, with a sigh. "We both had such different ideas of what marriage would be."

Gabbi looked up at him. "Same with Doug and me."

"Why can't people really talk?" he asked, though he didn't seem to expect an answer. "If we'd just been open and honest with each other to begin with, all sorts of heartache could have been avoided."

"Sometimes you don't know yourself well enough to be really honest," she said. She doubted Doug had. He had never been faced with something like cancer before.

"And sometimes you don't want to."

He looked down into her face with a gentle smile. She met his gaze straight on. She'd needed to be held to ease the ache in her heart, but now she wanted more.

Raising up slightly on tiptoe, she reached for his lips and found them. It was the meeting of a spring shower and an opening crocus. The whisper of the breeze on the budding leaves of a maple tree. It was the sun warming a bird into song.

There was no urgency, no impatience. No raging passion and no driving hunger. It was healing and calm. Soothing and rejuvenating. She felt stronger in his arms, more able to fight the battles of the day and win. She slowly moved away, wiping the last traces of tears from her cheeks.

"So, let's get back to that kitchen, shall we?" she said.

"Okay." He seemed to take a deep breath and then looked around, as if to orient himself again. "I was thinking, you could build an addition to the house and put your eating area there."

"I guess."

"It could be one of those air rooms. You know, those rooms that are completely glass-enclosed. Then you could put in more landscaping in the backyard."

Honesty. That's what he'd said had been lacking in his marriage. Thinking on it, it had been missing in hers, too. She'd been so eager to please that she hadn't really examined who she was and what she'd needed from a relationship.

"Maybe you'd prefer to discuss this some other time."

Panic suddenly seized her heart. She hadn't been paying attention. "I was just thinking about—" she said quickly. "It's a great idea. I like it. How much would it cost?"

"Let's take some measurements. The more detail you give, the more accurate the quote."

He moved around the tiny kitchen, calling out measurements to her to write down; then he pulled over the kitchen book and did some sort of figuring on a scrap of paper.

She lifted herself up on the counter and watched. He was such a nice guy, an understanding guy. She had the feeling there could be much more between them.

But when and how did you tell someone you'd had breast cancer?

She slid back down the counter and pulled over the daily newspaper she'd brought along. It was the Metro section. Articles about some residents' fight against train whistles in town, about an ongoing burglary trial and about last night's school board meeting. And tucked in the corner was a notice of a meeting of a support group—for breast cancer patients.

She shoved the paper away, goose bumps on her arms. Jeez, that was eerie. Ask a question in her mind and find the answer the next moment in the newspaper.

But Luke was still absorbed in his work, and her fingers had a mind of their own. They pulled the paper back. The meeting was Friday night at Memorial Hospital.

She would think about it.

* * *

"Go, go, go," Trisha had said. She would finish packing the stuff in her room, she promised.

So Gabbi went, went, went. But she wasn't so sure she wouldn't have been better off at home bundling up her books.

There were about a dozen women in the hospital's meeting room when she got there, some sitting in the circle of chairs, some getting coffee or soda from the table along one wall. Two women had brightly colored scarves wrapped turban-style around their heads, another wore an obvious wig. Chemotherapy. A seated woman still looked in shock, another moved stiffly, as if her surgery had been extensive and recent.

Gabbi thought about fleeing. She didn't belong here. She wasn't sick or afraid or in shock over the diagnosis. She could spend a couple of hours at the library rather than go right home and face Trisha.

Honesty. Seems she was willing to miss that boat a number of times.

She took a deep breath and a step further into the room. A woman in pink smiled at her. Gabbi came further into the room and noticed that most of the women actually looked more or less like her, though most of them were older.

A gray-haired woman in a blue shirtwaist came over. "I'm Andi LaVelle," she said, hand extended. "I'm a social worker with the hospital's outpatient oncology unit."

"Gabriella Monroe." She shook the woman's hand.

"This your first time with us? I don't remember seeing you here before."

"Yeah." Gabbi squirmed mentally. "I saw the notice in the paper and decided to come."

"Well, we're certainly glad to have you. Would you like some coffee before we start? Soft drink? Tea?"

"No, thank you."

As if she had Gabbi on an invisible leash, they moved over to the circle of chairs and took places. The other women drifted over also. Gabbi had hoped to remain anonymous, to sort of lurk in the background, but the circle format prevented that. Maybe they would just ignore her.

"Welcome ladies," Andi said as the group quieted. "Shall we join hands and begin?"

Gabbi felt a little self-conscious, but took the hands of the women on either side of her. The others were bowing their heads, so she followed suit.

"Let's take a moment to reflect on the blessings we have," Andi said. "Let's be grateful for our loved ones and our friends. For the care of the medical community and the sacrifices made by those who went before us. Let's especially remember Julie, who's scheduled for a needle biopsy tomorrow, and Ellen, who's back in the hospital."

Gabbi had no idea who these people were, but obviously most of the other women did. She felt their collective pain and realized how much some of these women depended on this group.

"Well," Andi said brightly as everyone dropped hands. "We've got some new faces here tonight. Would you like to tell us a little about yourselves?"

So much for anonymity. But Andi was looking at someone else, so Gabbi got a moment's reprieve.

"My name is Marcia Kuzlik and I'm fifty-five," another woman said. "I'm married with two grown daughters and had a partial mastectomy last month."

"Welcome, Marcia," Andi said, and the others echoed her.

Then all eyes turned to Gabbi. She swallowed hard. "I'm Gabriella Monroe and I'm thirty. I had a lumpectomy seven years ago."

"Seven years!"

"Wow!"

The women burst into a round of applause, making Gabbi feel strange and uneasy.

"A survivor!"

They looked at her with new eyes, with hope and pride, as if she had accomplished something precious. As she guessed she had.

"How big was your tumor?"

"Did you find it or was it through a mammogram?"

"It was about .3 cm, and I felt it." Gabbi wished they'd move on. She didn't mind talking about her cancer, but she never had before, not really, and old habits died hard.

"You're so lucky."

"More than lucky. You've got a guardian angel watching over you."

"You must live right."

"It wasn't all so perfect," Gabbi felt bound to tell them, but she couldn't mention Doug.

The woman next to her patted her hand. "We're not putting down all you went through, honey. It's just that you are what we wish we could be. Small tumor, found early and past that five-year mark."

"Let's move on," Andi said. "Before Gabbi runs away. I think Barb has something to share with us."

A youngish woman in a loose-fitting suit coat jumped to her feet. The grin on her face seemed to go coast to coast. "Show and Tell, ladies." She whipped open her coat and thrust her chest forward. "Which is me and which is Memorex?"

"Ooo." A ripple went around the room, accompanied by some applause and laughter.

"You got your implant!"

"Looks great!"

"It was so neat," Barb said, sinking back into her chair. "I wore this really low-cut dress last night, and Greg took me out to dinner. Everywhere we went I was turning heads. I felt so...so..."

"Whole," someone suggested.

Barb nodded. "It was wonderful! I was me again."

The other women nodded, as if they understood. Gabbi wasn't sure she quite did, but then she hadn't had such mutilating surgery. Doug was the one who had felt different, who had thought she wasn't the same person anymore.

"Anybody else with news?" Andi asked.

The woman in pink waved her hand. "I passed my first-year exam."

"Great!"

"Congratulations!" The words were almost lost in the applause.

One of the turbaned women spoke up. "I have some fuzz growing back in."

"Hurrah!"

"I took a shower in the open at the health club," someone else announced.

Another round of applause and murmurs of encouragement.

Marcia raised her hand timidly. "I start chemo tomorrow morning," she said.

The joy in the group changed to sympathy, so strong Gabbi could almost touch it.

"Would you like one of us there with you?" Andi asked.

"No, no," Marcia said quickly. "Joe—my husband—will be there. I'll be fine."

The turbaned woman with fuzz smiled over at her. "What time do you start? I've got a doctor's appointment tomorrow, and I could come in early. Sit with your husband, maybe. Help him to know what to expect and how to help you get through it."

"And to let him know your hair'll grow back," someone added.

Even Marcia smiled at that, though Gabbi thought her eyes looked watery. "That would be nice. Joe's just so worried...." She couldn't go on.

Andi passed a box of tissues down. "We've all been there, believe me," she said gently, then shifted gears to let Marcia regain her control. "Anything else? Anybody have anything they want to relate? Any questions?"

Gabbi said little, just watched and listened as the others talked about the difficulty of undressing in health-club locker rooms. About implants versus prostheses. About living with the fear of a recurrence. She was struck by how fears were accepted so easily and how everyone was willing to lend their strength when someone else felt weak.

She'd never attended a support group after her surgery. What with the divorce and deciding to look for work elsewhere, she'd treated her surgery the way someone might treat getting a wisdom tooth pulled. Something that had to be done, then not thought of again. Except it was obvious that she hadn't really *not* thought of it. It had been festering underneath the surface for years now, nagging at her at odd moments.

"Sometimes I think Wally doesn't find me attractive anymore," someone said.

Gabbi sat up a little taller.

"What gives you that idea?" Andi asked.

The woman shrugged. "He doesn't touch my breast when we make love. He used to, but he doesn't anymore."

"Maybe he thinks it's still painful."

"Stan treated me like I would break at the slightest touch for a while," someone else said in support. "He got over it."

"Have you asked Wally about it?" Andi asked.

The woman shook her head. "When I try, he assures me everything's fine. That he still loves me."

"Maybe he needs more time."

"Cancer rocks both people in a relationship, more if there are kids involved," Andi pointed out. "But if your relationship was strong before the cancer, it'll just get stronger. If you had problems before, the cancer just magnifies them."

Gabbi looked back into the past. Andi was right. A strong relationship would have survived the cancer. It wasn't the disease that killed the marriage, it was basic problems between her and Doug that would have surfaced eventually, anyway.

The group was starting to wind down. It was Gabbi's time to ask about telling a man you had had cancer, but she couldn't get the words out. Maybe it was all right, though. Maybe she'd had her answer in Andi's words. If the relationship is strong, it'll survive cancer.

If her relationship with Luke grew to be strong, telling him the truth wouldn't hurt. All she had to do was wait and see.

Chapter Six

Gabbi closed up the corrugated cardboard box and stood up. "Okay, fellas," she said. "This one can go."

One of Luke's recruits hoisted the box to his shoulder and carried it out of the kitchen. Gabbi looked around the room. It was done. All her cabinet doors stood open so she knew they'd been emptied. The house echoed with emptiness. Her footsteps sounded loud as she walked into the dining room.

"How're we doing?" she asked.

Luke looked up from the floor where he was dismantling the dining room table. "Almost done."

He removed the last leg and handed it to Adam, who wrapped the legs in a blanket. Trisha taped a plastic bag with the hardware to the bottom of the table as Luke got to his feet, wiping his hands on his jeans.

"I think that'll fill up this load," he said. Two of his recruits picked up the table and carried it out.

"We've only got a couple of boxes left," Trisha said.

"We'll put them in the car," Luke said. "Why don't you guys go get them?"

As Trisha and Adam raced off to get the boxes, Gabbi walked back into the kitchen. She closed each of the cabinet doors and checked the windows to make sure they were locked. She stopped at the sliding glass doors and stared out at the backyard.

Luke was really helping out today. He'd gotten some boys from the football team, besides himself and Adam. Then he'd taken over, supervising the loading and unloading of the truck. He was turning out to be a good friend. And she'd like him to be more.

She folded her arms across her chest and could mentally feel her scar. How would she tell him? And when she did, would it make a difference?

A cardinal hopped from a branch onto the patio, poking its beak between the bricks, looking for a snack. She was glad the weather was warm. The birds she'd fed all winter at her bird feeder shouldn't have a hard time fending for themselves.

"Regrets?"

She turned to find Luke in the doorway. His eyes seemed watchful, as if he could read into her heart, and she turned back to the outdoor scene. "No, not really. I'm just saying goodbye to my birds."

He came to join her at the door. "Give them your new address," he said. "Maybe they'll come visit you."

She just laughed and turned, finding herself in his arms. It was a great place to be, the right place to be, and she lifted her lips to his for a soft kiss. Her heart shouted out its excitement, suggesting all sorts of delights.

"Wooeee!" Trisha called out. "What have we got here?"

Gabbi jumped from Luke's arms to find both Trisha and Adam in the kitchen doorway, grinning at them. Gabbi's cheeks flamed.

"You guys gonna be here long?" Trisha went on. "Want I should drive the car down to the house and come back for you later?"

"You don't know how to drive, young lady," Gabbi said, grabbing up her purse from the counter. "You're too young."

Trisha's grin turned hard. "I'm too young to have my license, but what does that have to do with knowing how to drive?"

Caught again, Gabbi thought. Her suburban, middle-class upbringing was constantly leaving her open to attack.

But Adam was more concerned with other things. "Hey, Luke!" he protested in an almost whiny voice. "She's a year younger than me. How come she can drive and I can't?"

Luke exchanged glances with Gabbi that clearly asked if this was one of the magic moments in raising a child. Gabbi tried not to laugh. He just went over, turned Adam with a hand on the boy's shoulder and started both kids toward the front door.

"If you'd been listening," Luke said, "you would have heard that knowing how to drive and being allowed to are two different things."

Chuckling quietly, Gabbi followed them out to the front yard. The sun seemed especially bright, and she squinted. One of the boys Luke had brought was going to drive the truck to Gabbi's new house. Trisha and Adam piled in with him, leaving the other boys to ride back in one of their cars.

"Guess that just leaves us in here," Luke said, as he nodded toward Gabbi's car. The back seat was piled with boxes.

"Guess so." She stood and watched as the truck pulled slowly away. It disappeared around a bend in the street, leaving just the Saturday sounds of the neighborhood. She turned back to Luke. "I really appreciate your help today. It would have taken Trisha and I forever to pack up even the small things and then move them. We'd have had to hire somebody to move the larger stuff."

"Hey, no problem." He seemed uncomfortable with her gratitude. "We just want you moved in so we can use your basketball net."

"You could be using it now," she said.

He grinned, a teasing little-boy smile that did funny things to her heart. "Actually, we have, but I thought it sounded better to pretend we were waiting for you."

"Oh, did you?" She picked a dandelion and threw it at him. "Take that, you nasty bully."

"Hey." He put his hands over his head as if to protect himself and ran toward her car.

She ran after him, picking up the fallen dandelion on the way and throwing it again. She was ready to repeat the action when he stopped suddenly and turned. She ran right into his arms.

"Well, hello there," he said softly.

Her heart felt like purring, but she only let the thought dance briefly through her mind. There were more important things to think about, like his lips coming down on hers. Like the rush of fever that coursed through her at his touch. Like the wonderful way his body fitted against hers.

She was in heaven in his arms. Everything was perfect. There were no worries, no fears. She could fly to the stars or leap across rivers. She wanted to laugh and sing and shout. She wanted to nestle further into his embrace and dally there forever.

His lips moved against hers, rough and demanding, as if drawing strength from her. As if his hunger could only be satiated by the magic potion of her breath. Her heart sped and her breath quickened as she felt an answering hunger grow in her soul. But then the magic passed as Luke slowly let go of her.

"We'd better get going," he said. "I don't want to leave all those kids alone for too long."

She nodded and tried to catch her breath as she walked around to the driver's side. "I thought you said those kids were trustworthy."

"I trust them unconditionally." They got into the car at the same time. "Just as long as I can see them."

"Boy," Gabbi said, grinning at him. "I didn't know you were such a distrusting person."

He looked at her, his gaze penetrating. "The question is, do you really know me?" he asked softly.

Did anyone know anyone else? she wondered as she started the car. And how much did you need to know about someone before you knew you wanted to know them better, much better. She bit back a grin at her convoluted thought and started the car.

She kept her eyes on the road as she pulled out of the drive—not on Luke's hand resting on his knee so close to hers. And she concentrated on following the winding streets out the subdivision exit—not on the sound of his breathing. She saw a few people outside, but nobody waved. Even after living here since the beginning of summer, there was nobody she'd call a close friend.

She already had one at her new house.

"Are you going to miss this place?" Luke asked.

"No." Gabbi shook her head. "It was just a place to eat and sleep. With work and Trisha, I never really had time to become a part of the community."

She took one last look at the large houses, all turned to face the street, two- and three-car garages stretching out to the side. It looked like so many other subdivisions she'd lived in. Nothing bad but nothing special, either. Gabbi could have been dropped in Kansas or California, and, except for the weather, she would have noticed no difference.

"I've moved around so much," she said. "When I was a kid, we moved because of my father. Then when I graduated from college, I moved to follow the jobs."

"Yeah," Luke said. "You media people seem to be nomads."

Her heart skipped a beat, and Gabbi stole a sideways glance at Luke. His face seemed calm as he looked out the window. She wasn't sure whether that was a judgmental statement or whether he was just stating a fact as he saw it. It was hard to tell with Luke. He always presented such a placid surface to the world.

"Some of us are." She looked at him again. No reaction. "But then, a lot of us aren't. Some people stay in the same market for twenty years or more."

He just nodded.

"I've had enough moving around to last me a while. I'm staying put for a long time."

"That's good."

Was he saying that because he believed people moved around too much? Or was he making more of a personal statement? Did he want her to stay put? It was somehow important that he did.

"For one thing," Gabbi said, "I think Trisha needs the stability."

He shrugged. "Kids seem to adapt pretty well."

Gabbi remembered back to her own teen years. She'd attended two different junior high schools and three different senior high schools. In some ways, the moving helped her grow and mature. Toughened her up and made her self-reliant. But now as she looked back on things, she could see something missing. She'd never had any really close friends. The idea tried to push depression on her.

"This is a really great day." Gabbi tried to make the gloom go away. "It's like the start of a new life for us."

"I guess it is."

"Trisha's excited about moving, and so am I."

"Things will be different," Luke said.

"Things will be better," she replied. "Trisha will be closer to her friends, and I'll be closer to work."

He nodded.

"Next week, the adoption will be finalized and then we'll really be set." She flashed a smile in his direction. "A year ago I wouldn't have even thought I'd be such a settled-down old lady with a child and a mortgage."

"Well, maybe settled-down, but you sure don't look old."

"I don't feel old, either. How about a mature young lady?"

"Sounds good," he said on a laugh.

Being alone with him in the close confines of the car was almost like sharing a secret. She could reach out and brush his leg. She could take his hand, if she wanted. She felt she could almost read his thoughts in the tone of his laughter or the pause of his voice. She was half sorry when they turned down her street.

The truck had already arrived, and the boys, along with Trisha, were out in the street passing a football.

"Well," Luke muttered as she stopped at the curb. "At least they're not tossing any of your table lamps around."

"Boy," Gabbi exclaimed. "Why do you always expect the worst from kids?"

"I work with them every day." He paused as she turned off the ignition and set the parking brake. "And if you expect the worst, you will never be disappointed. Most of the time you're pleasantly surprised but never let down."

What a philosophy, she thought, the gloom creeping back. Is that what he expected from their relationship—the worst? Or did he expect anything at all?

Maybe in his mind they didn't even have a relationship budding. Maybe they were just neighbors, with no prospect of being anything more. The idea was almost enough to wash the sunshine from the day.

"Needs more oregano," one of the boys said around a mouthful of spaghetti.

"You want oregano on everything," another said.

Gabbi smiled and said nothing. She had made a pot of spaghetti sauce last night, so all she'd had to do after the move was heat it up, cook some pasta and serve it along with a bucket of fruit salad. It was incentive for them to set the dining room table up.

"I mean, he even puts the stuff on Becky Smithe's ears."

That remark brought loud guffaws, whoops and table-pounding from the other three boys. Gabbi was learning that louder meant better for teenager boys. Although Trisha wasn't too far behind.

"That's enough, gentlemen." The noise subsided down to a mild roar. "More than enough," Luke added.

This took the racket down to some mild chuckles. It was hard for Gabbi to believe how much control Luke had over the kids with his soft voice. She'd never seen him yell, but neither had she seen him need to. He got more than obedience: he got respect from the kids.

"I hear St. Joe is still interviewing for a head football coach," one of the boys said.

"Why don't you apply, Mr. B.?"

"Yeah, you're the greatest."

Gabbi sensed something in the air and glanced over at Luke. He had definitely tensed up.

"I'd have to give up one of the other sports," he said to the boys. "And I don't want to do that."

"No, you wouldn't," one of the boys argued.

"You can be a head coach in football and an assistant in basketball and baseball."

"Yeah, just like you are—"

"No." Luke stood up and began gathering the dishes. "I really can't."

Gabbi could see that the boys weren't satisfied, but she could also tell the subject was closed. Why wouldn't he want to be a head coach? He was so good with the kids.

"Come on, guys," Luke said sharply. "Let's clean up. It's time for you all to get home. I don't want your parents to think I've kidnapped you." He took his dishes into the kitchen.

"Yeah," Trisha said. "We don't want them to get their hopes up."

This elicited another round of laughter, but it was more subdued, registering in the semi-loud range on the Richter scale. Gabbi gave Trisha a sharp look, which the girl avoided. The boys stood and began stacking the paper plates.

"This is one weekend I wouldn't mind getting kidnapped," a boy grumped. "Mother's Day is such a bore."

Gabbi glanced at Trisha, but the girl didn't seem to be listening. She was mopping up the last of her spaghetti sauce from her plate with a piece of bread. Maybe Mother's Day without a mother had become commonplace. Gabbi was realistic enough to know it would take time for the girl to think of her as her mother. Luke brought in a plastic garbage bag and gave it to Adam, then took the serving dishes back into the kitchen.

"Yeah, my dad said I gotta make breakfast for my mother tomorrow." Another boy snickered. "Think I'll make cereal and milk."

Another of the kids was getting the bread from the table. "I gotta stay home all day."

Trisha took her plate around to the other side of the table. "Hey, Stretch," she said to Adam. "You in charge of plates?"

Adam just took it from her, dumped the silverware onto a tray and the paper plate into the trash bag. Trisha eyed him for a minute before turning away.

"I was gonna get my mom a portable disc player," one kid said.

"Really?" Trisha said, obviously impressed. Even Adam looked up. "That's pretty nice."

The kid laughed. "Yeah. Especially since mine broke."

The boys all roared, but Trisha just frowned. She gave a sideways glance toward Adam, but kept her glare intact.

"Boys," Gabbi said, but she was ignored.

"Think I'll get mine a bomber jacket," another of the boys said.

"I'll get mine a Porsche."

Trisha's frown was deepening by the second. She took a step closer to Adam, looking almost protective of the tall, thin boy, and had a certain stillness to her. Gabbi felt definite stirrings of concern. "Honey, how about if you take that garbage bag outside?" she suggested.

"Oops! Hey, there's another idea," another of the boys joked and pretended to reach for the bag.

But Trisha beat the kid to it. She grabbed it up, but then to Gabbi's horror, swung it around and walloped the smirking boy with it. The bag burst and paper plates, napkins and paper cups spilled out onto the floor.

"Hey!" the kid cried.

"You jerk-butt!" Trisha yelled, her anger in high gear. "You think you're so funny. I hope your mother gets you garbage for your birthday!"

Both Luke and Gabbi had moved at the same time, getting in between the two kids.

"Cool it, Mike," Luke said to the boy.

"That's enough, Trisha," Gabbi said.

"No, it's not! They'd be even dumber than they are now if their moms hadn't been taking care of them, and all they do is make stupid jokes."

"Trisha!"

"Man, that girl is nuts," the walloped boy said, rubbing the back of his head. "She's a mental case."

"I said to cool it." Luke's voice was tough. His look took in all the boys. "Not another word."

"She's right!"

They all turned to find Adam at Trisha's side. "You guys are jerks." He turned to Trisha. "Come on, squirt. Let's shoot some hoops." He grabbed Trisha's arm and practically dragged her from the room.

Gabbi felt stunned at Adam's defense. Luke seemed to share her speechlessness as he stared after the kids. The slamming of the screen door seemed to awaken him, though, and he frowned at the mess on the floor.

"Clean it up, gentlemen," he said.

"Us?"

"Hey, we didn't do it!"

"Make the nutcase clean it up!"

Luke leveled a look at them that Gabbi thought would have made guys a lot tougher and bigger than these obey him. "You were asinine and insensitive," he said. "Not to mention downright rude. Maybe you ought to think twice before you make fun of something others don't have."

"Don't have?" The walloped kid looked puzzled, then light dawned. "Oh."

"We didn't know." The others had the grace to look sheepish, and they all joined in to pick up the mess. Luke said nothing, but continued his fierce glare.

Gabbi slipped by him and went out back. She could hear the kids before she saw them.

"Ha, you couldn't hit the broad side of a barn," Trisha taunted.

Some scurrying noises were accompanied by a soft swishing sound. "Oh, no?" Adam sounded pleased with himself.

"Lucky shot."

Gabbi let herself out the gate, and the two kids stopped playing to look at her. "You guys okay?" she asked.

"Sure," Trisha said. "We're fine. Just hatched a little plot to get out of the clean-up. Right, Stretch?"

"Yeah, right."

Adam tried to look as self-assured as Trisha and came close. But he looked haunted, with his lips held stiffly and his gaze darting everywhere but at her.

Gabbi decided to play along. "Well, it worked. Everything's probably done about now."

"We were thinking of going to play ball at the park," Trisha said. "That okay with you?"

"Sure," Gabbi said. "Just be home before dark."

Trisha nodded toward the park and seemed to pull Adam along with her. "Come on, Stretch. We'll get a real game going." She glanced at Gabbi as they ran past. "See ya."

Gabbi watched until they disappeared around the end of the alley; then she turned back into the yard. Luke was coming out of the house.

"They all right?"

She nodded. "They went to the park. I think they needed some more space."

"Probably best." He slipped his arm around her shoulders as they walked back to the house. "That was quite a surprise. I heard the boys joking, and I'm afraid I didn't think much of it. Kids are always horsing around like that. They really didn't mean anything by it. They were just showing how grown up they were, showing they don't need their mothers anymore." He shook his head, and she could feel his anger at himself. "I should have been quicker to stop it."

"Maybe it was better you didn't," Gabbi said. "Hopefully the boys learned a lesson, and Adam actually spoke up."

"Yeah, but—"

"It's not like Mother's Day wouldn't have been on their minds, anyway. This way, they both got something out of their system."

He shrugged. "I guess, growing up without a mother, I never gave the day much thought."

She stopped on the back steps. "I doubt that," she said softly. "Not when you probably made cards and presents in school and ads everywhere reminded you of what you didn't have. You just turned off those feelings as you got older and convinced yourself it was just another day." Maybe some of those feelings were still turned off.

He looked away from her into some distant past. When he came back, his smile was strained. "Maybe you're right. I don't know." He forced more joy into his smile. "Anyway, there are four gentlemen inside who would like to apologize."

* * *

Gabbi sat down with a sigh and leaned back with her elbows on the wooden step behind her. "What a day," she said.

Luke turned to look at her. Her jeans were rolled up slightly and her short-sleeved shirt fit just right. She'd kicked her shoes off and had her legs stretched out before her. She was a masterpiece he could gaze at for hours without getting his fill of her.

"I've got the bare essentials unpacked," she said, keeping her eyes closed. "And everything else can wait a couple of years."

He and Gabbi were left alone in the softness that followed the hectic day of moving and Trisha's emotional outburst. "If a box can wait that long, just throw the damn thing out. You obviously don't need what's in it."

"Words to move by. You should have told me that before I packed. My trash pile would have been a lot bigger."

She looked up and smiled at him, then closed her eyes again. Luke was happy to see the pleasant remains of the smile on her lips. Bringing joy to those luscious lips and a sparkle to those eyes made him feel all-powerful. She was a dangerously heady experience. He looked away and let the shadow of that evening fall back over him.

"I really let things get out of hand there earlier," he said.

She looked at him, a smile dancing on her lips. "I see. You are so powerful that you can actually control teenage boys. I'm impressed. You must be some sort of god or folk hero, at least."

He had to laugh. "All right, so I'm not quite in those categories yet. But I should have had a tighter rein on them."

"They'll all survive. We just have to learn to listen better."

He knew she was right, but how did you listen when there were no words?

He looked around the yard and listened to the evening. Sparrows chattered as they bustled about, looking for a place to spend the night, and he could hear the belllike call of a male cardinal. The breeze rustled the leaves, sending wondrous scents of forsythia and lilacs through the air.

With his heart, that was how he had to listen. He had to learn to follow his feelings, not wait until someone told him point-blank. Listen to the sounds of the heart and the soul, not the words. Trouble was, he was okay at words, but totally out of it with feelings. He feared they'd lead him astray. Yet when had words been his friend?

"I'm going to have a glass of wine," Gabbi said, sitting up. "Can I get you some?"

Luke sat there and stared at her. He looked at her full lips and sparkling eyes. He smelled the sweet air of a reborn earth. It was all like a narcotic. He remembered how good a glass of wine tasted. He remembered how just one little glass could heighten your senses, multiply your pleasures. Just one glass. That's all he'd have to have. One teeny, tiny little glass and absolutely no more.

Fortunately, he remembered that there never was just one little glass. There was no bottom to the bottle just as there was no bottom to the pit that would await him.

"No, thanks," he said softly.

"Oh, I'm sorry. I forgot about your allergies." She stood up and mussed his hair before she went into her kitchen.

The light slap of her feet on the wood porch slowly faded away behind him, but Luke's body remained poised. Waiting for Gabbi's return, yearning for her return. Feelings. Go with your feelings.

He sighed and rubbed his eyes with both hands. If he went with his feelings, Gabbi might call the cops. But it wasn't just his body that was drawn to her. It was all of him. She was nice, funny, intelligent. The whole nine yards. Hell, more like twelve yards, fifteen, even. She was just one super lady.

He liked talking to her, walking with her. He liked just plain sitting with her and staring out into the evening as they were doing now. Of course, if he liked her all that much he should listen to his feelings.

The padding feet returned to his side.

"Hi, handsome," she said as she sat down. "Miss me?"

"Yes, I did," he replied, without looking at her.

"What did you say?"

"I said, 'Yes, I did miss you.'"

An impish grin flashed at him across the top of her glass. "That's what I thought you said."

He looked into those merry eyes. Luke knew that he should talk to Gabbi, tell her things. One of his problems was a reluctance to express himself. Jackie had told him that often enough, that she'd rarely had any idea what he was thinking. Maybe expressing himself was hard, but honesty shouldn't be.

"I don't really have any allergies."

Gabbi's smile slipped to halfway. Her brow wrinkled slightly. "Oh?"

Luke cleared his throat and checked out the far southwest corner of Gabbi's yard. "I'm an alcoholic."

The earth paused, and everything turned dead quiet. Luke didn't hear Gabbi leave, but he thought he felt her slipping away. Panic fluttered in his heart and he quickly turned to face her.

"I'm sorry," she said.

Luke shrugged in confusion. "About what?"

"I didn't know."

"That's okay. I have it under control."

"I shouldn't have brought this glass of wine out."

"It's no problem," he told her.

"But I didn't know."

"Gabbi."

She looked so worried that he felt compelled to put an arm around her shoulder and pull her close. It brought other ideas to his head. Ideas that would require action, slow and deliciously sweet. He put those thoughts from him. This was not the time to get distracted.

"I've lived with it a long time," he said. "I know how to handle it."

"I'm so sorry." She put her glass on the porch as far away from them as she could reach. "But I didn't know."

"Hey." He tilted her head up and placed a light kiss on her lips. "Number one, you didn't know because I didn't tell you, right?"

Her eyes seemed clouded, and he fought a desperation to dispel those shadows.

"Number two, I am not at all bothered to see someone else enjoy a beer or a glass of wine. I am not driven insane by the smell. It's just like hating apricots and sitting at a table with someone eating apricot pie."

"Is it that easy?" she asked.

"Sure." It wasn't that easy, but what else could he tell her? Honesty was certainly a good policy, but one didn't want to be a fanatic about it. "I haven't had a drink in years."

Gabbi didn't go away but she stayed silent, looking out over her yard. She also did not pick up her glass of wine. He hated to burst her little pleasure like that.

"When I was in high school," Luke said, "beer was our drug of choice. Someone could always get some, then we would drive out to a deserted area and drink."

"That sounds like the way things went when I was in high school." Gabbi paused. "Although a number of the kids were into other drugs."

"Yeah, we had that, too," Luke replied. "But not my group."

She took his hand, giving him hope that she hadn't drifted so far away, after all.

"I wasn't all that interested in academics, so after I graduated from high school I enlisted in the marines," he went on. "My father just about killed me. I had a football scholarship to Ball State."

"You shouldn't force things if you're not ready."

Luke laughed. "I think theoretically Matt would agree with you. But at the time, he had trouble being cool and understanding. Especially since enlisting in the marines then practically guaranteed that I'd be sent to Vietnam."

"And were you?"

"Yes." His voice was more clipped and final than he had wanted it to be, but there were some things he didn't talk about. Not even to someone who seemed so warm and open like Gabbi. He couldn't expect her to understand. She'd grown up in a world of order and fairness, of trust and honor. Everyone in her safe little world played by the rules. Those who didn't were punished.

She would never understand his torment. The pain of sending friends out on patrol and having them die. Of carrying the burden of their deaths with you forever. Of seeing their faces in your dreams until you were afraid to close your eyes and the only refuge was found in the bottom of a bottle.

Even Ron had never really understood, though he'd never stopped trying. He'd kept telling Luke it wasn't his fault, that he hadn't known what would happen. That he'd just been doing his job. Luke had known all of that. He'd even heard all the rigmarole about it being Dusty's time, that Stu was such a hotshot that he was living on borrowed time and that Ty never felt a thing. None of it had helped.

They'd been more than just his buddies, or even his family. They'd been his life, his sanity, part of himself in a world that made no sense. Where you could trust no one, not even yourself, because the things you saw weren't always what you saw.

"So did you take the scholarship when you came back?" Gabbi asked.

Luke looked at her, coming back from the hell he periodically slipped into. "They don't hold those kinds of things for you," he replied. "Besides, I'd been wounded and the drinking had taken a hold of me by then."

He didn't want to look in her eyes, but he was sure that she understood. "So I married my high school sweetheart and went to Indiana University here in South Bend. Got divorced and got my degree in secondary education."

"That's when you went into teaching and coaching?"

"Yeah." He nodded. "And while I was attending college, I helped my Dad out with his electrical contracting business. I still have my card, and I work for him during the summer."

"I imagine that helps the budget," she said.

"Yeah, financially I'm as comfortable as I want to be."

"Well, it looks like you straightened out whatever problems you had."

He nodded for a long moment, reliving pieces of the past. Ron hauling his pickled carcass home time after time. Ron trying to cajole him into sobriety. Anger. Rage. Broken glasses, windows and dreams. Finally, his weary agreement to try Alcoholics Anonymous because the unrelenting Ron had just worn him down.

And gave him back his life.

"I straightened out with the help of a really good friend." Luke paused. "Adam's father, actually."

"So that's why you took Adam in?"

"No choice to make. Ron trusted me." He ran his fingers through his hair and hoped that the despair in his heart didn't sound in his voice. He'd vowed when he got back from Vietnam never to hold someone else's fate in his hands again, and yet here he was. "I'm not sure why, but he did."

She tightened her hold on his hand. "Oh, I think I know."

He looked at her. She was so beautiful. There was something about her, something so sensuous. Desire nipped at the edges of his subconscious. He looked away.

Someone so perfect could never accept the real him. The man of fears and anger and distrust. She was all the light and beautiful things in the world. He was the shadow. He let his eyes take in the yard.

Dusk would be falling soon and the crickets were tuning up for their violin chorus. It was nice this time of the year. Pleasant and warm enough to sit outside, but too early for mosquitoes.

"Kids should be coming home soon," he said.

"Yeah."

Gabbi looked at her wine but didn't reach for it. He should tell her to go ahead and drink it. Tell her again that there was no problem for him. But she'd find that out soon enough herself.

"I guess we all have secrets," she said slowly. "Things in our past that we're not sure we want to talk about."

Too many images taunted him, and he got to his feet. The darkness threatened to overcome him. He felt the need to run.

"And most of them should stay there," he said with a nervous laugh. "I wouldn't have bored you with my dirty laundry, except I felt bad about my allergy story."

"Oh." She looked slightly disconcerted.

"Come on," he said, reaching down to pull her to her feet. "Enough of all this seriousness. Get your glass of wine and let's go inside. I've got a hankering for some lemonade."

Chapter Seven

"Want to go out and shoot some baskets?" Luke asked Adam late Sunday morning.

"I got homework," Adam said as he trudged toward the stairs.

"Don't look at me," Matt said quickly, as if fearing Luke would turn his attention to him next. "I'm reading the paper." He proceeded to open up the funnies so that he disappeared from view.

Luke frowned. He felt antsy, as if they should be doing something, but he didn't know what. The front doorbell rang, giving him a reprieve. It was Gabbi and Trisha, both dressed as if they'd just come from church. Their car was out in front.

Gabbi wore a smile and that sense of barely contained energy. Trisha looked thoroughly uneasy. Luke suspected it might have something to do with the dress she had on. He'd never seen her in one before.

"We're here for Adam," Gabbi said, leaving Luke absurdly disappointed. "But you can come, too."

An off-handed invitation, but he was all too willing to accept. He took a few steps toward the stairs and called up for the boy before turning back to Gabbi. "What are we doing?"

"Mother's Day."

"Mother's Day?"

Adam stopped, partway down the stairs. "Huh?"

"No 'huhs' allowed," Gabbi said brightly, looking around Luke. She must have spotted Matt in the living room. "Hi, Matt. You're welcome to come along, too."

He got to his feet. "Don't mind if I do. Got nothing else going."

What about reading his precious paper? But Luke didn't challenge him as they all trouped out to Gabbi's car. Adam looked concerned. Luke felt unsure himself, but Matt was relaxed and easy.

"So what is this?" Luke asked as they settled into the car. He was in front with Gabbi, the others were in back. Gabbi handed him a box to hold. He peeked inside. There were some pieces of folded paper, little candles and some droopy pink roses.

"You'll see in a minute." She drove west, then turned north along the river. When she reached the public access launching area, she turned in and parked the car. "Okay. Everybody out."

She led them all over to the gentle grassy slope and nodded for them to sit down. It was kind of nice here along the river. Quiet and peaceful, and there was something about the constant movement of the water that promised tranquillity.

"Today's Mother's Day," Gabbi said quietly. "The day we traditionally remember our mothers and honor them. I sent my mom some flowers and called her this morning, like I do every Mother's Day, but I got to thinking yesterday how Mother's Day isn't just for mothers, it's for all us children, too. A day to think about our mothers and what they taught us and how well we're measuring up to their hopes and dreams for us. And to thank them, wherever they are, for all they did for us."

Luke glanced at Adam. His face was solemn, his eyes seemed glued to Gabbi's face. Trisha looked pained, as if she was at the doctor's office and about to get a shot.

Gabbi opened her box and took out some of the papers. They had been folded into little boats. She handed one to Trisha, one to Adam and one to Luke. He frowned at her, but she wasn't paying attention. She had turned to Matt; he nodded and took one, too.

"These boats are going to carry our love and our gratitude to our mothers," she said.

Luke wasn't sure he wanted to play some silly game. "How come you don't have one?" he asked.

"Because she gave me hers," Matt said. "Stop being a grump and listen."

Adam cracked a slight smile, and Trisha sent a definite smirk his way.

Gabbi went on. "The first thing we want to do is put a candle in," she said as she passed out squat little white candles. "And think about one memory of our mother that is special."

Matt put his in and smiled. "Whenever I smell bleach, I think of my mother. She worked as a washerwoman in a laundry and that was her perfume. The smell makes me remember her hugs and how safe and happy I felt around her."

He looked over at Luke, obviously passing the baton. Luke wanted to pass. This wasn't his sort of thing, baring his soul in front of others. Yet Gabbi's eyes were on him, telling him how important this was, and he looked at the two kids. Adam's eyes held his pain and loss. Trisha's held a bravado that said nothing touched her, yet even there he saw a shadow of uncertainty.

With a sigh, he put his candle in and closed his eyes, willing a picture of his mother to come forward. "She came to my school play in second grade," he said slowly. "I had the lead, Abe Lincoln, and she made this stovepipe hat for me. She'd helped me practice my lines every day after school, but I figured she'd be too sick to come to the play, but she was there. She looked so proud of me." Stupidly, his eyes got all misty and he looked out over the river, taking a deep breath.

Damn. He should have stayed home.

"My mom used to call me Peanut," Adam said in a little voice. "And whenever I had a hard test, she'd put a little bag of peanuts in my lunch. They were my Peanut Power." His voice almost died completely.

Luke took another deep breath. What was the purpose of all this? To make them miserable for the rest of the day? He shouldn't have come. He should take Adam and leave.

Trisha sighed loudly, obviously not about to give in to all this emotionalism. "Once when I was about six and it was winter, my mom was helping me get ready for school. I had my mittens on already so she had to zip my coat for me, and she zipped it up too high and pinched my neck." Trisha burst into giggles.

"Ouch," Matt said. "Bet that smarted."

"A little, but I didn't cry." Trisha grew more solemn. "She did, though. She felt so bad about it."

Great, another step closer to group depression.

Gabbi pulled the droopy-looking roses from the box and handed one to each of them. "We're going to put rose petals into the boat for all the things she taught us and all the dreams she had."

Matt sprinkled some petals into his boat. "My mother thought honesty was most important."

"My mom always said she just wanted me to be happy," Adam said.

Trisha dropped her petals one by one into her boat. "The most important thing to my mom was education. She really wanted me to get good grades and go to college." Her voice was quiet, thoughtful.

Luke felt everyone's eyes on him. He stared down at the stupid flower. The petals fell slowly into his hand. "My mom always said to do your best. She wasn't so concerned about winning and losing, but about doing your best."

He could see her eyes, so gentle and understanding. She liked it when his teams would win, but all she really cared about was his effort. Even today, when he wouldn't really try for something, he'd feel her eyes on him.

Matt let the rest of the petals fall. "She taught me to be loyal and trustworthy and to honor my responsibilities."

He took the packet of matches from Gabbi and lit the candle, then set the little boat onto the river. The current caught it, pulling it away from the shore. "Thanks, Mom," he said quietly.

Adam took the matches and stared down at his boat. "She liked me to laugh. She was always telling me jokes. She told me not to think about myself, but to figure everything I was afraid of, everybody else was afraid of, too." He lit his candle and set his boat out to join Matt's. "I love you, Mom," he whispered, then handed the matches to Luke.

He felt really weird. He hated this kind of thing. Okay, maybe it was good for Adam, but Adam was still a kid. He wasn't. It felt as though he was taking off his armor, piece by piece, until he was naked.

He felt Adam's gaze on him, though, and knew there was no ducking out. Luke took a deep breath and carefully lit his candle. "She taught me compassion. And to take the blame when it's due as well as the praise when you earn it."

He set his boat into the water and watched it inch away from him, suddenly seeing it as his mother inching away from him with her death. As if a hand had tightened around his heart, he felt strangely hurt and alone the farther the little boat went. He held his breath as it collided with a stick, then relaxed as it went by. "I'm trying, Mom," he whispered into the air.

"Jeez, this is dumb," Trisha muttered as she took the matches. "And these stupid boats are polluting the water."

"I know," Gabbi said and just waited.

Trisha glared at her, then frowned at the little boat in her hand, then shifted her weight with an enormous sigh. She wrecked the first match, the second one lit, but fell into the grass and she had to laboriously dig it out and wet the tip in the river. When she saw no one was getting up to leave, she sat back down and lit her candle. She put it into the water and stared after it a long moment.

"My mom thought letting somebody know you loved them was the most important thing," she said in a frowning rush. "She was always working 'cause she had lousy jobs, and she couldn't spend much time with me, but she always wanted me to know that she loved me." She paused. "That everything she did was for me."

Trisha took a long, deep breath and stared out at the river for what seemed several lifetimes. "Then she worked so much that she just got so tired and sick and died." Her voice was shaking, fighting back the tears, even as her shoulders were set in a stubborn denial that anything was wrong. "I'm trying to be strong, Mom." She gulped in air. "And I'm sorry I got mad that time when you couldn't afford for me to play softball."

The four little boats were in the middle of the river, being pulled along toward the Michigan border. They all just stood and watched as the lit candles flickered in the sunlight. Luke could feel Adam's sniffling and slipped his arm around the boy's shoulders. Adam leaned into him. Trisha was trying to be tough and kicked at the dirt, but apparently Gabbi wasn't fooled. She took the girl's hand and stayed at her side until the little boats were lost in the sunlight's glare on the water.

"They probably sunk," Trisha muttered. "And burned some poor little fish."

"The candle'd go out, dummy," Adam said. His voice was almost normal, but Luke saw a single rose petal in the boy's hand. He slipped it into his pocket and looked around quickly. Luke averted his eyes just in time.

Once the boats were gone, the kids turned away. Matt walked to the car with Trisha, surreptitiously handing her his handkerchief. Adam trailed along, lost in his own thoughts. Luke picked up Gabbi's box for her.

"That was very nice," he said, surprising himself that he really meant it. "I think it helped the kids."

"Even if it hurt the fish?" Gabbi asked with a laugh.

"Even at the expense of the poor fish."

He looked at her as the morning sunlight lit a fire in her eyes and wondered how the gods had let such a marvelous person come into his life. Was this some sort of test or had his luck changed?

Gabbi hadn't quite known how to react to Luke's confession Saturday night, but did know that she had let a chance go by to tell him about her cancer. She had sort of tried to, though not very hard, she admitted to herself. She could have pushed harder after he hadn't noticed her feeble attempt to bring the subject around to her secrets, but her heart hadn't been in it.

Maybe it wasn't the time, she'd told herself, and she should stop worrying about it. They were friends, getting to know each other. Such confidences weren't necessary at this stage.

"I really appreciate your coming with me tonight." Gabbi smiled at Luke. "Trisha appreciates it also. She's been so antsy this week as the final adoption hearing gets closer that she's been driving me crazy."

Luke took his eyes off the road for a moment and flashed her a smile full of understanding and untold mysteries. "That's okay," he said. "If I wasn't with you, I'd probably just be cruising the Strip."

"I didn't know cruising was in anymore. I thought malling was the activity *du jour.*"

"For the junior high set, yes. For the rest of us, it's cruising." Luke shrugged. "We're always a little behind here in the Midwest."

Gabbi laughed and slid over closer to him. "I can't imagine spending hours just driving up and down one street."

"They stop. Sit around in the parking lots. Talk and get into fights."

"Oh," Gabbi murmured, wondering if Trisha would be pulled into that culture as she got older. Hopefully, she wouldn't. Maybe her interest in sports would occupy her enough.

"But I hear the police are really cracking down on the cruisers." He turned to smile at her. "So I'm the one who owes you. If it wasn't for you taking me out, I'd probably wind up in jail."

Gabbi just smiled at his joking. Truth be told, Trisha really didn't have to do much pushing to get Gabbi to include Luke in her plans. She liked being around him, and found he came into her thoughts unbidden. But for the last few days, so had that uncertainty over her silence.

He'd confided in her, really dug down deep in his soul and told her his deepest, darkest secret. Yet she hadn't reciprocated. It wasn't because he'd changed the subject, but because she'd been too afraid.

God, if he had enough faith in her to tell her he was an alcoholic, shouldn't she have told him about the cancer?

But deep in her heart, she wasn't sure why he'd told her about his alcohol problem. Was it a sign that he felt their relationship was deepening? Or did he just prefer openness about it? Maybe it was something he routinely told to his friends and co-workers, just so there was no misunderstanding about it. She didn't know what to think, and decided thought was something to be avoided for the moment.

"This is neat riding in a truck," she said brightly. "You get to look down on ninety percent of the population. That's something a person my size rarely gets to do."

"If you want me to, I'll tie you down on the roof," Luke said. "That would put you higher than everybody except the semis."

"That's okay."

Luke had called for her in his pickup. He had then embarked on a twisted route that took them through downtown, an area of offices, banks and municipal buildings, and around the edges of a warehouse section.

"I presume you know where you're going," she said.

"Oh, sure," he replied. "The Biegers were family friends."

Gabbi wrinkled her nose and looked out the passenger side of the truck. "Remind me to punch you when we get there."

"Okay."

She didn't really want to punch him, but she'd take any way she could to get her hands on him.

They were going to the Bieger House, an old mansion that was used for various community events. Tonight the Michiana Women in Communications were hosting a mystery dinner where professional actors, along with guests, would put on a mystery play as the dinner progressed. As a member of the group, Gabbi had suggested Luke join her.

"You do know you're going to have to play a part in this production," Gabbi reminded Luke. "A small part."

"Do we get to pick?"

"I doubt it." She turned to look at him. "But if we could, what part would you like to play?"

"The corpse."

"Why?"

"I'm not too good at speaking, singing or dancing."

"Aw, poor baby."

"Lying around I can handle really well."

"Come on," Gabbi said. "Certainly as a coach, you've given speeches."

"Yeah, but they're always the same two." He stopped for a red light. "A speech for the beginning of the season and one for the end of the season."

"How about those pep talks at halftime?"

"The head coach does that."

"Is that why you don't want to be a head coach?"

He turned to look at her, and his placid blue eyes seemed to harden just a bit. Someone honked behind them, and Luke quickly turned to pull through the intersection.

"I don't want to be a head coach for a lot of reasons. Time involvement is probably the main one."

"I can't believe you'd spend that much more time than you do now."

"I like what I'm doing now," he insisted, his voice just a touch defensive. "I can be friends with the kids and watch them grow. No hassles. No pushy parents."

No responsibility. The thought leapt out at her, but thankfully she controlled her mouth for once and didn't say it. Somehow, though, once the idea came, it wouldn't leave. It took root and began to sprout almost immediately. Did he have an aversion to responsibility?

Until Adam came along, he hadn't much in his personal life. And if he avoided head coaching positions, then he hadn't had that much in his job, either. Of course, as an alcoholic, he might be leery of responsibility. Maybe it was the pressure that used to drive him to drink. But still...

They rode in silence the rest of the way to the mansion. The front lot was already full so Luke pulled the truck over to the civic lot where he parked the vehicle, then came around to help Gabbi out.

She shouldn't be so judgmental, she scolded herself. First of all, she had no idea her thought was right. And even if it was, she didn't know him all that well, didn't know what had made him who he was, and had no right to find him wanting.

"I'm sorry about intruding," Gabbi said as Luke locked the car door.

"Hey, don't worry about it."

His features were relaxed, and his eyes were again calm as a lake on a summer's day. Gabbi's own worries faded. He wasn't angry with her.

"I should be used to it," Luke said. "Matt's always on my case about something."

"He's your dad. He's allowed to. I'm just an old busybody and shouldn't interfere."

"Hey, didn't we discuss this 'old' stuff before?"

He brushed her lightly on the cheek with his lips, then gave her his arm. Everything was fine. She was just so hyper about her own past that she worried about everybody else's. Maybe she should concentrate on her present and let the rest take care of itself. Words Gabbi definitely intended to live by. They walked to the front of the building, up onto the porch and into an enormous foyer.

"Gabbi, I'm so glad that you could come." A tall, redheaded woman came toward Gabbi and gave her a hug, then smiled in the general direction of Luke as she handed them sheets of paper. "Here are your parts. You two are the young lovers."

"How far can you go before you're not young anymore?" Luke asked.

The woman was already moving away to greet another couple. "You're just right," she said over her shoulder.

Gabbi scanned the pages. Luke was Lance Forthright, a world-famous inventor and suitor of Letitia Purity, daughter of the town banker.

"It says here that you're rather shy," Gabbi said.

"Great. I don't have to talk all that much." He flipped through the pages. "Looks like you do most of the talking. I can take that."

"Actually, the professional actors handle most of the lines," Gabbi said and looked around them. "Gee, can you imagine living in a place like this?"

The walls were paneled in dark wood that matched the beams that crossed the high ceilings and framed a design painted in greens and reds. The floor was marble, the molding around the doorways and windows was thick and elaborate. A staircase that any bride would kill to come down rose from somewhere farther back.

"Just like where I grew up." Luke laughed. "Except it was a bit smaller. And had a bit less wood. And a little less marble. But we did have walls and a ceiling."

"Maybe even windows and doors?" she suggested.

He frowned at her. "Hey, were you living there, too? How come I never noticed you?"

She laughed and slid her arm through his, and he pulled her close. One thing she did admire about Luke was his acceptance. He must not have an envious bone in his body. He seemed so very content with what he had. She wished she could say the same for herself.

At times, she seemed so consumed by ambition, by a need to rush out and grab whatever she wanted. Was it the brush with death that made her see the need for urgency in life or had she always been so driven?

A bell rang from the interior of the old mansion, rescuing her from her thoughts. They followed the crowd into a large, banquet-sized dining room. Place cards, with their names on one side and their stage names on the other, indicated where they should sit.

A woman in a long black dress moved to the head of the room. "Good evening, ladies and gentlemen," she said. "I'm Pam Lauber, and I will be your director this evening. These folks to my right will be your main entertainers. I say 'main' because all of you have some part in our performance tonight."

The men and women were dressed in period pieces from the turn of the century. Gabbi took Luke's arm and gave it a squeeze. Partly because she liked being close to him, but partly because she wanted him to feel comfortable since he didn't seem to be involved much in these kinds of creative things. She gave him a kiss on the ear.

Smiling, he turned toward her. "Practicing?"

"I want to do well," she replied. "You never know. There might be a big Hollywood producer in the audience."

"Whoopee!"

A wine steward came by just then and poured a measure of white wine in her glass before she could protest.

Luke reacted faster, covering his glass with his hand. "Ice water will be fine for me."

Gabbi frowned at her wine.

"It's okay," he whispered in her ear. "Drink what you want."

"All right now, what's going on there?"

A voice broke into their cocoon, and she and Luke both started. The director was staring at them, a big grin on her lips. Actually, everybody in the room was staring at them. And smiling. Gabbi's treacherous cheeks glowed with warmth.

"We were practicing," Gabbi stammered.

"That's right," Luke agreed. "Just practicing."

"I don't mind you practicing," the director said. "But I would prefer that you stick to the script. Perhaps you'd like to join us on page seven."

Her cheeks still blazing, Gabbi turned to that page. Luke was doing the same.

"Now," the director said. "If Lance Forthright would like to read his line..."

Luke looked down at the script, then cleared his throat. "Letitia, lovely Letitia," he said. "Come with me, my love. Let us run to paradise. An island far from the maddening crowd."

Gabbi grinned at him. "Okay," she said.

"No, no, Letitia," the director shouted as the crowd burst into laughter. "Follow the script, please."

With her cheeks blazing and laughter echoing in her ears, Gabbi looked down at the script. She was supposed to say her father wouldn't want her to. "But Dad won't care," she explained to all. "He's out playing golf."

The laughter erupted again and the director fought for control. "All right, folks." She turned to Gabbi. "Letitia, how are we going to get your father murdered if he's out playing golf?"

"Hit him with a runaway golf ball?"

The room laughed, and Gabbi just grinned at Luke, leaning a bit closer to him. Running away to paradise sounded very tempting. But, then, was running away necessary?

Anywhere Luke was seemed pretty close to paradise as it was.

"What do you think?" Gabbi asked, stopping in front of a wooden cabinet.

Luke had convinced Gabbi to drive to LaPorte with him after work to scout out the Slicers baseball team for the upcoming playoffs, and on the way home she'd spotted this estate sale. It wasn't exactly his thing, but then, baseball wasn't hers. Trouble was, stopping wasn't enough. Now she wanted opinions.

He frowned at the cabinet. "I don't know," he said. "What is it?"

"It's a cracker bin."

"We keep our crackers in a tin can."

Gabbi just laughed and shook her head.

It was one of those days that Matt would call an "Indiana sample." Today was a sample of what July would be like. Hot and more than a tad humid. Gabbi was dressed in shorts, sandals and a sleeveless blouse. Her face was almost without makeup. Luke's arm moved up of its own volition and went around her shoulders.

"What would you do with it?" he asked.

"Probably keep napkins in it."

This time Luke shook his head. "If you want something to hold napkins, then you should get a napkin bin."

She took his arm and leaned against him. "All I'm asking is, what do you think of it as a piece of furniture?"

"It's okay."

"Just okay?"

Jeez, what did he care what the damn thing looked like? He wasn't buying it. "If you want the thing, get it."

"I was just wondering what *you* thought of it."

"I'm in between. It's not so ugly that it disgusts me. On the other hand, it's no big deal if I never see it again."

"You don't want to make a decision, do you?"

Why had it suddenly become such a big deal? "Since it won't be in my house, I don't see that I have a right to make a decision."

"How about an opinion?"

"I gave you my opinion," he replied.

"You're really slippery, aren't you?"

"Let's take a walk." He took her arm in his and felt the shivers of passion race down his spine. Her skin was so smooth, so silky. Yet just the slightest touch could ignite a hunger that ate at his soul.

He cleared his throat, hoping he could still manage to speak. "If you decide you want it, then we can come back."

"But someone else may buy it in the meantime."

Luke stopped. "Well, if that would break your heart, then you ought to buy it now."

She looked back at the cracker bin, wrinkling her nose as she shook her head. "Nah, I don't think so."

Hah, he thought. She doesn't really know if she likes it, either. "Fine. Then let's take a walk. It'll clear the cobwebs." He wanted to get her alone, without the distractions of stupid furniture. He felt unreasonably jealous that all her attention was on a cracker bin. Did she even eat crackers?

"I don't have any cobwebs." Her voice was a tad sharp. "I'm just not sure I want that piece of furniture."

"Well then, let's just walk around and look at the other stuff," he said. "You might find something you really like."

"All right."

They walked toward the back of the yard surrounding the old farmhouse. Cabinets, tables, old rockers and benches were spread across the lawn for the estate sale along with milk cans, churns, lamps and framed pictures of dour old ancestors. He turned to stare at the old, two-story farmhouse up on the slight incline. Its windows were darkened and curtains drawn, as if its eyes were shut.

"My Dad rewired this house about thirty years ago when he was just starting his business," Luke said. "And the house was old back then."

"I don't know if I could do this." Her voice sounded weary all of a sudden. There was a trace of sadness that he didn't understand.

"Do what?"

"Put my life out here for people to pick over."

"It's not their life. It's just old stuff no one wants anymore," he said.

"But some of it is really old. They're selling their family history."

Luke shrugged. "I guess it's not important to them."

"I don't suppose any of the family is here," Gabbi said.

"No," Luke replied. "From what I overheard, all the heirs live out on the West Coast someplace."

"I think it's sad."

"I thought you said that you moved around a lot yourself," Luke said. "Sort of a standard issue, suburban American."

"Maybe that's why I think this is all so sad. I don't have anything that was handed down through generations of my family. If I did, I certainly wouldn't leave it out on the yard for strangers to pick over."

Luke could see that Gabbi was serious, so he kept his mouth shut. She'd been like this before, the night they'd been planning the kitchen. She'd gotten all nostalgic over redoing someone's dream kitchen. Now it was over someone's discards.

"If this is what their lives boiled down to, then they didn't have much," he pointed out. "Most people's legacies are in the love they shared, the strength they had and the people they helped. If you leave all that behind, who cares about some old furniture?"

"I guess." She turned to stare up at the house. "I hear they're going to wreck the house."

"Yeah." Luke looked out at the surrounding maze of apartment houses and discount stores. "Apparently the area has a desperate need for more parking space."

Gabbi shook her head. "I think we're all going to miss things like this when they're gone."

Luke just shrugged. "I wish it were that easy." On one hand he could see the good parts of preservation, but as a tradesman, he could also see the good in the jobs that development brought. At times, it seemed like a no-win situation.

"I'm going to buy that cracker bin," Gabbi announced. "You have room on the truck, don't you?"

"Sure," Luke replied. "Plenty."

"My house isn't all that old, but I think it'll be a nice place for an old piece of furniture like that."

Luke smiled as he followed her. She was always surprising him. One moment a modern, no-nonsense career lady, the next moment, a soft, sensitive woman feeling emotions that he'd never expected. Looking at the world through her eyes was changing him, making him a different—better—person.

"Is that it?" Trisha cried, leaning against the airport's huge plate-glass window as if it could help her see the taxiing plane better. "I think I can see Doris at the window."

"Oh, yeah?" Gabbi swallowed hard. Her stomach was churning and her hands were sweaty. She knew it wasn't the glare of sunshine off the tarmac or the plane. It was her parents' impending arrival.

"I'm gonna fly someday," Trisha was saying. The big plane stopped at the gate, and the ramp swung out toward the door. "Maybe I'll even be a pilot."

"I think pilots need to stay out of fights and do well in school," Gabbi said.

Trisha pretended not to hear, but her excitement level deflated slightly. Did that mean the girl was taking her words to heart? Gabbi could only hope so.

People began to deplane at a nearby gate, and Gabbi wandered slowly over. This was crazy to be so jittery, but then her parents did that to her. They loved her dearly, she knew, but they also gave the impression that they were never quite sure of anything she accomplished.

"Al! Doris!" Trisha cried and waved wildly. She stayed behind Gabbi, though.

Gabbi went forward and was enveloped in first her mother's hug, then her father's. She was momentarily stifled, but then escaped and looked for Trisha. The girl was still hanging back slightly.

"You, too, honey," Gabbi's mother said. "You aren't escaping. Not now that I'm almost your grandma."

Trisha allowed herself to be hugged, but didn't look totally comfortable. Once she was released, Gabbi's father took a moment to pat her on her shoulder. Then both of Gabbi's parents turned toward her, as if they'd done their duty.

Gabbi bit back a sigh, determined not to say anything in front of Trisha. But why did her mother have to make Trisha feel she'd been on trial? Why did her father treat Trisha like a stray dog Gabbi'd taken in? Why had they bothered to come for Trisha's final adoption proceedings if they weren't going to share in the excitement?

Gabbi had considered Trisha her daughter from the moment she'd arrived in her house, but her parents had made it clear in subtle ways that she wasn't part of the family until the legal system made her so. For Trisha's sake, Gabbi fought back the surge of annoyance.

"How was your flight?" she asked her father.

"Long." He looked around them. "So where do we get our luggage?"

"Down this way."

She led them down the corridor with Trisha trailing along a few feet behind them. The girl was pretending to be checking everything out, as if the Michiana Regional Airport was the most fascinating place she'd ever been. Gabbi tried to slow her steps to allow Trisha to catch up, but that didn't work.

"You're looking wonderful, darling," Doris said to Gabbi as she fiddled with the collar of Gabbi's shirtwaist dress. "I wish you wouldn't wear such pale collars, though.

You're still a beautiful girl. You shouldn't be afraid to call attention to yourself."

"I'm not, Mom," she said.

"She wears lots of bright clothes," Trisha called out, her voice verging on belligerence. "Luke likes that dress."

Oh, great. Trisha had done it now.

"Luke? Is that your gentleman friend?"

Gabbi heard Trisha's snicker and knew she was fully aware of what she'd done. "He's a friend of mine," Gabbi said slowly. "And since he's male, I guess you could call him my gentleman friend."

"He's around all the time," Trisha announced.

"That sounds serious," Al said.

"He lives behind us. So any time he's at home, he's sort of around."

Gabbi was never more relieved to see the baggage claim area. And ready to send flowers and candy to the airline for having the luggage unloaded already. Her father grabbed a suitcase from the rack.

"Only one?" Gabbi asked. "Aren't you guys staying until Monday morning?"

Her mother just smiled sheepishly. "We were going to, but your dad was invited to play in the Pine Crest tournament this year. So we need to go back early Sunday."

"Oh." Gabbi told herself not to take it personally. It was only a day less. Her father loved golf and had been trying for years to get an invitation to that tournament. "Congratulations," she told him.

They walked out to the car, occupied with watching for traffic as they crossed the roadway and then weaving through the row of cars to theirs. They put the luggage in the trunk, then all climbed into the car. Trisha and Gabbi in front; her parents in back.

"Wait till you see our new house," Trisha said. "It's really neat."

"We're anxious to, dear," Doris said. "I can't imagine what it's like to live in the city itself."

"It's not like there's an elevated train running nearby," Gabbi said.

Trisha turned to face Gabbi's parents. "We do have train tracks not too far away. And sometimes at night you can hear a train go by."

"Oh, my." Doris's sigh was not one of excitement. "Maybe we should have gotten rooms at a hotel. Your father needs his rest for the tournament."

"He won't hear a thing."

"Unless the motorcycles race down the alley," Trisha noted.

Gabbi gave her a look. "There are no motorcycles. Trisha is teasing you."

Trisha just grinned, and they drove the rest of the way home in silence. Gabbi pulled up to the front of the house.

"This is it," Trisha said. A dare not to like it was in her voice.

"Why, it's darling," Doris said. "It's not very big, but it's cute."

"Nice trees," Al said.

It was a hit. Gabbi breathed a sigh of relief and took them inside. Apparently Trisha felt they'd passed some test also and happily showed them around, ending with her room, where they were going to stay. From the expressions of approval, it appeared that no one minded the boxes still stacked in most of the rooms, awaiting unpacking. While her parents were settling in, Gabbi went down to put some coffee on.

She started some brewing, then discovered Trisha hadn't taken the garbage out after dinner, so she picked up the bag and hurried out to the garbage can in the alley. When she opened the gate, she discovered the alley wasn't empty. It wasn't the motorcyclists that Trisha had invented, but Luke. He was painting the back of his fence. Seeing him made all her little worries seem distant.

"Hi, there," he said, standing up when he saw her. "You look like springtime come to visit."

She couldn't help but look down at her creased dress, then up at him.

"Uh-oh, something wrong?" he asked.

"My parents are in," she said. "And my dress wasn't quite up to my mother's standards for me."

He looked her over from head to toe, a soft grin covering his face as a slow heat took over her body. "Looks pretty good to me," he said. "Though I wouldn't object to something with less length or less shoulder or more cleavage."

Her smile dimmed, and she turned to shove the garbage into the can. She made good use of the moment to calm her suddenly volatile emotions. "Trisha had another fight in school today," she said.

"Is she going to be suspended?"

"No, she and her opponent are going to have to wash windows after school for the next five days." Gabbi turned to face Luke and leaned against the fence. "The principal said a suspension would just give them time to lie around the house and watch television. He said his way would give the girls work they didn't like and the school would reap the results of their cheap labor."

"Makes sense to me," Luke said.

"Me, too. Trisha will remember washing windows more than she would a suspension."

Gabbi heard her voice drift off as she lost track of what she was saying. Luke wasn't that close, but not that far, either. She could see the way his chest rose and fell with each breath. And she felt a sudden longing to lay her head against him, to set her breathing to his even rhythm. She looked away.

"The fight was with her best friend," Gabbi said.

"That's not abnormal."

"I guess," she replied. "When we're tense and uptight, most of us will lash out at those closest to us."

"That's true."

His voice was so soothing. She should tell him about her parents, so concerned about her appearance, so worried that she will never find a man again now that she's settled with a house and child. But to make him understand, she'd have to tell him more.

And there wasn't time to do that now. She had to get back inside.

"With the adoption being finalized tomorrow, I guess she's kind of scared," Gabbi said. "So she strikes out.

That's really different from me. When I'm scared, I go into a little hidey-hole and keep everyone out at arm's length."

"Me, too," he said. "Only arm's length sounds too close." He'd kept his voice light as if he were joking, but Gabbi could see something in his eyes that made her believe he was telling the truth.

"I wonder why we react the way we do," she said lightly. "Well, I can see why Trisha does. She's afraid to show weakness. But why don't I get up and fight my fears?" She was asking him more than he knew.

"Because it wouldn't be ladylike?"

Maybe. But not in the way he thought. Was she afraid to tell him about her cancer because she'd already violated her parents' and Doug's idea of what a lady was? Beauty and breasts, two of the main definitions of a woman according to some people. Was Luke one of them?

"If fear of being unladylike is my excuse, what's yours?" she asked.

"Fear of leaning on someone," he said. "Fear of believing what I'm told because it might be a lie." He looked away a long moment, then turned back to her. Or at least his eyes did. "Everyone told me my mother would be fine. No one thought an eight-year-old should be told the truth."

"I'm sure they did what they thought best," she told him.

He shrugged. "How about when I lied to myself, saying I could drink when I wanted and stop when I wanted?"

"You were sick."

He just shook his head, as if all her excuses were just that—excuses. "Sometimes," he said carefully, "you just learn not to lean on anyone or let anyone lean on you."

The terrible finality of his voice saddened her. She wanted to take him in her arms and hold him close. She wanted to wipe all those hidden memories from him forever. She wanted to bring him joy and sweetness and sunshine.

Unfortunately, her parents were waiting. She had to go back in the house.

Chapter Eight

"This adoption is hereby declared final." The judge grinned down at them and slapped her gavel. "I now pronounce you mother and daughter. You may give each other a hug if you like."

Gabbi turned, about to lift her arms, but Trisha just stood as if rooted to her spot. Poor kid. She was all pale and her hands were quivering.

"Honey," Gabbi said softly as she stepped closer.

"Well," Trisha said, her voice coming out in almost a squeak. "I guess you're, like, stuck with me now."

"I wouldn't have it any other way, kid." Gabbi took Trisha in her arms.

Trisha folded in and put her own arms around Gabbi's waist. "I'm gonna be good. I'm really, really gonna try." She took a moment to snuffle. "But I can't really and truly promise anything."

"A real try is good enough," Gabbi assured her.

They parted to the sound of clapping and cheering, and turned to those around them: Gabbi's parents, Doris and Al; Luke and Adam; Pam, Claire and Jim from the radio station; Jody, their social worker, and Mitch, their adoption counselor.

Doris rushed forward to hug Trisha. "Welcome to the family, honey," she cried.

Gabbi's father hugged her once she got free of Doris. "Welcome."

Trisha was surrounded by well-wishers but was holding up under the hugs and kisses pretty well. Luke slid up to Gabbi's side.

"Congratulations," he said, enveloping her in a light, quick grasp. "You're a special lady."

His words brought her warmth and a special sweetness, not because she thought adopting Trisha was some great humanitarian gesture, but because of that look in his eye. She wanted to bask in his gaze, but knew this wasn't the time.

"I'm glad you were able to come," she told him.

"We wouldn't have missed it for the world."

There were other groups in the courtroom, waiting their turn, so Gabbi ushered everyone out into the hall. They found a relatively quiet corner.

"Thank you for coming," Gabbi said to them all and pulled Trisha to her side. "Trisha and I are happy to be able to share our special day with you. But the party's just starting. We have reservations at Hannah's in New Buffalo for dinner, and you're all invited."

Gabbi's co-workers declined, citing family responsibilities, as did Jody and Mitch. After another round of congratulations, they left.

"Well, now what?" Al asked.

"It's too early to eat," Trisha said. "How about we play a little basketball? You know, like gals versus guys."

"Oh, not your grandfather and me," Doris protested quickly.

"So, two-on-two then."

"I don't think any of us are dressed for basketball," Gabbi said.

"Besides, Adam has a tournament tomorrow," Luke said.

Trisha frowned at them. "Are you guys chicken or something?"

Adam gave them an angry glare.

"Trisha," Gabbi said, trying to fill her voice with warning.

"Well, they must be," her daughter said. "They're like always dodging our challenge."

"I am not!" Adam snapped. "We played last weekend."

"Why don't we get going?" Gabbi said. "If we get to New Buffalo early, we can walk around the stores."

"Stores?" Trisha whined. "Who wants to go shopping?"

"Trisha." The name came out strongly, but Gabbi didn't care. "Do you want to go to New Buffalo or would you like to go home and study?"

"Jeepers. Why don't we get hostile?"

"Trisha. New Buffalo or your room. Those are your choices."

"Okay, New Buffalo. I mean like jeepers, creepers." She shuffled ahead and joined her grandparents.

Gabbi smiled woefully at Luke. "High as the sky one minute, crashing to the ground the next."

"Welcome to the world of teenagers."

Gabbi looked around him at Adam. "I can't believe you're that changeable," she said.

The boy shrugged without even the hint of a smile, then increased the pace of his shuffle slightly so that he was walking in between Trisha and her grandparents and Luke and Gabbi.

"He seems down," Gabbi said. "You two didn't miss a game because of the proceedings, did you?"

"Nope, just a practice."

They started down some stairs, and somehow their hands naturally found each other. Some things just seemed so right, so normal.

"I would have understood if you couldn't have made it," she said.

His hold on her hand tightened. "This was more important than any baseball practice or game, even. Family and belonging. What more is there?"

What more, indeed? Maybe that was the key to why she liked being with Luke so much. She felt as if she belonged. There was a strange way that they seemed to read each other's thoughts, to know each other's needs and to be there. She glanced at him quickly. His jaw spoke of strength, yet his eyes said he was gentle, compassionate and kind. He was everything she'd wanted Doug to be.

Did that mean he was her ideal man?

The idea both tantalized and frightened her. What was she getting herself into? Was this just friendship or were they racing pell-mell in another direction?

She was glad when they reached the outside door. "We're in the parking garage," she said.

"I'm down the street," Luke replied, nodding in the other direction. "We'll meet you there."

"Great." She smiled brightly, but was glad of the respite from the wild thoughts his presence generated. She needed to catch her breath, in more ways than one.

With her parents and Trisha, Gabbi turned toward the municipal parking garage. They crossed the street and entered through the pedestrian ramp.

"I wonder what's wrong with Adam," Gabbi said to Trisha. "He doesn't appear to be in a good mood."

"He's just an old grump," Trisha said as she skipped backward. "He ought to get himself a cane and grow a beard." She had apparently regained her good humor.

"I'm not sure Adam can grow a beard yet."

Trisha was now hopping. "Maybe not, but he can sure do grumpy good."

"Maybe something didn't go well at school." Gabbi pushed the button for the elevator.

Trisha just shrugged. "Bet I can beat you guys to the car."

Gabbi shook her head as she watched Trisha race up the ramp a ways.

"Are you sure she ought to be going up by herself?" Gabbi's mother said worriedly.

The elevator came and the three of them got in. "She needs to run off some of her energy," Gabbi said. "And she'll be fine. She's a lot more aware than you might think."

"She never seems to stop," Gabbi's father admitted. "You were a lot quieter."

"Spent a lot of time fixing your nails and doing your hair," her mother remembered, a smile in her voice. "Curling irons were a real challenge to you."

What an accomplishment to boast of. "I'm not sure Trisha's way isn't better," Gabbi said.

"Taking care of your appearance is always important."

Unless your appearance defines who you are. The elevator stopped and they got out.

"I like your Luke, dear," Gabbi's mother said. "He really seems nice."

"Trisha said he's a teacher," her father said. "They don't make much, do they?"

"Since I'm not asking him for a loan, I didn't think that mattered much." He wasn't "her Luke," anyway.

"Does he know?" Doris asked. Her voice was carefully casual.

Gabbi just glanced her way and kept walking. She didn't have to ask what her mother was talking about. "No, Luke doesn't know," she said. "I never told him."

"And why should you?" her father said.

He wasn't making a statement about their relationship, Gabbi knew. His words reflected his attitude toward her cancer.

"Would you tell somebody you had your hair cut ten years ago? Or your teeth cleaned?" he said. "And it's not like you're any different. You're still just as pretty as ever."

Gabbi didn't bother to argue or try to explain. She was different because of the cancer. Maybe not appearance-wise, but it changed something deep inside her. She didn't take life for granted anymore, or believe that happiness was something to be waited and hoped for, but something to achieve now. She tried to have this discussion any number of times though, and her parents, her father especially, just never seemed to understand. Maybe they couldn't deal with her mortality because they hadn't dealt with their own yet.

As expected, Trisha had beat them to the car. She was in the aisle ahead playing airplane, running in wide circles with her arms out. Gabbi was finding out that a high energy level along with a low maturity level sometimes made for bizarre happenings.

"Calm down," she said, "or I'll make you run home."

"I bet I could beat you."

"Get in the car," Gabbi said with a sigh.

Once she was in the car Trisha turned quiet. Maybe the kid was finally running down. Gabbi paid their parking fee and then turned onto the street.

"Since Adam is a little down today," she said, "it would be nice if you didn't bug him anymore."

"I don't bug anybody."

"Trisha."

"All right," Trisha mumbled as she slouched down in her seat.

"Thank you," Gabbi said. "I appreciate that."

"But he better not bug me."

Gabbi stared straight ahead at the street before her. She hadn't really and truly thought things would be easier after the final decree, but she wouldn't have minded a little break.

The breeze off Lake Michigan held just the right touch of warmth, and the setting sun was turning the sky a marvelous palette of reds and golds and oranges. The water darted up on the sand, like fingers trying to grab at their feet. Gabbi let her hand slip into Luke's. Ahead of them on the beach, Adam and Trisha were walking with Gabbi's parents, though Trisha spent much of the time darting around.

"Someone certainly is high," Gabbi noted. "You'd think with all the dinner she ate, she'd be as sluggish as the rest of us."

"It's just the May goofies combined with adoption-day highs," Luke said.

"The May goofies? Is this another little nugget of joy that I should be looking forward to?"

"It's spring," he said with a shrug. "School's almost over, and their young minds just kind of short out."

"Goody."

"It'll pass."

"But will I survive?"

"Sure, just don't let it get to you."

There were a lot of things she needed not to let get to her. She guessed she could add another to the list. And this one might be a lot easier to ignore than things like the feel of Luke's hand in hers, or the way her eyes sought him out whenever he was near.

She glanced his way. He seemed so unaffected by everything. Did that include her nearness? She didn't like thinking that and turned toward him.

"Are you this calm and understanding when you have the little dears in the classroom or on the playing field?"

He grinned. "Usually."

"What do you do when you lose it?" she asked.

"I never lose it."

"Excuse me." She let her voice be teasing, but a nagging little urge awoke in her heart. An urge to see Luke lose control, even just a bit. "What do you do when the kids have pushed you to, but not over, the line of losing it?"

"I give them the famous Luke Bennett stare." He demonstrated for her.

He looked so cute and about as threatening to her as a teddy bear with a pout. She couldn't help but laugh.

"I don't appreciate that."

"Sorry." She tried holding it in but failed and began laughing again.

"I bet a little swim in the lake would sober you," he said.

Gabbi looked out at the water. Lake Michigan was calm today, but she knew the water would still be extremely cold.

"Bit of a grump, aren't we?"

Luke turned an exaggerated scowl toward her. "Not me."

She laughed again and fell silent, enjoying the sand beneath her feet, his hand in hers, the freshwater smell, the blue sky. Her parents laughing with Trisha. In fact, everything around her. She couldn't ask for a more perfect day.

Adam's frowning face was the one cloud in the sky. "Adam seems down today."

"He doesn't like missing practice."

"Boy," Gabbi said, "he's a dedicated player, huh?"

"Yeah." Luke shrugged. "Actually, he's sensitive about being the only freshman on the team, and with me coaching, he doesn't want anybody to think he hasn't earned his spot."

"He seems like a good player from what I saw."

"He is. He just has to relax and believe in himself. He worries too much about what others think or what they might say."

She saw herself in his words. "I guess that's something we all have to work on."

They walked on in silence for a while. Surprisingly, for a Friday evening, the beach was almost deserted. Another couple was strolling in the opposite direction, and a man with two small children was playing ball farther up the beach.

It was just starting to get dark: the colors seemed to lose their intensity and a haze had settled over the land. There was something so magical about this time of day as they went toward the secrets of the night. Gabbi hated for the time to end, though she knew they had to head back to the cars.

As if her parents had read her mind, they turned around and headed back toward the parking lot at the far end of the beach. Trisha rushed toward her and Luke, and Al looked as if he were demonstrating a golf swing to Adam.

"Hey, know what, Mom?" Trisha cried. "Michael Jordan plays golf! And Al played on a golf course that Jordan once played on. Isn't that the greatest thing ever? Al's going to teach me to play when I go stay with them in the summer."

She was gone again before Gabbi had a chance to respond. Mom. Trisha had called her Mom.

Luke slid his arm around her shoulder. "Well, looks like it's really official now. How does it make you feel?"

"I'm not sure," she said, her voice cracking. "I always said love would be enough to turn her around, but it's kind of scary. Kind of scary, too, how easily she said it, as if it weren't anything special."

"Perhaps she's been practicing in secret," he suggested. "Don't we all worry how to say things right and practice our conversations just to make sure we don't screw up?"

Maybe. Or maybe we're just too chicken to even practice. The shadows grew longer, and the water darkened to a murky churning. Its fingers were no longer teasing, but threatening.

"Your parents are nice," Luke said after a moment. "They seem to really like Trisha."

"I guess," Gabbi said. "Up until today, I would have said they weren't accepting her at all."

"Maybe they and Trisha have a lot in common. They all want to be absolutely certain before they make any emotional commitment."

"Nobody wants to take a risk." She was talking about more than just Trisha and her parents, she knew.

"Who's to define what a risk is for someone else? We all have our own nightmares to battle. Maybe even waiting is still a risk for Trisha. Can she ever really be certain you're hers? Things can happen, as she well knows."

That was true. Each person had their own definition of risk. Gabbi had to move at her own pace, do things in her own way. She took a deep breath and found the encroaching darkness was magical, not scary. Luke the magician.

"You're pretty relaxed," she said, leaning closer into his side. "And here I was sure you would have gotten the third degree somewhere along the line."

"I did," he admitted. "After dinner when you and Trisha went to the washroom."

"And did you pass?"

"What do you think?"

His laughter relieved her, told her that he hadn't been annoyed at her parents' prying. That he hadn't assumed she'd led them to believe their relationship was anything more than it was.

They walked along in silence. Gabbi gathered in quiet tufts of joy, as if she were picking cotton and weaving the pieces together into a blanket of total contentment.

Moving was certainly a chore. Gabbi had had a lot of help getting everything over here, but it all had to be put away, and she was the only one who could do that. And since her parents had taken Trisha to Chicago for the day, this was the time to really get into her chores with a passion.

Passion. An interesting choice of words. She closed her eyes and thought. But unpacking boxes wasn't the image that came to mind. It was more like the image of Luke's strong shoulders. His easy smile and his lips coming down on hers. It was his hands, so gentle as they eased fire into her soul.

She opened her eyes with a start. This wasn't accomplishing anything. She marched into the living room and grabbed the top box off the pile. Rather, slid the top box off. These were books and not the lightest thing in the world. She opened the box and took out a handful, shoving them onto the built-in shelves on either side of the fireplace.

A knock at the back door interrupted her industriousness. She walked through the kitchen. It was Luke.

"I have a front door, you know."

"What's the matter?" he asked. "Don't you like me anymore?"

Gabbi looked up and down his lean body, finishing with his deep, quiet eyes. "Like" couldn't adequately describe what she felt for him. There were no words to describe the yearning, tight feeling in her body. She didn't say anything, afraid she wouldn't be able to control the words that might spill off her lips.

"Who comes to your front door?" Luke said. "The mailman, bible sales people, sometimes the police."

Gabbi let herself smile.

"Friends and neighbors use the back door. And the better the friends, the more they use the back."

"Hey, I let you come in, didn't I?" she said. "Now what? Are you going to stand here all day and yak?"

He followed her into the kitchen. "Sounds quiet. Where is everybody?"

"My parents took Trisha to Chicago," Gabbi replied. "They're going out to eat, and then go see the Bulls play."

"How'd they get tickets?" Luke asked. "It's the playoffs."

Gabbi shrugged. "I didn't ask. I was too busy trying to keep Trisha on the ground. She'd do anything to see the Bulls, probably even wear high heels."

"Your mother isn't making her do that, is she?"

Gabbi shook her head. "Not this time."

"So whatcha doing with all your free time? Want to go canoeing?"

The idea of being alone with him on a peaceful stretch of the St. Joseph River was tempting, but she shook her head. "I've got to work on unpacking," she replied. "I'm doing the living room."

"Need any help?"

"I don't think so, but you can keep me company."

Luke stopped in the doorway, gazing at the shelves. "How is a little shrimp like you going to reach the top shelf?"

"I'm going to use the stool."

"That's too dangerous," he said, shaking his head.

"How else am I going to put my books away? Bungee jump from the roof and swing in through the picture window?"

"I'll do it. You hand me the books and I'll put them away."

Sounded simpler than the bungee jumping. "Okay."

He climbed up the stool, and she handed him the first bunch. "What's this?" he said. "*Word Origins*. Sounds fascinating."

"It is." She put the next stack on a lower rung.

He had flipped open the book. "Do you know the origin of the word *romance?*" he asked.

"No."

"From the word *romans*." He frowned down at her. "That's not very exciting, is it? If you're feeling romantic, are you feeling like wearing a toga and olive leaves?"

The look in his eyes did funny things to her stomach, made it twist into knots and spread a delicious tingling all through her. She wondered briefly what it would be like to let that tingling spread, to feed it until it consumed her and she found peace and joy in Luke's arms. She looked away from him. Safety demanded she keep her head. She put another stack of books next to the others.

"How about *gymnastics?*" Luke asked.

She shrugged. It sounded safe enough. "Tell me."

"Train naked. Want to practice some gymnastics?"

She felt her cheeks turn red and hot with the immediate agreement of her body. "Where are you finding these things?"

He held up the book, his gaze all innocent. "In here."

"Maybe we should go on to some of these," she said, as she patted the stack of books.

He shook his head sadly. "And I had you pegged as someone eager to learn."

"Just eager to have my new house set up."

He took the next stack and put them on the shelves, then pulled out another one of the books even as he did so.

"Not again," she moaned. "Maybe I ought to be doing this myself."

"I'm determined to show you the joy of learning," he said, climbing off the stool. "Once a teacher, always a teacher." Book in one hand, he took her hand in his other one and led her over to the sofa. "Now pay attention, there'll be a test afterward."

Truth be known, she didn't really want to organize her house. She wanted to feel alive again. She wanted to be whole and completely a woman. She wanted to feel attractive and loved and able to generate passion in a man. A bravery crept into her heart that she hadn't known was there.

"All right," she said as she settled herself on the sofa next to him. "I'm all ears."

His eyes took in her face and her gentle curves, her smile and her bare feet curled up next to her. "Oh, I don't think so," he said softly. "I definitely think you're wrong there."

She smiled back with a surprising headiness. Doug's rejection of her was long in the past and forgotten under the potency of Luke's gaze. Doug was the long, distant memory, Luke was here and now. He was real. He was what mattered.

"So," he said as he opened the book in his hands. "Do you know when ice cream was introduced to the United States?"

"No. I have to admit, I don't." She snuggled up closer to him, laying her head against his shoulder, and closed her eyes. Up close to him, where she could feel their hearts beat in unison, she let her dreams run wild.

It had been so long since she'd really given herself to a man, heart and soul. She knew she and Luke had been heading in that direction, even if the movement had been in fits and starts, and she was ready. Her heart wanted to belong to someone, even if just for an evening. Her lips wanted to taste the sweetness of love.

And as for her scars—well, they weren't a worry at this point. She refused to let them keep her from love.

"Hey, what are you doing?" Luke asked. "Going to sleep on me?"

She opened her eyes and smiled at him. "Nope, just relaxing."

"Looked like sleeping to me," he said in mock grumbling, tossing the book aside. "Maybe we should have planned something a little more vigorous than a history lesson."

She looked into his eyes, loving the glimmer of passion that she saw. She let her arms slip around his neck, not bringing him closer, but not letting him move away, either. "Got any suggestions?" she asked.

He raised his eyebrows at the touch of her hands, then bent slightly to plant a kiss on her arm. A shiver raced through her, igniting a long-buried cord of desire.

"Maybe," he said. "You got any other plans for the afternoon?"

"Besides unpacking?" she asked. "Not a thing."

He slipped his arms around her waist, pulling her closer into his embrace. "So I get to be activities director, do I?" he murmured with a smile. "This could be a good time to continue our sports lessons. We haven't had one in a while."

She ran her fingers lightly over the back of his neck, ruffling the short hair there. "And what sport do you suggest we study now?" she asked. "Wrestling?"

He frowned. "That sounds so violent. I was thinking of something a bit less brutal."

"But a contact sport?"

He smiled. "Oh, definitely."

He leaned closer then, as if drawn to her warmth and laughter. Their lips touched, and heaven smiled on them. She tightened her arms, sliding deeper into his embrace. It was as if the clouds had parted and allowed the sun to smile down on her. It was as if the gods up above had decreed that she would be happy.

She let his lips linger against hers, then pressed closer, needing his touch to set her heart free. The shadows of the past wanted to reclaim her, wanted to drag her back into their cell, but Luke's magic was too strong. His touch was too wonderful, and the smile in her soul melted all her heartbreak from years past.

They pulled apart just slightly, so that she still rested in his arms. It was a time to catch her breath, to let sanity return if she so desired. She didn't, not if sanity meant to stop and live in timidity and fear of love.

"So what's this sport called?" she asked, teasingly. "And what rules should I know about?"

His hand brushed the curls from her forehead, but his touch was so gentle that she barely felt it. Rather, she sensed his closeness, felt an excitement take hold of her.

His hand slid down her cheek ever so tenderly, leaving a trail of fire behind it. She wanted that hand to roam farther, to explore other areas with its fiery touch, but it stopped to cup her chin possessively. He leaned forward to take her lips again, but only in the most breathless of kisses.

"It's known as cuddling," he said. "Or nuzzling."

"And the rules?"

"Very few." His lips took over from where his hand had strayed, and he rained gentle kisses along her cheek, over toward her ear and then down her neck.

She arched against him, relishing the quiver of pleasure that followed each brushing touch, the current that raced through her, making her alive with hunger. She felt so much a woman, so desirable and so desiring. Her heart seemed to be shouting out its joy, crying out its needs.

"Use of hands is freely allowed," Luke whispered, as his hands slid back around her. They didn't just hold, though, they pulled her close. They spread out, covering her back with their possession.

"And use of lips is encouraged," he went on, even as his mouth meandered along the base of her neck. The feel of his lips on her skin seemed to weave a tighter and tighter spell around her soul. Breathing became harder, thinking was all but impossible as her spirit cried out for more.

"And who wins?" she asked, a breathless question murmured into the air.

"Everybody," he said. "Everybody."

His lips had taken hers again in suffocating demand. There was no past or future, just now, and the hunger that rose up in them both. He seemed to pull the very breath from her, even as she took life from his appetite.

His hands slid under her T-shirt, and her cool skin flared up into flames. His touch was rough, but spread the magic of their needs. She pulled his shirt from his jeans so that she could feel him. His skin was covered with a mat of hair, so delightfully delicious to run her fingers through, but underneath the hair lay a steel wall of muscle. Muscles that would hold her tight and keep her safe. Muscles that would be enough to possess and protect her from all the nightmares that might be hiding up ahead.

His hands found her bra and unclasped it. She felt a moment of panic as the past came rushing back to claim her. Its mocking laugh seemed to ring in her ears, but she wouldn't give in to its pain. She was free and whole and not about to hide away any longer. She moved closer into Luke's arms, closer to the heart of his desire and almost gasped in joy as Luke cupped her breast.

His hand brushed against the scars, but there was no slowing his caress, no question hanging in the air to be answered. As if as one, they lay back on the sofa, his weight on her a wonder. When he pushed her T-shirt up and took first one nipple in his mouth, then the other, she gave herself up to the ecstasy of passion. She felt newborn and newly loved.

With slow and careful movements, they stripped off each other's clothes. Her T-shirt and bra were first to go, so Luke could touch and kiss her breasts as if they were the source of all her joy and hunger. For a time she let them be, but then grew more needy. The fire within her threatened to consume all and she reached up to unbutton his shirt, then push it back and out of her way.

She let her fingers dance among the hairs on his chest, then let her tongue take their place. She treasured the gasps of bliss that came from Luke's mouth. She felt strong and powerful; she felt giving.

But the delights could only be reveled in for a moment, before other cravings began to make their demands felt. Luke helped her slip off her shorts and panties, then wiggled out of his own jeans and underwear.

He lay against her then, hard and strong and, oh, so masculine. She closed her eyes and let the tide of passion wash over her. He slipped between her legs where the core of her yearnings lay, where the fire that was engulfing her lay ready to rage over them both.

She took him into her, giving him her heart and soul along with her body. The fire flared up, greater and greater, until a blinding rush of light surrounded her. The sky was exploding along with the very essence of her. Upward they soared, locked in each other's arms for eternity, until the heavens collided and their destiny was set. Then ever so slowly, they floated back to earth.

For a long time they lay still, locked in an embrace. Then Luke lifted his head ever so slightly and kissed her. Kissed her lips, then her chin, then down to her breast.

He raised up a touch more and ran his fingers lightly over the scars. "What happened here?" he asked, his voice a thready whisper. "You in an accident?"

"Yeah." That was it. An accident, that was all it had been.

She closed her eyes, cuddled closer to Luke and let the stardust settle around her heart. Their love had been enough to set her free again. It had been enough to give her life and hope and wondrous joy. No silly old scars were going to take that away from her—not today.

* * *

Gabbi took a slow, deep breath, savoring the sweet scent of clean, damp earth. It was night now, with the moon playing peekaboo in a partly cloudy sky. But even at this time, just after midnight, there was a scurry of activity in her backyard. Luke had said the tracks indicated that raccoon, possum and rabbits visited her yard on a regular basis.

She smiled and took another lungful of the pure air. Her toes wiggled on the damp film covering the steps she was sitting on. In addition to cooling her feet, the dew had also dampened her shorts and was cooling her butt, not that she cared. Gabbi liked everything about her new home. Her house, her yard, her neighbors. She chuckled deep in her throat. Especially her neighbors. Well, some of her neighbors, since she didn't know most of them yet.

Luke Bennett was one fine dude. A quiet dude. But that was just the old story of still waters running deep. Luke had a great deal of depth to him. Gabbi could feel her cheeks warm in the cool night air. And he had other qualities, as she'd found out just a few short hours ago.

She stretched her hands up high over her head and yawned. Pleasantly tired, but not sleepy, she leaned back. Trisha and her new grandparents had gotten home about an hour after Luke had left, full of stories about their day and full of weariness. They were sound asleep now, but Gabbi couldn't let the shroud of sleep come over her just yet.

For a quiet man, Luke was surprisingly full of passion and fire. He came to her needfully and demanding. Yet along with his fierce desire and need, he brought consideration. A thoughtful consideration that Gabbi, before she'd met Luke, would have argued no longer existed. His quiet mask hid a huge kettle of emotions, boiling and bubbling from the very depths of his soul. And yet Gabbi had a strange feeling she'd only scratched her man's surface.

Her man. It hadn't been all that long ago that she would have laughed cynically at the thought of being able to savor those two words.

Yet, along with the joy came an uneasiness. The old honesty issue raised its head again. Luke had been totally honest with her. He'd discussed his previous marriage and he'd told her about his problem with alcoholism. As for her—

Suddenly the newly awakened earth was just cold and damp. Gabbi wrapped her arms around herself and shivered. She should tell him. She should be totally honest with Luke, as he had been with her.

Yet she couldn't. She was afraid. She was afraid, because deep down in her heart she didn't trust Luke. Every other man in her life had loved her for her beauty. She couldn't believe that Luke was any different.

A cloud mass dashed across the face of the moon. Gabbi took the resulting darkness and carried it into her house with her.

Chapter Nine

"Oh, hi." Gabbi was taken aback as she walked into her office Monday morning. Her producer had told her that a student from St. Joe High School was going to spend a few hours with her as part of the school's World of Work program. She hadn't expected to find Adam, and his glum face, waiting for her.

"You don't look like Jenny Somers," Gabbi said, forcing a short laugh up past her throat.

"Jenny's sick."

"And you're her replacement?"

"Yeah."

He didn't look all that happy about it. She wondered if he'd been drafted to fill an opening. "Are you interested in radio and television?"

Adam shrugged. "I don't know."

"Or are you just interested in getting out of class?" Gabbi hoped her smile showed there were no hard feelings if he was using this job visit as an excuse to get out of algebra or whatever else was not near and dear to his heart.

"No."

It looked as if he'd been taking chatting lessons from Luke and was now trying to outdo his mentor.

"Well, whatever your reasons," Gabbi said, "I'm glad to see you."

He nodded solemnly, apparently accepting her happiness but not wishing to take any responsibility for it.

"So, do you have any questions?"

"Nope."

"Okay."

The people running the World of Work program recommended a two- to three-hour visit. Given Adam's apparent interest level, Gabbi figured that they might need ten to twelve minutes, at most.

"Well, why don't we go into the studio?"

"Okay."

At least he wasn't going to be argumentative.

They walked toward the back of the station where the studio, engineering and her producer's office were located.

"Engineering is back there," Gabbi said, indicating a room with several knobs and dials visible. "And Jim is our engineer." The bearded Jim waved at them.

"What does the engineer do?" Adam asked.

"Mostly he sits around and hopes nothing goes wrong." That got no rise at all out of the teenager. Oh, well. "He checks on stuff and makes sure it's in working order. And he establishes the link when we get a feed from another station or a central broadcasting facility."

Adam nodded as Gabbi pulled him to a young woman at a desk.

"Pam here is my producer," Gabbi said. "She does just about everything except go on the air and sweep the floor at night."

Pam smiled, but Adam just blinked.

"She keeps track of our on-the-air schedule, researches discussion topics, schedules my outside speeches and mans the phone when we're live and taking calls."

He nodded again.

"Okay, let's go into the studio."

He followed her into the glass-enclosed room like a gangly puppy.

"We'll be going on the air in about fifteen minutes. Let me explain a few things to you and you can sit in during a live show. Okay?"

"Yeah, sure."

Gabbi wondered for a moment if Adam had asked for a visit to the broadcast booth at Covelski Stadium and they gave him her instead. He did say he was replacing a sick classmate. Maybe he had to take her before they would give him to a sportscaster. She sat down in her seat and indicated he should take the guest chair.

"When it's time, I put these earphones on, kick off my shoes, lean back and let 'er rip."

He nodded solemnly.

"Pam signals me when a caller is ready, and I just hit the flashing button."

"Does the person talking go through you or does it go directly to the radio?" he asked.

Gabbi stared at him a moment. There wasn't anything wrong with the question. She was just surprised to see Adam demonstrate any interest.

"It goes directly to the radio circuits."

A little smile played on his lips. "What if—" He shrugged. "Like—" He shrugged again. "Like, you know."

She did know. "What if someone says something they shouldn't say on the air?"

"Yeah," he replied, nodding vigorously.

"It's Pam's responsibility to catch that. There's a seven-second delay between the phone lines and the radio circuits."

"Seven seconds, huh?"

"Yep."

He nodded again and then, apparently satisfied, leaned back in his chair. It looked as if maybe the visit wasn't a complete waste for Adam. Now he had a solid piece of information to take back to his peers.

Since it didn't look as if there would be any other questions, Gabbi went into her normal program start-up routine. She checked the equipment with the engineer. Then Pam came in and went over the commercial breaks with her.

There were the normal advertisements, two newsbreaks and three special public-service announcements.

Adam didn't say anything the whole time, but he appeared to be awake. The boy still looked a little down, but there wasn't any time to chat. Jim was counting down the time with his fingers and then the red On the Air light went on.

"Happy lunchtime, Michiana," she said into the microphone. "This is Gabbi Monroe, your host for 'Gabbin' with Gabbi,' WNDN-AM 740 on your dial. Welcome to today's show. If you have any outside things you want to do today, then do them early. Danny Walz, our weatherman, says there's a nasty front moving in from the west this evening. Lots of rain and thunderstorms."

She switched to the first prerecorded ad, checked the spot off her to-do list and turned toward Adam. At the moment, he looked almost interested.

"Got anybody you want to say hello to?" she asked.

His eyes grew big. "This is a woman's show," he stammered.

"Sure, but anybody can listen."

He just stared at her.

"Got a special girlfriend? I know she should be in school now, but maybe you can say hi to her mother."

"No." He shook his head violently. "No, I don't have anybody."

Judging from Adam's reaction and the color that flooded his face, Gabbi guessed he had somebody special, but the object of his affections probably didn't know of his interest. Jim signaled that she was about to go back on.

"Welcome back, ladies. We have with us today a special guest from St. Joe High." Gabbi took a moment to watch tension muscles stretch in Adam's face. "But he wishes to remain anonymous."

She turned away as relief rushed to his face, filling in the stress lines. Poor guy. It was hard being fifteen.

"Our subject today is daycare," Gabbi said into the microphone. "Tell us your experiences, your opinions, your needs. Our number is 555-2778."

Following that announcement, Gabbi pushed the button for her second prerecorded ad spot. It was a short one, but it gave her time enough to smile and wink at Adam. He responded with a small smile. It was hard to believe, but he appeared to be even quieter than Luke.

The rest of the show proceeded uneventfully. There was little controversy, no one had to be cut off, and they didn't forget any of the paid or unpaid announcements. All in all, it was a good day.

"Well," she said, turning to Adam once she'd signed off. "How did you like it?"

"It was okay," he replied, nodding.

"See a career for yourself in broadcasting?"

"No."

"No? How come?"

"I couldn't figure out enough stuff to say. I mean, like there's a lot of time that you gotta fill in with nothing but talk."

Gabbi got up from her chair, and they left the studio. "We all have different talents. You just have to try different things until you find something you like."

He nodded at that display of wisdom. Probably nothing his teachers hadn't already told him.

"You have any plans for lunch?"

"Uh, yeah. Donny Symanski is gonna pick me up. We thought we'd stop in at Mickey Ds on the way back to school."

"Oh, okay."

"Donny drove me down." He seemed uncomfortable.

"That's fine," Gabbi said. "I usually eat in unless I have to give a speech or meet with somebody."

"Donny's a senior. He has his own car."

He stood there, not even looking as if he were going to make a move, and Gabbi wasn't sure what she was supposed to do. Did he want an escort to the reception area? Was she supposed to formally dismiss him?

"Well." Gabbi stuck her hand out. "It was nice you could drop by."

He shook her hand. "Yeah."

Yeah. Okay. "You can wait for Donny in the reception area," she said. "You can see if anybody drives up."

"He ain't gonna be here for another half hour."

"Oh." Gabbi took a deep breath. "I don't suppose you brought any work with you?"

He shook his head.

"Well, there's a bunch of magazines out front. I have some stuff to—"

"Gabbi, can I ask you something?"

"Sure."

"Is it hard to adopt a kid?"

The words spilled out quickly, like brawlers thrown out of a bar. Once he spoke, Adam looked away. Gabbi blinked, thinking it was a funny kind of question. Certainly Adam knew he was too young to adopt anybody. Maybe he wanted Luke to get him a brother.

"Sort of," she replied. "You have to apply to an agency. Then they have to do a background check, make sure you'd be a good parent. After that they try and match you up with a kid most suitable for you."

"A teacher would probably pass this background check thing real easy, right?" Adam asked, turning back to face Gabbi.

She shrugged. "I suppose so. They want to make sure that you're not a criminal, that you like kids and can work with them."

Adam looked away. "I thought so."

Something seemed wrong. "What do you mean, you thought so?"

He shrugged but wouldn't look at her.

One thing Trisha had taught Gabbi was patience. She waited.

"Luke doesn't want me."

Gabbi felt a wave of shock wash over her. She couldn't believe it. "Did he say that?"

"No."

"Then how do you know? Has he done anything to indicate he doesn't like you?"

"No."

"Are you two having some problems?"

"No, we get along fine."

She took a deep breath. Another thing she'd learned from Trisha was that conversation with a teen could be like being blindfolded and feeling around for something in a pit full of snakes.

"Then why do you say he doesn't want you?"

"He won't adopt me."

Gabbi didn't know what Adam's legal situation was. "Maybe he can't."

"Yes, he can."

Maybe. There might be some impediments that a fifteen-year-old wouldn't understand.

"Have you talked to him about it?"

"Yeah."

She stared a moment at Adam.

"Sort of."

"Sort of?"

"Yeah, kind of."

She wondered what that meant. Tight-lipped as those two were, it could mean they had shared a total of three words between them on the subject.

"Have you talked to Matt about it?"

"Sort of."

Another sort of. Gabbi wondered why Adam was telling her about this situation. She wasn't a normal confidante of his. Another lesson from Trisha. Kids don't tell you anything unless they want you to do something.

"Do you want me to talk to Luke?"

He shrugged. "If you want."

If I want. Gabbi sighed. She probably didn't. But the kid was obviously troubled. "Okay."

"I think I'll wait outside." He grinned slightly. "You know, like I gotta get in my outdoor thing before the storms come."

Gabbi watched as he went to the door. He gave her a wave and a broad smile before he stepped outside. Goody. That's just what she wanted. A serious little chat with Luke.

Luke wasn't exactly a Chatty Charlie. He seemed to keep a lot of things locked up inside.

But there might be a simple answer to why he didn't legally adopt Adam. He called him his foster son, and he'd indicated that taking care of him was something Adam's father had wanted Luke to do. And the boy's father had been an attorney, so she assumed that Luke and Adam's relationship satisfied whatever legal requirements the state had. So maybe he couldn't adopt the boy. That was probably it. She turned and walked quickly toward her office.

Yet. She shook her head. Luke had this way of keeping things at arm's length. Things and people. She'd felt that herself. Could Luke really not want to adopt Adam? Rats. She didn't want to find out.

"Hello?" Luke called into the house from the back door. "Gabbi?"

"In the dining room," she called back.

He went inside and found her kneeling on the floor in front of a china cabinet, unpacking a box of table linens. Her hair was disheveled, her face slightly flushed, and a smudge of dust was across her cheek. She'd never looked more beautiful.

"What're you doing?" He reached into the box, then handed her a stack of napkins.

She gave him a look he deserved. "Unpacking." She put the napkins into a drawer.

"Okay, dumb question. How about, are you ready for a break? I feel like taking a walk."

"Help me finish this box and you're on."

It only took a few minutes to unpack the rest. The trays and serving dishes went into the side section, the tablecloths into the middle section and some candlesticks into the other side.

"Box number twenty-three unpacked," she said with satisfaction and broke the tape on the bottom to fold the box up. "Only 895 to go."

"What are you doing, a box a day? Hey, you'll be done in no time."

She grinned and took his hand. "So we're taking a walk, are we?"

Right now, with her hand in his and that smile lighting all sorts of yearnings in his heart, taking a walk was the last thing he had in mind. But he shook his thoughts free and took the box from her.

"Trash?" he asked.

She nodded. "Since I am never, ever moving again, I won't need to save my boxes."

The idea of her living forever in the house behind Luke ought to have pleased him. He'd be able to look out each morning and see her leave for the station. He'd be able to sit on her back steps with her and watch the evening settle over the town. But the idea left something incomplete, an emptiness in his heart that he had no idea how to fill.

Still hand in hand, they left the box in the alley and strolled down to the street. Without discussing it, they both headed down toward the river, walking silently. The air smelled of freshly cut grass and lilacs. Every yard they passed seemed to be in full bloom. Tulips, lilacs, peonies. Some people had already planted their annuals, impatiens mostly because they bloomed so well in the dense shade of the area.

Besides the colors and scents of spring, the neighborhood seemed to be a riot of sounds and movement. Kids were riding bikes and roller-skating. Laughter was adding its own special spice to the air. In spite of the threat of storms approaching, the area was alive. Or was it because of the threat?

They crossed Riverside Drive and walked down the grassy embankment to just above the river's edge. The current was reasonably strong, but steady. A few leaves and sticks were caught under a low-hanging branch, trying to escape the relentless pull of the river. How long could they delay the inevitable?

What was the inevitable for him? Giving in totally to Gabbi's charms or failing her at some crucial moment? Or both?

Gabbi sat down on the grass, and he sat next to her.

"Thanks for showing Adam around today." He leaned over and gave her a light kiss on the cheek, trying to escape his stormy thoughts. "He was really excited about it."

Gabbi stared at him. "Excited?" Her mouth hung open, and amazement filled her face, overflowing her eyes.

Luke had to laugh. "Hey, you gotta be able to read the signs with Adam."

"Well, he seemed reasonably interested," Gabbi said. "But excited—"

"Believe me." Luke took her hand and stared out over the water. "He was. He couldn't talk about anything else all through dinner."

Dark clouds were hanging on the far horizon. A faint streak of lightning danced briefly in the sky.

"Gonna storm tonight," Luke said. "Matt says his bursitis is telling him it's going to be a beaut."

"Why do you think Adam feels he can't talk about anything else?"

Luke suppressed the sigh that wanted to escape. He had sought her company out because he didn't seem able not to, but then his own melancholy tried to follow. Now, when he seemed almost able to escape that, she wanted to bring storm clouds of her own around.

"There isn't anything Adam can't talk about," he said cautiously.

"Do you think Adam feels that way?"

She was usually so straightforward. But now she seemed to be backing into a subject, instead of putting it on the table straight out.

"I think so," he replied. "But you never know for sure what another person is thinking. Especially a fifteen-year-old boy who's rather on the quiet side."

"Have you ever thought of adopting Adam?"

He came to a stop. "Huh?"

"I said, have you ever—"

"I heard you, I heard you." He turned toward the water again. Man, what the hell brought this on? "No, I haven't."

"Oh."

It was a simple word, but the tone was foreboding. Although he wasn't sure, Luke thought that it contained a load of blame. But blame for what? He wasn't hurting anyone.

"Would you like to?"

He stared out at the horizon. The storm was probably still out over Lake Michigan. Too bad it wasn't closer. Like about thirty seconds away. Then they would have to run for their houses. And even then they'd get soaked to the skin. So wet they'd have to take their clothes off and dry each other with great big bath towels.

"I never really thought of it."

Gabbi didn't reply, and he felt a need to explain. "Adam's an older kid." Hell, that was a stupid remark. Especially considering that Gabbi had just adopted an older child. "I mean, Adam had his own parents."

Damn. This conversation was like quicksand. The more he explained, the deeper he got. All adopted kids had other parents at some time in their lives.

"Ron just asked me to take care of Adam. See that he got through school and into adulthood. Nothing was said about adopting anybody."

She still didn't say anything. Luke found the silence uncomfortable, although there was no reason to. Probably had something to do with the low air pressure and the incoming storm.

"I don't even know that Adam would want me to adopt him. I mean, whose name would he take? Would that screw up his inheritance in any way? It's a complex issue."

"I don't know about all the issues," Gabbi said. "But I do know that Adam wants you to adopt him."

He turned toward her again. "You know?"

Gabbi nodded. "That's all he wanted to talk about when he was at the station." Her face, her eyes, were so serious.

Luke looked away and sighed. It had sounded so simple when Ron had asked him to take care of Adam. Just look after the kid if anything happened to Ron and Laura. No big deal. Take care of him until he was old enough to be on his own. After all his old buddy had done for him, Luke couldn't say no. And to be perfectly honest, neither of them thought the need would ever come to pass.

"This has sort of snuck up on me," Luke murmured. "Guess Adam and I will have to have a chat or two."

"I think so."

You think so. But Luke quickly swallowed his initial flush of irritation. It wasn't as if Gabbi hadn't been around the mountain herself a few times. She'd had some hard moments, what with her divorce and all. And then taking on a challenge like Trisha.

But an adoption was permanent. And Luke wasn't a permanent kind of guy. He wasn't into long-range plans and lifetime commitments. He liked taking things day by day. It kept him away from booze and it would keep him on the straight and narrow in everything else.

"I'll talk to him. We'll hash it out. Do what's best."

A distant rumbling drew their attention. The rain was getting closer. Swell. Why couldn't the storm have come when he really needed it?

"We'd better get on home," he said as they got to their feet.

"Yes, we'd better."

Things didn't seem quite as sunny now, and it had nothing to do with the storm approaching.

"How are the pancakes?" Luke asked as he watched Adam wolf down his stack the next morning.

"Okay."

"As good as Matt's?"

Adam shook his head, probably because his mouth was full.

"How come?"

"Matt's the greatest cook," Adam replied.

"What's different between his and my stuff?" Luke asked. "We both use the same recipes."

Adam mopped up the remains of the syrup with his last forkful of pancake before popping it in his mouth.

"He's the greatest," Adam said. "I mean, like what more can I say?"

"Nothing that I can think of."

He watched the kid drain his milk and then finish up with a full glass of orange juice. Luke's eyes wandered to the clock over the sink. They still had a few minutes before they had to leave. Better to get it over with before they got into the day's activities. He cleared his throat.

"Gabbi said you guys had a nice chat yesterday."

Adam nodded. "Yeah, she's a neat lady. She told me all about radio broadcasting and different stuff like that."

"That's good," Luke said, nodding. He cleared his throat again. "She also said you talked about adoption with her."

Adam blinked and stared at him for a moment. Luke's stomach tightened as he waited. He wondered if Adam would get mad and explode, go off stomping to his room, or both.

"Yeah." The kid's words came out slowly. "I thought about Trisha when I saw her. And that made me think of adoption."

"I see," Luke replied. They both took a turn staring at the clock and out the window beneath it.

"Adoption is a pretty complex kind of thing," Luke said.

"Yeah."

"Especially with older kids."

"Yeah."

"And even more so where, like in your case, a person is sort of taking over for a friend of theirs."

"Uh-huh."

Luke had always considered himself a straightforward guy. Someone who said what was on his mind. He didn't believe in beating around the bush, but this personal stuff wasn't as easy as telling a kid how to lower his dribble or when to swing at a ball.

"I should be getting ready to go," Adam said.

Luke glanced at the clock again. They had a lot of time. "You know your father and I were close friends?"

Adam nodded.

"And, as his son, you're carrying on Ron's name for him."

"Ah, yeah. I guess."

"Well, that's what kids, especially sons, do. They carry their father's name into the next generation. And then when you marry, your son will do the same for you."

Adam stared at him.

"You understand?"

"I guess," Adam replied with a shrug, "but what difference does it make?"

Shoot. Now what? How did one discuss these things with a kid? Should he talk about a sense of having a part of you live on with someone who, like all teens, probably considered himself immortal? Or should he tackle the subject from the basis of property and how different things were passed down from father to son? Luke doubted if Adam cared about either.

"I don't know," Luke said. "Some things are kind of hard to understand until you get older."

Adam's stare turned into a bit of a glare. Damn. That was a dumb remark. After all his years of teaching, Luke should know that teens hated to be talked down to.

"I meant, different things are important to you at different times in your life."

"Oh."

Yeah, oh. Luke couldn't think of any better reply to his words, and he wasn't fifteen anymore.

"I really like you, Adam." The kid stared at him, and Luke could feel his stomach tie up into a million, zillion knots. "Actually, it's more than just liking you. I love you like you were my own son."

Luke paused. This emotional stuff was like dealing with nitroglycerin. One wrong move and *bam!* everything's blown to hell. Adam still looked cool, though.

"But I was your father's best friend," Luke went on, taking a long moment to check out the floor. The tile on the kitchen floor was starting to look a little worse for wear. "So I don't really want to take his name away from you. The name your father gave you."

Adam's face wrinkled in confusion.

"That's what would happen," Luke said, leaning forward. "If I adopted you, then you'd take my name. You'd become Adam Bennett."

"Oh," Adam replied.

Oh? Did that mean he understood? Luke waited in silence while Adam stared down at the table, frown lines creasing his forehead.

Finally the boy looked up. "I just remembered something."

"Yeah?" Something Ron had told him?

"I promised Sam Burke I'd help him with his algebra this morning."

They stared at each other for a long moment.

"Then I guess we'd better get going," Luke said.

"That's what I thought."

Adam slid out of his chair and hurried up to his room while Luke remained, staring out the window above the sink. A pair of sparrows were quarreling outside. Luke felt like telling them to shut up. What the hell did sparrows have to argue about?

But then he decided that you never knew unless you were one. For instance, as a teacher, he had considered himself an expert on kids. Now as a parent, he saw how dumb he really was.

Sighing, he stood up. At least now if Gabbi asked him if he'd talked to Adam, he'd be able to say he did. Not that he was sure what he accomplished, if anything. He didn't know whether the issue was dead or whether it would rise up and bite him in the ass when he least suspected it. His newfound knowledge of kids told him that the latter was most likely.

"Back in the old days there used to be a bunch of mills along here," Luke said.

Gabbi heard Luke's words, but they didn't seem to penetrate. She just stared across the East Race of the St. Joseph River. There was something going on at the convention center, with people milling around on the building's riverside patio. A part of her longed to be there, to be safely lost in the middle of a crowd. His silence finally jolted her.

"I'm sorry," she said. "My mind was drifting off. What did you say?"

"I was just playing tour guide," Luke replied. "Nothing important."

Moving closer to him, Gabbi put an arm through his. How could she wish to be anywhere else? She loved being with Luke, and would love it more when she didn't have a guilty conscience nagging at her. They leaned against the rail together and shared a silent view of the water rushing past them.

Luke had called her when he'd gotten home from school. It had been too wet to practice, so he'd suggested they take a bike ride along the Rail Trail, a hiking-biking path built on an old railroad right-of-way. Neither Adam nor Trisha had wanted to go, so it had just been the two of them. They were pausing here next to an old factory that had been refurbished into an upscale restaurant, catching their wind for the return trip home.

"I didn't mean to ignore you." She gave his arm a squeeze. "I'm just a little out of it today. It's been a hectic week or two."

"Next time, you need to plan your moving a bit further from your final adoption hearing."

"I'll remember that," she said, leaning her head on his shoulder.

Next time. Next time. Next time. She wasn't planning on a next time in terms of moving, or a next-time adoption. Trisha was enough for her. The only next times Gabbi was hoping for involved Luke.

But what was he hoping for? She'd been a turmoil of seething emotions since they'd made love the other night. Ecstasy. Joy. Guilt. Fear. Hope. Total, absolute confusion. Yet he seemed the same as ever. Hadn't he been touched by the experience, or was he just better at hiding his feelings?

Neither were issues she really wanted to explore. "You were talking about some mills," she said.

Luke nodded toward the old factory building near them. "When South Bend first started," he replied, "factories like this one needed power, so they located here on the river. The water drove whatever machinery was needed."

"Hmm. Interesting."

His face lit up with a smile. "Oh, I'm an interesting kind of guy."

The laughter in his eyes touched her, sent a riot of feelings scurrying down into her depths. She squeezed his arm. They were moving too fast. Maybe they should step back. Slow things down.

"I suppose all this water power is going to waste now," she said.

"Oh, no. They hold kayak races here, that kind of thing."

Gabbi laughed. She loved his sense of humor. He could lighten any moment for her. Doug could do that, too. He always had something clever to say, yet his retorts seemed more staged then Luke's. Did that mean that Luke was giving more of himself to their relationship?

"I had a short talk with Adam this morning," he said.

"Oh?"

"We didn't have a lot of time, but we did talk a bit about adoption and his situation."

She had the feeling that "talk" might mean one thing to Luke and another to her. "Did Adam feel any better?"

"Hard to say." He stood away from the railing. "I should be getting back home. It's my turn to fix dinner tonight."

Gabbi pushed away from the railing. "Yeah, mine, too." She couldn't help but feel annoyed with herself as they walked back to their bikes.

"What's Trisha doing?"

"Visiting a friend who just got a puppy."

"I guess a fenced-in yard like yours must need a dog."

"I'm waiting until the summer," Gabbi said as they started pedaling. "I'd hate to leave a puppy alone for a good part of the day."

"Cats do well in that kind of environment."

"Don't tell Trisha," Gabbi said with a laugh. "She'll just want both."

Gabbi went ahead as they rode single file up the street. It was a pleasant ride and got even better once they got up on the bluffs high above the river. A canopy of trees sheltered them from the world as they rode along the paved path. They passed an occasional bench provided for weary hikers, since this path was intended someday to go up into Michigan and eventually all the way over to the lake.

Plan for the future, even if it's still a long way off, was the message the path told her. Put in rest spots even if there's no need for rest now. What did she need to do now for her own future?

They turned off the path and made their way around the park before heading for home. The trip back was taken a little faster, causing Gabbi to break into a minor sweat. It felt good.

"Why don't you take the bike home?" Luke said. "We don't need it."

"Trisha and I should be getting our own. We just haven't had a chance to go shopping."

"I'm sure you'd prefer a girl's bike, but keep this one until you get your own. In fact, we have two more at home. Why don't you keep both of them? One for you and one for Trisha."

They pedaled down the alley between their homes, and Luke helped Gabbi put the bikes in her garage. He was sharing so much of himself and his life with them. Why couldn't she share just a piece of herself?

She needed to know her fears were silly, that he was as strong as he seemed and as true as the day was long. She needed to feel that wall of safety his arms provided to know everything would always be fine. A major false assumption, if there ever was one. She turned to find him watching her.

"What kind of rent are you going to charge us?" she asked.

"I don't know," he replied. "I haven't thought of it."

He was there for the taking, his arms ready to give her all the safety and security she wanted. She stepped in closer and put her arms around his neck, pulling his lips down to hers. His arms slid around her, pulling her into his cocoon of warmth and stability. She was protected here. She was guarded.

His lips moved against hers, and the yearnings of last Saturday returned. She wanted to feel his strength. She wanted to run her fingers through the mat of hair on his chest and know the steel that lay beneath it. She wanted his hands on her, stroking her softness, adding to her needs. Pressing closer and closer to him, she reveled in the way his arms tightened around her, yet she longed to be closer still. To be one with him again, not just in body but in heart and soul.

She pulled away slowly, and they stepped back out into the alley. "Well, let me know when you've decided," she said, trying to maintain the earlier joking atmosphere. "I'm willing to pay anything that's fair."

"Oh, I'll think of something," he said.

He stood there, his body muscular and strong, a healthy flush to his cheeks and an invitation swimming deep in his eyes. Gabbi swallowed, suddenly seeing all sorts of pitfalls ahead of them. Was she ready to swim? And without a life jacket?

"See ya," she said with a wave, followed by quick steps toward her yard. Coward, a little voice shouted.

Luke shut the gate and leaned back against it. Oh criminy. Mother Nature wanted to insure the existence of all her species, so within each she put a powerful desire to mate. Man then took that simple desire and wrapped it in all kinds of emotions, romantic and otherwise. Filling a simple need with such enormous complexity that man himself didn't understand it anymore.

Hell, he thought as he walked toward his house, he should have been a monk.

A powerful smell of meat, tomatoes and chili powder greeted him as he stepped into his kitchen. "What are you doing?" he snapped at Matt, who was stirring a big pot on the stove.

"Making you guys a batch of chili," his father replied. "Dinner tonight, and then you can freeze the rest."

"I was going to cook tonight," Luke protested.

Matt tasted his work. "You were off with your lady friend."

"We weren't going to be gone that long."

"You should spend more time with her." Matt went to the pantry and pulled out a package of noodles. "She's doing you a world of good."

"Huh?"

"You're more relaxed," Matt said. "Not as grumpy as you usually are."

"We're just friends."

"Gotta start somewhere." Matt pulled a pot from the cabinet and filled it with water.

"There's nothing serious between us."

"Why don't you go set the table?" Matt said. "I don't want to do everything around here."

Damn. Luke took his newly relaxed mood and stomped into the dining room to set the table. Hell. Were things so obvious? He must look like some geeky little high school kid stumbling around and grinning for weeks after his first kiss.

Chapter Ten

Gabbi and Trisha climbed toward the top of the bleachers, but instead of sitting down Trisha cupped her hands to her mouth and shouted, "Yo, Stretch."

Luke smiled and waved, but Adam ignored them, concentrating instead on practicing catching with another boy from his team.

"Boy, oh, boy," Trisha said, laughing. "That really frosts his lids."

"Frosts his lids," Gabbi repeated. "What in the world is that?"

Her daughter just rolled her eyes heavenward, obviously calling on the gods to send Gabbi at least a minimum of intelligence.

"I can see that you're irritating the poor guy."

"That's what I said," Trisha replied, looking very put upon.

"Why do you want to do that?" Gabbi asked.

"He needs it."

Gabbi leaned back and stared at the field. There were times when it was better to say nothing.

"May and Clarisse are here," Trisha said, indicating two girls that Gabbi recognized as her daughter's classmates coming through the gate. "I'm gonna sit with them."

"Okay." Her eyes went back to the field as she watched the teams prepare for the game. Luke was moving among the kids and, judging from the smiles he was getting, loosening them up with jokes and wisecracks. With his firm demeanor and graying temples, he looked the part of a man in charge. Yet his youthful attitude made it easy for him to relate to the kids.

"Gabbi Monroe?"

She looked at a tall, slender blond woman standing a level down and nodded. "Yes."

"I'm Laura Kurek," the woman said, sticking her hand out. "We live one block east and the next street south of you."

"Oh, yes." Gabbi took her hand. "Hi."

The woman sat down. "Come to see a coaching legend at work?"

"You mean Luke?"

"Who else?"

"Actually, we came to see Adam."

"Sure."

Gabbi could feel her cheeks grow warm, but she plowed on with her explanation. "Adam lives across the alley from us, and my daughter wanted to see him play."

"Oh, yeah."

"They're friends. Sort of. Adam and my daughter."

"That's nice," Laura said.

Gabbi felt like a fool. She hated it when she stammered. A communications professional like herself should be cool under any and all circumstances.

"Let's bring it on in, guys," one of the coaches called out, and all the players ran to their respective sidelines.

Gabbi quickly hunched over and stared at the activity on the field. Nothing exciting, but at the moment, she'd be willing to watch paint dry instead of talking about why they came to a high school baseball game. Laura was still sitting by her side.

"How do they decide who gets to bat first?" Gabbi asked.

She wanted to know, but she was more interested in diverting the woman's thoughts to something neutral. It wasn't really what the woman said. It was more her attitude. In either case, Gabbi didn't want to get into any kind of discussion about her and Luke and Adam and Trisha or anything of that sort. Good thing that thought hadn't been put into words. Even Gabbi herself didn't understand it.

"The visiting team always gets to bat first," Laura replied.

"Oh."

They watched the two teams gather around their respective coaches. The St. Joe boys listened to the words of a short, bald man who was, most likely, the head coach, but they saved a good bit of attention for Luke, who roamed the outside of the circle, patting a back here, dropping a word there. Gabbi thought it was obvious that the kids respected him.

"He's really a great coach," Laura said. "Explains things well, relates to the kids and is able to motivate them."

"Oh, that's nice."

"He's just an all-around good teacher."

"I've heard that."

Both teams broke at a cheer, with the St. Joe players scattering to their positions across the field and the visitors sending their first player to bat.

"My son plays football," Laura said. "He said that if it hadn't been for Luke, the whole team would have gone down the tubes this fall. Their head coach had some health problems and Luke really stepped in."

"Oh," Gabbi said.

"I don't know why Luke's never been a head coach," Laura said. "Especially in football. Everyone says he could coach at the college level if he wanted to."

Luke did seem a little old and experienced to still be an assistant. "He coaches the year around. Maybe he wouldn't be able to do that if he assumed full responsibility for one of the teams."

"I suppose."

The crack of bat to ball brought a pause in their conversation, and they watched as the ball floated up high over third base. Adam caught it, and the first batter was out.

"That Adam's a good little player," Laura said. "Only a freshman and he's already starting on the varsity."

"He's down on himself because he hasn't hit a home run yet this season," Gabbi said.

"Yeah, he's real competitive," Laura replied. "His father was like that. And so was Luke."

Was or is? Gabbi wondered if Luke was any different from when he was a teen. Of course, he had to be. Life changed people, and he'd taken some hits during the years. Vietnam. A divorce. Fighting alcoholism. And losing his best friend to an auto accident.

"It's probably politics."

"What?" Lost in her thoughts, Gabbi had forgotten about Laura.

"You know, the reason Luke's never made head coach," Laura said. "I bet it's politics. He probably doesn't shine up to the right people."

"Could be." Gabbi watched the batter swing and miss.

"Say, I gotta be going. Season's almost over and I have to talk to some of the other mothers about the team banquet."

"Oh, good luck."

"It's no problem. A bunch of us have done it before." Laura stood up and patted Gabbi on the shoulder. "Nice meeting you. And whenever the two of you are out walking or cycling in the neighborhood, drop in."

"You mean me and Trisha? Thank you, we will."

"Sure, bring the kids along."

With a quick wave, Laura was gone, long legs stretching to catch up with another woman who was heading toward the exit. Gabbi frowned slightly. What was this nonsense about the two of them dropping in for a visit? Were she and Luke an item in the neighborhood? Jeez, the place really was like some small village where everyone knew everyone else's business.

While Gabbi was lost in her thoughts, more of the visiting team were struck out. At least two more, because the teams were changing sides. St. Joe was now up at bat, and the visitors were in positions on the field. Her mind was about to wander again when she noticed that Adam was going to be the first one up to bat. His body language spoke of tension, his face was set with determination, and he gripped his bat like a battle-ax. Poor guy. He wanted so badly to hit a home run.

"Yea, Adam!" she shouted.

He flashed her a quick smile and ignored the hooting sounds that Trisha and her girlfriends were making. Gabbi told herself to have another little chat with Trisha about being positive and encouraging.

Adam hit the first pitch, and it sailed high out into the far left field. Gabbi jumped up, thinking this was going to be Adam's home run, but it hit the top of the fence and bounced back onto the field. The opposing player was there to pick it up, and Adam had to slide into third base.

"Way to go, Adam!" Gabbi cheered.

Even Trisha and her little section cheered. She saw Luke congratulate him, but the boy's face still wore a frown. Poor kid. It was hard learning that sometimes what you wanted and what you could get were two different things.

Gabbi settled back down in her seat. Had she ever learned that or was she still trying to resist accepting that fact as truth?

Was she wanting a man she could lean on when what she had fallen in love with was a sunny weather friend?

The fans, the stands, the game itself, all disappeared. Fallen in love with? She wasn't in love with Luke, was she? She couldn't be. She had her life all planned and love wasn't part of it.

Yet in spite of all her big plans, she had fallen into that same trap again. Love and all its baggage.

She stared over at Luke where he stood, waving a runner around the bases as he kept one eye on the outfield and the ball. Why hadn't she realized how dangerous he was? His gentle and accepting air had made him seem so safe, yet they were the very reasons her heart had fallen for him.

What was she going to do now? Did she run, figuratively speaking, of course, or did she pretend nothing had happened?

Somehow the idea of letting the love grow, nourishing it and reveling in all the joy it would bring, didn't even seem an option.

Luke turned the faucet on and off a few times. It didn't leak anymore. Another job well done by Super Handyman. He gathered up his tools and wondered what else he should do. Saturday morning was a normal fix-it time for him, but he didn't really feel like doing anything. He could definitely feel a load of the grumps coming on, and he paused to lift a blind and look out at the house in back.

He wasn't really spying, and he wasn't a dirty old man. Well, a little smudged maybe, but not really dirty. He just liked to check out the neighborhood. Make sure that everything was in order.

Although he had to admit that he'd been checking out the house across the alley a lot more since the new owner moved in. His eyes just naturally roamed over to where Gabbi was. It was as if they were magnets and she was steel. There was no activity going on across the way, so he let the blind drop.

He really should get a life.

Luke leaned against the wall. Actually, it wasn't as if he didn't have a life. Between teaching, coaching and taking care of Adam and himself, he thought he had a full plate.

Then Gabbi had come along. He still taught school, coached and took care of Adam and himself. Nothing was left to slide. But his life seemed a lot fuller than it had been.

And a lot emptier.

A flash of color from across the alley caught his eye, and Luke raised the blind again. Gabbi and Trisha were out in their yard, struggling with a ladder.

Well, not really struggling. That Trisha was as strong as an ox. She was five foot six and still growing. The kid was going to make a hell of a forward on a basketball team or a damn good soccer goalie.

They put the ladder up against the house, then had a short discussion before Gabbi scrambled up. Trisha stayed below and steadied the ladder. Looked as though they were going to clean the debris out of the gutters. Maybe he should go over and help them.

Luke let the blind fall and turned away from the window. If they'd needed any help, Gabbi would have gone out and hired someone. She wasn't one of those helpless pieces of fluff who needed a man to do everything for her.

He picked up his tools and went downstairs. And now that he thought about it, that was the main reason he liked Gabbi. She wasn't a clinging-vine type. She was a strong, competent woman, fully able to take care of herself.

After dropping his tools on the kitchen counter, Luke went out his back door and into his yard. It was a nice day, and he didn't have anything pressing to do, so he might as well go over and visit his neighbor. After all, that was the kind of neighborhood it was—friendly.

They heard him as he stepped through the gate. Gabbi called out a welcome greeting, while Trisha hollered, "Luke. Come here, quick."

Worried, Luke hurried over to the ladder.

"Here," Trisha said. "Grab this."

He put his hand on the ladder, and Trisha let go.

"Trisha," Gabbi called down. "What are you doing?"

He looked up. Gabbi was wearing shorts, a T-shirt and sneakers. He hadn't remembered viewing her from this angle before. But Gabbi was like a fine sculpture. No matter which way you looked at her, it came out good.

"Nice view, huh?" Trisha had a grin on her face. "I mean, if you're a guy."

"Trisha, what are you doing?"

"Nothing," she replied, looking up.

"Then why don't you go and clean your room?"

"We just moved in."

"We've been here long enough," Gabbi said. "And that room hasn't been cleaned yet."

Trisha looked at Luke, bewilderment filling her face. "She's serious, isn't she?"

"Sure sounds like it," Luke replied.

"I can't believe it."

"Trisha."

"I cannot believe it," the girl said, shaking her head as she walked toward the back door. "It's just freaking unbelievable."

"I guess I'm the horrible stepmother."

Luke went back to looking up the ladder.

"What do you think?" Gabbi asked.

"I think she's right."

"What?" Gabbi glared down at him.

"It's a great view," he said, pausing to let a grin fill his face. "If you're a guy, that is."

She took a handful of debris and threw it down on him.

"Hey," he protested.

"That's what you get for being a smart aleck."

"You're really a mean little thing." Luke brushed dirt from his face and shirt. "Didn't your mother ever tell you that you can catch more flies with honey than vinegar?"

"So what?" Gabbi snapped. "I don't want any flies. They're filthy little things."

"You're not a very reasonable person," Luke muttered.

"You better start being nice to me," Gabbi said as she threw more debris on his head. "Or you're going to be in big trouble."

"Would you cut that out?"

"No." Some more dirt and junk rained down on his head. "Not until you start being nice."

"I'll show you nice." Luke started to climb up the ladder.

"Luke," Gabbi shouted. "Quit fooling around."

"I'm fooling around?" He paused to look hurt. "You're throwing dirt on me and now I'm the one fooling around."

"I'll kick you."

"Don't fool around," Luke ordered. "It's dangerous up here."

"It wouldn't be if you were on the ground holding this ladder like you're supposed to be."

Luke eased himself around Gabbi and onto the roof. Then he leaned over slightly and kissed her. She was so outraged and worried and beautiful. "See, it's not so dangerous."

Gabbi laughed. "Not up here it won't be. I can guarantee that."

Her eyes danced with laughter that awoke a hunger in his heart. He wanted to lean forward again and take a long, lingering taste of her lips. He wanted to sweep her into his arms and let that fire grow. But he just leaned back, looking out over the neighborhood.

"Nice view," Gabbi said. "Isn't it?"

"Actually, the one from below was better."

"Hmm. Be careful, fella. Flattery is liable to get you everywhere."

"You mean like a date for dinner?"

She looked confused, taken off guard. "I can't tonight."

"Oh?" He tried not to sound as disappointed as he was.

"I, ah... I have this... I have these people I have to meet with."

Luke looked at her. It was obvious she wasn't comfortable telling him more. Did that mean she had another date? The sun might as well have fled.

"As long as I'm up here," he said. "I might as well help you clean these gutters."

He moved down and began dumping the debris and dirt on the ground below. Damn gutters looked as though they hadn't been cleaned in years.

Why wouldn't she tell him where she was going?

"I hope we didn't ruin your evening," Andi said once the waiter had left with their orders.

"Oh, no," Gabbi replied. "Not at all. I didn't have anything planned." She let Luke's invitation dance briefly in her memory, but then shut it out. Andi LaVelle from the cancer support group had called earlier in the week and asked Gabbi to join her and a few others for dinner, and Gabbi had accepted. First come, first served. Maybe Luke shouldn't assume they were going to spend every Saturday evening together.

"We sometimes like to have our board meetings and planning sessions over dinner," another woman explained. Gabbi remembered her as Barb-with-the-implants from the meeting. "Gives a reason to get out and treat ourselves."

"I think it's a good idea," Gabbi agreed. Was this a board meeting or a planning session? Either way, why was she here?

The other woman present, a middle-aged woman named Nancy, smiled sympathetically at Gabbi. "Although Saturday evening meetings are harder on you young singles."

"It's no problem."

Barb grinned at her a moment. "I hope you left that nice coach fella with something to do," she said. "You leave a young man like that at loose ends and he's liable to get into trouble."

Gabbi froze for a moment. What? Did they know about Luke? They couldn't. She and Luke hadn't exactly been discreet, but they hadn't advertised their relationship, either. There was no reason for the whole city to know that they were occasionally seeing each other.

"I have a cousin who coaches at John Glenn High School in Walkerton," Barb said. "He knows Luke Bennett really well."

"Walkerton?"

"That's a little south and west of here."

Like about twenty miles southwest. Well, it looked as if the whole city didn't know about her and Luke. The whole county did.

"Want to hit the salad bar before we get down to business?" Andi asked.

Gabbi quietly followed the others to the restaurant's extensive salad bar. She couldn't believe this. There were somewhere around 250,000 people in the county and they all knew about her and Luke. Was Luke out telling everyone about them? She found that hard to believe. The man wasn't exactly a talker.

She filled her plate with tossed salad and balanced a slice of freshly baked bread on one side and some fruit slices on the other. Everyone smiled at her as she sat back down.

"You're probably wondering why we asked you to join us," Andi said.

"The question had crossed my mind."

Barb laughed as she spread her napkin in her lap. "I knew you'd be suspicious. In fact, I'm surprised you agreed to

Andi's invitation. 'Course, you're new to the group. Any of the rest of us would have known to just refuse flat out."

The others laughed, though Andi stopped before the others. She leaned across the table. "We're the Outreach Committee," she told Gabbi. "Our main function is to reach out to the general community to educate, support and inform."

"As you can imagine, it gets kind of hard to come up with new ideas," Nancy said. "There's only so many people you can reach with pamphlets and public-service messages."

"So we thought of you," Barb said.

"Me?" Gabbi wasn't sure she understood. She speared a piece of lettuce, playing for time.

Barb nodded. "We knew who you were when you came to the support group, but you didn't mention your radio show, so we didn't."

"But it would be the perfect forum to discuss all sorts of issues related to breast cancer," Andi said.

Gabbi said nothing for a long moment, taking the time to carefully chew the suddenly rubbery lettuce. Her fingers felt icy cold all of a sudden. "I did a show on breast cancer last year," she pointed out. "In October, when the cancer society has its mammogram drive."

"But that wasn't from the perspective of a survivor," Nancy pointed out.

The icy cold spread up her arms, and Gabbi reached for her coffee, taking a sip. It didn't help warm her.

"We thought that a show focusing on actual cancer patients and survivors would really help," Andi said. "Some women are so afraid of the disease, they don't get checkups of any kind."

Gabbi clutched her cup, hoping the warmth inside would somehow seep into her fingers and her heart. "It sounds interesting, but I'm not real sure about it," she said slowly.

There was a long moment of silence as the others exchanged glances. Gabbi felt as if she'd just told a little kid there was no Easter Bunny. She bit her lower lip and tried to fight the feeling of panic that was rising.

"I mean, it's not like I don't want to help other women," she said. "It's just that—"

"You haven't told people about your cancer," Nancy said softly.

Gabbi could feel her face blaze and she looked down into her cup. No inspiration there. The panic threatened to overwhelm her.

"I've told some people," she said, glancing around the table as quickly as possible. "It's not like I'm keeping it a secret."

Wasn't she?

"Hey, it's okay," Andi said quickly. "It was only a thought. And maybe we can still do it, just not with your input."

"Sure," Barb said. "There are enough of us around that we could cover most of the bases."

Gabbi couldn't stifle that voice in her mind, though, the one calling her a coward, a chicken. "I told my daughter, of course," she said. "And my doctors know. But it's just hard to tell other people. Friends. Co-workers."

"Hey, we understand, honey," Nancy said. "Margie Schumaker was like that. Scared to death to tell anyone."

Nancy and Barb began picking at their salads. Andi just smiled at Gabbi. "We really didn't want to put you on the spot."

"I don't know how you all can be so open about it," Gabbi said. "Aren't you scared what reactions you'll get?"

Nancy shook her head. "I thought the cancer was enough to be scared of. I didn't have any fear left for telling people about it."

"Not everybody handles it that way," Barb said quickly. "Nancy's tougher than a lot of us."

"And older," Nancy admitted. "I was fifty-two when my lump was found. I'd had my kids, was on my second marriage and had a lot of things sorted out."

"I was twenty-three," Gabbi said. "Fresh out of college, with a degree in broadcasting and..."

"Married?" Andi finished for her.

Gabbi just nodded and took a moment to butter her bread. She even nibbled at it before she found her voice again. "We had jobs at the same TV station in St. Louis.

On-the-air reporters. My specialty was late-breaking news stories. Doug's was politics."

"On-the-air reporters," Barb repeated with a touch of awe in her voice. "You know, I always wondered, how do you keep your hair looking so good when you're standing in the middle of a snowstorm doing some report? A gallon of hair spray?"

Gabbi smiled. "You have to have the right hairstyle, one that isn't too elaborate, and you need to position yourself right in regards to the wind."

"Jeez," Barb muttered. "I wouldn't last a minute in that job. I'd look like a piece of tumbleweed and get fired."

Gabbi took a deep breath. "That was sort of the future Doug predicted for me once I found the lump. Not the tumbleweed, but that I would never look good enough to keep my job."

Silence fell over the table. Andi finally sighed. "Nice guy. Safe to assume he's history?"

Gabbi nodded. "Of the ancient variety."

"How long did he stay after your surgery?" Nancy asked quietly.

"I was out of the recovery room, if I remember correctly." Gabbi tried to make a joke out of it.

No one laughed, but she wasn't surprised. The pain was still there for her, but it wasn't nearly as bad as it had been. Everyone here respected that pain, though, no matter how hard she tried to joke about it now.

"Some guys are real jerks," Barb said as they all went back to their salads. "I was lucky. Greg hasn't budged from my side. Sometimes I wish he'd give me just a little more room."

"No, you don't," Gabbi said.

Barb's teasing manner disappeared. "No, I don't," she agreed. "I can't imagine what it would have been like to go through the surgery and the treatment alone."

"That was the easy part," Gabbi said. "And I wasn't really alone. My parents were with me, and a million doctors and nurses and technicians. It was later, when everything was over but the long wait between checkups, that it hurt. You want to start over, but you're afraid."

"But that was seven years ago," Andi said. "You must have met other guys who haven't given a damn about your surgery."

Gabbi didn't say anything. Her eating slowed, and she sipped carefully at her ice water.

"You haven't?" Andi said. "Does that mean you've been meeting only the jerks in the world or that you haven't chanced a relationship?"

Gabbi put her fork down. "It's so terrifying." A knot in her stomach tightened. "You need someone so much just to be there and care about you. To let you know that you're still all right. And when the one person that you should be able to lean on, runs, it's really hard to trust again."

"But when you find someone else, it's worth the risk," Nancy said.

Gabbi just shrugged. "I'll take your word for it."

Barb frowned at her. "You haven't told Luke, have you?"

Gabbi's face must have reflected her sudden fear, because Barb reached out and took her hand. "Hey, no one but you is going to," she said quickly. "It's your show, but don't underestimate him. He's got a reputation around town as a real top-notch guy."

"And don't worry about it," Andi said. "When you're ready to tell him, you will."

"I've been trying," Gabbi admitted.

Nancy shook her head. "Quit trying and just relax. When it's time, you'll know."

Gabbi took a deep breath and let it out slowly. Surprisingly, a lot of her fear and tension left along with it. "Well, let's get back to that show idea. I'm not sure I'm ready to add my two cents, but who do you think should be on it?"

They spent the next hour in a lively discussion of what the show should entail and who should be asked to participate. Their dinners came and were devoured as any tensions that had been present earlier were forgotten. Gabbi felt as if she'd gained some friends by the time she was driving home. And some sound advice.

Relax and let it happen. The best advice she could have gotten.

Her car nosed its way into her alley, and Gabbi hit the garage door opener. The lights went on as the door rolled up, and she eased her car in, hitting the button again to close the door behind her.

A shadow moved across the lights in the kitchen window, and Gabbi smiled as she stepped out of the garage. It was nice to have someone waiting for her.

"Hi," Gabbi said as she stepped into her house.

"Hi." Trisha went over to the telephone and dialed. "I made iced tea for you guys," she told Gabbi.

"Us guys?"

But Trisha was talking into the phone. "She's home. Bye." She hung up.

"Who did you call?"

"Luke."

"Luke? Why?"

"He's coming over." Trisha took two glasses out of the cabinet, put in some ice cubes and poured iced tea.

"Why is he coming over?" Gabbi asked, suddenly worried. She had so many conflicting emotions, she wanted time to sort them out.

"To visit you," Trisha said sharply as she put slices of lemon in each glass. "Why else?"

"Oh." What good would time do? Did she really think if she allowed enough time, inspiration would come?

"You want to go and change," Trisha said. "Put on some shorts. Luke likes you in shorts."

Gabbi wished she could have gotten Trisha when she was a little younger. Just a few years. Enough for her to have learned which buttons to push to slow the kid down. The way things were now, once the girl got something in her head, there was no slowing her down.

"That's okay," Gabbi said. "I'll just wear what I have on."

"Then take your shoes off," Trisha said. "Relax a little. Otherwise he's gonna feel like you called him to a meeting or something."

"I didn't call him," Gabbi pointed out.

Trisha started to roll her eyes, but a soft knock on the back door interrupted her. "Come in," she called.

Luke stepped into the kitchen. "Hi."

He was wearing shorts, a knit short-sleeved shirt and loafers without socks. Gabbi stared at him a moment, rocked by an unexpected wave of desire. Why was she so afraid? He was rock-solid, his arms would be strong enough to hold her through the scariest night. She just had to tell him the truth when she was ready, that was all.

"Want to sit out on the porch?" she asked.

"Sure."

"Well, see you guys," Trisha said. "I'd sure like to visit, but I have some homework to do."

Homework? On a Saturday night? But before Gabbi could make a smart-aleck remark, Trisha was gone. Shaking her head slightly, she followed Luke out to the back porch where they sat down in their usual place.

She took a sip of her tea, then sat there gazing up at the stars. She loved starry nights. The little specks of light, light years away, made her feel comfortable and insignificant all at the same time.

"Tired?" Luke asked.

"Sort of."

"I shouldn't have come over."

"No, don't be silly." Gabbi put her hand on his thigh and he wrapped his arm around her shoulders. She closed her eyes and let the warmth and safety enclose her. "I'm happy to see you. I'm just not in a chatty mood."

"That's okay," he replied. "We can watch the stars together."

Her insignificance level stayed about the same, but her comfort index went way up. There were so many things they did together that were fun in their own way. Everything from dances to sitting on the back porch stoop. He could handle the news; she knew it, but tonight wasn't the time. She wanted to hold on to her quiet mood and treasure it.

Chapter Eleven

"Ms. Monroe, we can take you now."

Gabbi put down the magazine and followed the woman through the swinging door.

"You can change in here," the woman said, indicating a tiny dressing room with lockers along one wall. "And then come on down to room one."

Gabbi entered the dressing room and changed into a cotton gown. She put her clothes into a locker and took her purse with her as she went down to room one. After six years of mammograms, she was familiar with the routines.

"Hi, Gabbi," said the technician who followed her into the X ray room. "How've you been?"

"Great, Mary Ellen." Except for falling in love. "Wonderful." Except for having to tell Luke about her cancer. "I've got a daughter now. Trisha's adoption was final a couple of weeks ago."

"Wow, that's great." Mary Ellen placed Gabbi in front of the machine and slipped the X ray plates in place. "You having any soreness with your breasts? Anything unusual?"

"Nope, they're fine. No need even for these tests."

The technician just laughed. "Wouldn't it be great if it was that simple? I feel great, therefore I must be." She shook her head and positioned Gabbi's left breast on the cool metal surface. "Tell me if this gets too tight," she said as she lowered another piece onto the breast to compress it.

"How could I complain about something that could be conceivably saving my life?"

The other woman shrugged. "Not everybody has your perspective on it. You'd be amazed at the number of women who are forty and haven't had a baseline X ray taken. Or the women over fifty who don't have yearly exams." She stopped moving the piece. "That okay?"

Gabbi nodded. It was tight, but not all that bad. The discomforts of mammograms had been greatly exaggerated. And when you weighed it against the risk of not having them, it was almost a joy.

Mary Ellen went behind a screen and took the first shot; then she repositioned Gabbi and repeated the process. Due to her medical history, Gabbi had more shots taken than another woman might have, but she was done in a half hour.

"See ya next year," the technician said as she carried the last plate from the room.

"Right." Gabbi got dressed and glanced at her watch. She still had plenty of time before Trisha got home from school. Maybe she could get her grocery shopping in.

She walked through the radiologist's lobby, then out into the hall, where she literally collided with a solid mass of a man.

"Well, hello," a familiar voice said.

Good Lord, what was Luke doing here? She felt her world spin slightly, and he grabbed her arms to steady her as if her wobbliness had been from the collision.

"Hi," she said, her voice quivering with her worries. "What are you doing here?"

He held up a handful of some sort of pamphlet. "At the end of each academic year, we do a presentation on the dangers of steroids to all the athletes. Doc Haslett—" he nodded down the hallway "—gives us a bunch of handouts."

"Oh." She wished she had met him in the elevator or the downstairs lobby. Or in her backyard. Anywhere but right here, where she was almost forced into an explanation. Suddenly any other time or any other place would have been better to tell him about her past.

"And you?" He glanced around her at the door she had obviously just come out of.

You'll know when the time is right. "I just had my yearly mammogram," she said, trying for lightness in her tone.

"Oh?" They started walking toward the elevator. "I wish those things had been around in my mother's day. She might be alive today if they had been."

"She had breast cancer?" Gabbi asked.

He nodded as he hit the call button for the elevator. A shadow had come into his eyes as he slipped his arm around her shoulders. "I'm glad to see you taking care of yourself," he said, pulling her close. "I couldn't lose two people I care about to that disease. Watching my mother die was more than enough for one lifetime."

Gabbi just looked away, her heart falling into her toes. Now what? If she told him, he would surely leave. She could feel it in her bones. The fear of the disease coming back would drive him from her. Oh, maybe not dramatically and with sudden heartbreak, but he would pull away. And just as surely, she'd be without him.

What were her choices? Tell Luke and lose him. Keep quiet and live a lie.

"Where is that elevator?" she grumped. "Do they think we've got all day?"

"You all by your lonesome?" Gabbi asked as she let herself into Luke's yard. "Or is everybody hiding until you get the work done?"

He looked up from where he was pulling some errant grass from between the bricks on his patio. His eyes lit up when he saw it was her.

"Nope, I'm all by myself. Adam's at the library for the evening, working on a research paper, and Matt's bowling. How about you?"

She shrugged. "Trisha's at soccer practice, then they're having a team dinner at the coach's house. I wasn't quite sure what to do with myself," she admitted.

"Well, you came to the right place 'cause I'm sure what to do with you." He opened his arms and she went into them, straight and sure as if she were going home.

He held her loosely for a long moment before smiling down into her face. "So how about some dinner? I've got some great hot dogs, and if you ask right, I might be able to find some potato chips."

"What a treat." She didn't want to leave his arms, though. She'd felt lonely and alone when she'd been wandering around her house, and now that she found some place that felt like home, she wanted to stay.

As if he sensed her mood, he left one arm around her shoulders as they walked into his house. The kitchen was shadowy, a refuge against the world. They leaned against the counter, his arm still lightly around her shoulder.

"It seems like Trisha's never home," she said. "She's growing up already."

"Kids tend to do that."

"Yeah, but I've hardly had her," Gabbi said. "I thought we'd have a couple of years of constant companionship before she started to leave the nest."

Luke just laughed and planted a soft kiss on her forehead. "I think we've got a case of the blues to contend with here. It's time for Dr. Bennett to dig into his bag of tricks and find some cheering-up medicine."

"Well, doctor, the patient is ready and willing," she whispered up into his lips.

The laughter in his eyes died as his gaze locked with hers. Time stood still, and then, ever so slowly, he pressed his mouth onto hers. They clung together, taking and giving joy and hunger, hope and promises of tomorrow.

His arms slipped more completely around her, pulling her into his world of warmth and safety. She came to him, needing more than his touch. She needed his soul, too, this time. She needed to belong fully, to know that she had a place in his heart as well as in his arms.

The lips spoke words of love, making promises of forever as their hands stoked the fires of passion ever hotter, ever higher. His hands moved under her blouse, his touch impatient and demanding, but not demanding enough for her.

"Want to go upstairs?" he asked, his voice thready and quiet.

They went up without speaking, their hearts about to explode with love. Together they lay on the bed, hands on the other as their souls begged for joining, for finding that peace in the other's possession. Passion grew as they touched and kissed, as their spirits mingled in hunger. Then they were one and life was perfect. Their love was everything. It was enough.

Gabbi stepped into the house and slipped off her shoes. It felt so good to be home. She'd had a long day of preparations for a series of shows she was doing with the wives of local politicians and needed a break.

After dropping her purse on the kitchen counter, she padded to the front of the house to get the mail. Nothing exciting there, so she went back to the kitchen and poured herself a glass of iced tea, wondering where Trisha was. She should be home from school by now.

Sipping her drink, she went into the den to check the answering machine. The flashing light indicated there were three messages. Gabbi hit the Play button and dropped into a chair to listen.

There was a long pause at the beginning of the first message and then a "Hey, Mom. Are you there?" Another even longer pause, then, "Ohh, fudge ripple! I hate machines."

The dial tone came on, and Gabbi patiently waited as the machine went into the next message. She knew what would be next. Had it taken Trisha three messages to get all her thoughts out?

"Hey, Mom." This time there was no long pause. Trisha had steeled herself to talk to the answering machine. "We've got track practice right after school today. Okay? So I'll be home around five. Okay? Mrs. Severino is gonna give me a ride. Okay?" A short pause, as if she were waiting for Gabbi to answer. "Bye, Mom."

The kid did really well. Gabbi got to her feet. Only two messages this time. She was about to turn the machine to Reset, when its beeps and wheezes reminded Gabbi that there still was another message to play.

"Gabbi, this is Dr. McAndrews." The woman's voice hit Gabbi like a sledgehammer. "Please call me as soon as you can. I'll be in my office until six this evening. After that, you can reach me through my answering service."

There were beeps, squeaks and whirring sounds. An electronic voice came on, telling her there were no more messages. Gabbi heard them all, but she remained standing stiffly, staring at the far wall. Cold fingers had closed around her throat.

Oh, God. Dear God, something was wrong. It had to be. Otherwise the nurse would have called, asking Gabbi to set up an appointment at her convenience. That was the way it had gone for six years now, ever since she'd moved here from St. Louis. No fuss. No bother.

But today it had been the doctor. The doctor with her cool, professional voice telling her to call today. And not just today. As soon as she could today.

Gabbi put her glass down next to the phone and took a deep breath. She thought briefly of running. Not even packing or anything. Just dashing out the door and running as far and as fast as she could.

She shook her head. That wouldn't do. She'd at least have to stop and slip on her shoes. Her feet would never be as tough as Trisha's.

And once she stopped for the shoes, she'd stop for other things. Most of all, she'd stop to think. Stop to remember that she wasn't alone anymore. She had a daughter now. A daughter whom she'd promised to raise. A daughter whom she had said she would guide and lead into womanhood.

The scene before her blurred. A yucky yellow kind of blur. She hadn't gotten around to painting the den yet. She was going to paint the walls green. A soft, peaceful kind of green.

The film covering her eyes coalesced into a teardrop. One for each eye. And then more teardrops formed. Then the tears grew into a little thin stream that took on a life of its own as it flowed down her cheeks.

They hadn't painted Trisha's room, either. She'd wanted blue. A light blue that would go really well with the Indian blanket on her bed.

And she wanted a panda. A giant stuffed panda to sit on her bed. They'd seen the one she wanted at the mall a couple of weeks ago, but they hadn't bought it yet because the store always had a big sale in June.

The tears turned into torrents, driven along by sobs. Fear had clenched itself tightly around her lungs, and she could barely breathe. How the hell did she know she was going to be around next month? Why did she have to be so damn cheap? Now her kid would never have her panda. She sank back onto the chair and sobbed.

Several lifetimes later, her clock told her only a couple of minutes had passed. Gabbi got up and went to the bathroom to splash cold water on her face. She took several deep breaths and stared fiercely at her image in the mirror.

"Up and at 'em, old girl. You've been through this before and you won. You'll do it again." Then, throwing her shoulders back, Gabbi marched resolutely back to the phone to dial her doctor's office.

"Dr. McAndrews's office." The receptionist was her usual chipper and perky self.

"Hi, Debra. This is Gabbi Monroe. I'm returning the doctor's call."

There was a moment of hesitation. Was it a long moment? As she was put on hold, soft music came dancing through the receiver and Gabbi breathed a small sigh of relief. She was probably just being paranoid.

"Ms. Monroe?"

Gabbi swallowed. The doctor's voice was cool and professional. No "Hi, Gabbi, how are you?" Not a touch of chummy in it. She must have reason to be paranoid.

"Good afternoon, Doctor. How are you?"

"I'm fine." The doctor cleared her throat, and Gabbi held her breath. "Thank you for calling so quickly. The radiologist and I have reviewed your X rays and there might be a problem."

There was a little spot on the film? "You want me to retake the mammogram?"

"Ah, given your history, we believe another procedure would be better."

There was a big spot on the film. "You want me to have a biopsy?"

"Yes. We believe that would be best. When is your next period due?"

"In a day or two," Gabbi said. "Do you want to do it now or wait until afterward?"

"Afterward will be fine. Let's tentatively schedule you for the biopsy at ten o'clock next Friday morning," the doctor said.

"Okay."

"See you then, Gabbi." The doctor paused, not hanging up. "I don't want you living the next week in total fear," she said quietly. "I'm reasonably sure this is nothing to worry about, but we have to be certain."

"I know." Gabbi tried to sound calmer than she felt. Tried to sound as if fear hadn't taken hold of her.

"Take care, Gabbi." The doctor hung up this time, and Gabbi slowly lowered the receiver into its cradle. She stared at the wall again.

This time there was no blur, no tears. Just a tiredness. The needle biopsy was done as an outpatient procedure. If you passed, you went home. If you flunked, you won a stay in the hospital's oncology ward.

Was she an optimist or pessimist? Should she take Friday as a sick day? Or should she go whole hog and schedule a week's vacation? If she took a sick day, the station would just replay one of her old shows. If she went the vacation route, they would have to set up for a replacement. She'd have a week to worry about the outcome of the test, but she really needed to decide how much time she'd take off.

And who and how much she would tell.

Chapter Twelve

Gabbi sat and stared off into space for several eons, at least, before she finally rose to her feet and went back to the kitchen to pour out her tea. Then she stood, staring out the window at her backyard. The lilies of the valley were in full bloom now, tiny little bells of a flower that poked forth bravely from deep green leaves. Her eyes burned slightly, but no tears came. She was dried out for now.

It was eight days before her scheduled biopsy. That was a long time to mope and live in fear. She needed to be active. She needed her life filled with things to do. She needed to be fully scheduled. Straightening her shoulders, Gabbi marched resolutely to the phone.

"WNDN-AM, Pam speaking. May I help you?"

"Hi, Pam. This is Gabbi." The words came out brisk and sure. That was good, very good. That degree in communications and all those years of radio and television were certainly coming in handy.

"Yeah, Gabbi."

"I want to take next Friday off."

"Okay. You and Trisha got something big planned?"

"Yeah." She guessed it was technically true. "We'll need to decide which of the shows to rerun."

"Right," Pam replied. "And we need to let the advertisers know."

"I wanted to give you time to check those things out," Gabbi said. "Then we can review our course of action tomorrow."

"Sure, that'll be fine."

"Real good, Pam. See you."

Gabbi hung up and leaned against the wall, as exhausted as if she'd run a marathon. She had handled it well, hadn't given a single hint of problems, but she was a little shaky now. Like somebody who'd been asked to hold a car up while an accident victim was being pulled away. Her emotional muscles had been strained. It was going to be a hard eight days, but she'd get better as time progressed and she got into her act.

The biggest problem was handling this with Trisha. Gabbi had to get her fear under control before she said a word to her daughter. The kid would take her cue from Gabbi, and she wanted to make sure it was the right cue. She wanted to present it simply. Maybe say it was like when you went to the dentist for a checkup and he found a cavity; you made a later appointment to have it filled. That was a good analogy.

Gabbi glanced at the clock on the microwave, feeling as if she were just awakening from a long sleep and needed to reorient herself to the present. It was not yet five o'clock. Too early to start dinner. Maybe she should catch up on her reading.

She went into the living room, where she had first flipped through the magazines, then looked at some newer books, but nothing caught her eye there. She thought about cleaning her cabinets, but since they'd just moved in a few weeks ago, that wouldn't be much of a challenge.

She sank into a chair and stared at the fireplace, now empty like her heart. The minutes dragged by as if they were days, the days turning into decades and millenniums. What should she tell Trisha? How should she break the news to her? It would be dishonest to hide the fact from her daughter, but Gabbi also didn't want to upset the child.

And what about Luke? On Tuesday she had felt she couldn't tell him about her past bout with cancer because of his mother. Now, when it might be returning, there was definitely no way she could tell him. A shadow on an old X ray was one thing. That same spot on a new X ray was a far different story.

A car door slammed, causing Gabbi to rise slowly from the chair. She reached her front window in time to see a dark mane disappear around the corner of the house. The car sat in front and waited.

There was a commotion of scrambling feet and banging doors in back. By the time Gabbi reached the kitchen, Trisha had burst on the scene.

"Mom," Trisha said breathlessly. "I'm in a history play tomorrow." Her daughter paused to take a breath. "And Angie's in it, too, and—"

"Angie?"

"Yeah, Angie Severino. She's out in the car with her mother." Trisha nodded toward the front of the house, as if there might be multiple cars parked all about. "Her mom said we could practice it at their house, and then she said she'd give us dinner. She's making lasagna, you know. So, can I go? Huh?"

Her daughter's eyes sparkled, her T-shirt hung out over her pants, some of her hair was slipping over her face and her fingers were spotted with ink. She was so beautiful that Gabbi wanted to cry.

"Mom?"

Gabbi just smiled, locking all her pain inside her heart. "Sure, honey. Call me when you want to be picked up."

"Mrs. Severino said she'd bring me home."

"Whatever."

Trisha stared at her a long moment. "Are you okay?"

"I'm just fine," Gabbi replied. She must not have locked things up as tight as she'd thought. "I was reading a magazine and I dozed off. I'm just a little dopey, that's all."

"Thanks. I gotta go." Trisha turned and hurried to the back door, where she stopped and turned. "You eat a good dinner now."

"I will," Gabbi promised.

"I'm gonna check on you, you know."

"I know."

Trisha turned to leave, then stopped again. "Oh, can you run that movie on top of the TV back to Adam? I promised him I'd return it today, but I'm not going to have a chance."

"Sure."

"Thanks a bunch, Mom. Bye." She dashed out the door.

Gabbi just stood there, basking in the waves of positive energy that Trisha had left behind. She wrapped her arms around herself, trying to squeeze closer into the energy, like a homeless man trying to get closer to an oil-drum fire.

Kids Trisha's age were so self-centered, so into their own thing. Sometimes that could be a problem, but today it was good. Trisha had gone dashing off without noticing that anything was amiss.

And her full schedule would give Gabbi time to regroup without having to defend herself against Trisha's worry and questions.

She just had one little errand to do and then the whole evening was hers to set her goals in place once more. She took a deep breath, willing positive energy into her whole being. Then she picked up the videocassette from the television and walked to the back door.

"You don't care about me!" Adam shouted. "You don't care about me at all."

"Adam." Luke stepped forward and tried to put his hand on the boy's shoulder, but Adam just dashed out the back door, slamming it hard behind him. Luke sped after him. "Adam, wait. Damn it, will you wait!"

The boy stopped in the yard to glare back at Luke. "Why should I?"

"Would you listen to me, please?"

"Why should I listen to your lies? If you don't want me around, you should just say so."

"Adam—" He had barely begun his sentence when Adam took off and ran around the corner of the house. Hell, there was no use chasing him. The kid could outrun him on one leg.

"Damn!" Luke exclaimed, as he turned and punched the frame of the screen door.

"Why did you do that?"

Startled, he spun around and saw Gabbi standing in the middle of his yard.

"Because it feels so good when I stop," he snapped.

She just stared at him as he rubbed his bruised knuckles. He looked down and saw that the skin was broken in a number of places. He took his handkerchief out, wrapping it around his hand.

"What are you doing here?" he asked.

"I came to return Adam's video," she said.

"Oh." He winced as he pressed the handkerchief to his knuckles.

"Shouldn't you go after him?" Gabbi looked worried.

Luke felt the need to look away. "He's probably going over to my father's," he said. "He always does."

"Always?"

Hell. That made it sound as if Adam was always getting mad and running away. That wasn't the case at all. They got along really well. Most of the time.

"Once in a while he gets mad about things. When he does, he likes to talk things over with my dad. He'll stay there awhile, talk, have dinner, and then Matt will bring him home."

Luke was sure that was what would happen. It always did. Although this time could be different. He'd never seen Adam as upset as he had been today. He couldn't understand why the kid was making such a big deal about this adoption thing. It wouldn't change anything. Adopted or not, Luke would still love him and take care of him. Help him become a man just as Ron had asked.

"Where does Matt live?"

"Just over the river and a bit north," Luke replied. "It's a little over a mile. Running, Adam can make it in ten minutes."

They stood there, neither wanting to speak. Suddenly there was this huge chasm between them and no bridge in sight.

"You should probably clean those cuts," she finally said.

"They'll be okay."

As if she'd suddenly made up her mind, she walked across the yard toward him. "Come on. Let's take a look at your wounds."

"I told you I'll be fine. This isn't the first time in my life I've broken some skin."

"You men are all babies."

He glared at her.

"You're willing to punch somebody or something, but then you're afraid to have a cut cleaned and dressed."

"I'm not a baby," he protested, but Gabbi was already dragging him into the kitchen.

She put the video on the table and pulled him over to the sink, taking the handkerchief off. "Oh, you did a nice job there."

He clenched his jaw as she ran water on the wounds. Then she squirted some liquid soap on the cuts and rinsed them again.

"Why did you punch the door?" she asked, patting the hand dry with a paper towel. "Was it being bad?"

Punching the door was a stupid thing to do, but Luke wasn't in the mood to admit it.

"I bet it hit you first, didn't it?"

He wasn't interested in the teasing lilt in her voice, but since she was looking at him, he didn't have the top of her head to glare at. So he glared at the cuts on his knuckles instead.

"Do you have any gauze and tape?" she asked.

"Yeah," Luke replied. "In the corner cabinet by the refrigerator."

"Here." She handed him a clean sheet from the roll of paper towels over the sink. "Dry it well."

Luke pressed the paper to his knuckles, staring at Gabbi as she went to the cabinet and searched for the supplies she wanted. She stood on her tiptoes to reach the upper shelf. That put a nice curve to her calves, which completed the very pleasant curves that started up near her shoulders. He quickly looked down at his hand once she turned around and came back to him.

Her small fingers were deft and quick as they covered the cuts with gauze and then wrapped his hand in adhesive tape.

"You're pretty good at this stuff," he said.

"Thank you." She went back to the cabinet and put the supplies away.

Luke had another chance to take in her curves. "If you ever get tired of radio," he said, "you could probably get a job as a cut man at the boxing matches."

Gabbi didn't crack even the tiniest smile. Strike one.

He flexed his bandaged hand. "You want to send me a bill for this?"

"Why was Adam so angry?" she asked.

Luke shrugged and went back to concentrating on his bandaged hand.

"You don't want to adopt him, do you?"

"I didn't say I didn't want to."

"But you didn't say that you did."

Strike two.

Clenching his jaws a moment, Luke stared out at his yard. They were just playing with words. Damn. Give him a ball of any kind and he was great. But women were different. Give them a bunch of words and they would play with them. They started as soon as they could talk.

"Ron never said anything about adoption," Luke said. "He just wanted me to take care of Adam until he was old enough to take care of himself."

Gabbi didn't reply, turning her attention instead to the scraps of towel on the counter. She picked them up and threw them in the trash underneath the sink. Luke found her silence a louder accusation than her words.

"I went through all the papers Ron left after I talked to Adam the last time."

She didn't reply. Her lips were closed and her face was unreadable.

"He didn't mention adoption at all. No place at all."

Gabbi still didn't say anything.

"Well, damn it!" Luke could feel the irritation building within him. "He was a lawyer. A good one. So he would have thought of it. Ron thought of everything. That's the kind of lawyer he was."

Turning her back to him, Gabbi tore a piece of paper towel off the roll and used it to wipe up the water around the sink. Women sure knew how to play the game. They knew when to use words and when to use silence.

"I mean, maybe Ron didn't want me to adopt Adam. Has anybody thought of that?"

"Ron is dead," Gabbi said softly. "Maybe you ought to be concerned about what Adam wants."

He couldn't believe it. The irritation flared up into anger. "Just because Ron is dead doesn't mean that his wishes should be ignored."

"Do you really believe that Ron didn't want you to adopt Adam?" She appeared to be getting hot under the collar, but Luke didn't think he'd gotten his third strike yet. He thought that maybe he was just hitting some foul balls.

"He would have said something," Luke insisted.

"Adam's saying something," Gabbi replied. "Adam is saying exactly what he wants."

Adam was a kid. He didn't understand. It wasn't that simple. "I'm not going to steal Ron's son away from him just because he's dead."

"That's one of the dumbest remarks I've heard."

The expression on Gabbi's face more than backed up her words of disdain. There was no doubt about it now. That was strike three. Luke looked away. "You don't understand."

"No, you don't understand," Gabbi snapped. "Adam wants the security of belonging. He wants to know that you'll always be there for him." Her eyes darkened and her face grew still. "It's what we all want. Just to know somebody will always be there for us. No matter what we do, no matter what happens."

"Nobody is always there for anybody," Luke snapped. "Life isn't some stupid fairy tale. It's people, real people doing the best they can. And the best for some of us real people isn't always very good."

"So you don't want to make the commitment because you might want to duck out of it someday in the future?"

He just shook his head, not bothering to deny her accusation. He was tired of having his words twisted. Tired of having to explain his deepest fears and motivations. Tired of this whole argument. He should quit arguing with the umpire and walk off the field.

He was giving all he had to Adam, but in doing so, he would not cheat Ron. No one seemed to understand the debt he owed Ron, no one but himself. Gabbi sure didn't, but she led such a simple, straightforward life. She didn't know about failing and the fear of failing again. She achieved her goals as if she bought them at the goal store; her confidence and her belief in herself made things easy. She never agonized over letting people lean on her; she took on their burdens and gave them her strength.

"That promise I made to Ron means more to me than anything else in this world," Luke said finally.

"It doesn't mean that much to Adam."

"He doesn't understand."

"I don't understand."

His anger had reached its boiling point. Luke could feel the heat behind his eyes. "You don't have to understand. It doesn't concern you." His voice echoed in the kitchen. His anger made the words hang in the air, taunting them.

Gabbi looked straight at him, pinning him to the mat with her eyes. "Well, excuse me. But I think it does. I think it's central to everything right now. Maybe I need to know where we stand, where we're going from here."

She took a deep breath and looked away. "Or maybe we ought to just agree that we aren't going anywhere. That relationships are burdens and you obviously aren't interested in taking on any more burdens."

She turned on her heels and stomped out the back door, slamming it hard behind her. Luke winced at the sound. He hadn't been just put out. He'd been ejected, thrown out of the ball game. There would be no more chances to make good. Walking to the table, he dropped his body into a chair and his head into his hands.

It seemed as if a lot of people, people important to him, wanted him out of their lives. He wished he were better with words, wished that he could explain things to them. But he couldn't do it back in Vietnam and he wasn't any better now. For one of the few times in his life, Luke wished that he knew how to cry.

"What's the matter with you?"

Startled, Luke came halfway out of his seat. He was so immersed in his pain that he hadn't heard his father come in. "Nothing."

"You look pretty awful," Matt said.

"I'm fine." Luke held up his bandaged hand. "I just hurt my knuckles a little bit."

"I didn't even notice that."

Luke made a face.

"Where's Adam?" Matt asked.

"Probably at your place."

"You guys have a discussion?"

"No." Luke remembered Adam's face all contorted in pain before he stomped out of the house. "We had an argument. One of those shouting and screaming matches. It ended with Adam slamming the door and running out of here."

Matt looked at the floor and shook his head a moment. "Who bandaged your hand?"

"Gabbi did. She came over just as Adam was leaving."

His father grunted.

"She's not happy with me, either."

"Oh?"

"Yeah, she stomped out of here, same as Adam. Slammed the door behind her just like he did."

Matt put his hand over his mouth and, with his thumb and forefinger, brushed back the hairs of his mustache. "Looks to me like you got some deciding to do."

"Deciding?" Luke frowned at his father. "Deciding about what?"

"Whether to get involved or not. You know, get in the game or sit off on the sidelines."

"I don't understand." He was already out of the ball game, but he didn't want to discuss that with his father.

"You can't do relationships halfway, Luke. It's an all or nothing kind of thing. You can't keep folks out on the edge and touch them just when you feel like it."

Luke could feel his mind swirling around as if it were caught in a whirlpool. And it probably was. Getting involved with others was the same as jumping into a whirlpool. You were drawn in deeper and deeper. You were banged around, and pieces were chipped off as you went down.

"I'm speaking from experience, Luke."

He closed his eyes and clenched his jaw hard. Damn it. They'd done fine. Or at least Luke thought they had. Now, after all these years, he finds out that his father had once yearned for another woman. Well, if he felt that way, he should have gotten married. In fact, he still could. It was his life. All he had to do was leave Luke out of it.

"I better get on home," Matt said. "Adam's probably waiting there."

"Yeah, he probably is."

His father went to the back door and out. Suddenly there was a loud bang.

Luke jumped up nearly to the ceiling. "What the hell?" he shouted.

Matt popped his head back in. "I'm not really mad at you," he said. "But things happen in threes. So I thought I'd just slam the door and get that over and done with."

"Gee, thanks." Luke's stomach was still quivering.

"Now you can go over and visit your lady. Sit down and have a nice little chat with her. You owe it to her."

Luke glared at the door, which Matt now gently closed behind him.

Gabbi sat at her kitchen table and stared at the cup before her, shivering in spite of the steam rising from the surface of the brown liquid. By the time she'd reached home, she was filled with anger, depression, sorrow and fear. She'd thought some hot tea would bolster her spirit, but it just sat before her and cooled. She hadn't taken a single sip.

She and Luke were through.

It was funny, really, when you thought about it. Here she was facing a possible return of her cancer, yet the thing breaking her heart was that she no longer had Luke.

She had been trying so hard to hang on, to convince herself he would be there for her. Or that it didn't matter whether he was there or not because they were just friends. She'd gone from *When should she tell him?* through *How could she tell him?* to *She could never tell him.*

He had been a good friend, but he had too many ghosts from his past hanging on to him. He would never be free of them and all the guilt they were buried with. Whatever he had left to give, he had to give to Adam, not her. It was only right.

A rap on the back door pulled her out of the depths. Gabbi just sat for a moment, hoping it had just been her imagination. There was another knock. This time louder. Sighing, she pushed herself up out of her seat and went to the door. Who would be knocking at her back door?

Deep in her heart, she knew that was a dumb question. There was only one person who had made her back door his point of entry. Tension twisted the muscles of her stomach when she saw Luke standing out on the porch. Maybe if she ignored him, he would go away.

But Gabbi harbored that thought for only a moment, not long enough for it to take root. Forcing her reluctant body forward, she opened her door.

"Hi," he said.

His tanned features looked drawn. She wanted to just take him in her arms and hug him to her bosom. Run her fingers through his hair and kiss the worry lines away. It took all her strength to keep her arms down at her sides.

"Hello."

Giving him comfort would accomplish nothing for either of them. Sure, it would give her a momentary sense of usefulness, but Luke would still be Luke. He would be nice and polite, but he would still dance on the periphery of her needs. Hers, his and Adam's.

"Can we talk?" he asked.

"Do you want to come in?" she asked.

"It's nice out here," he replied. "Why don't we take our usual seat?"

She came outside and took her place on the steps. He sat down next to her, and neither one said anything for a long time. Gabbi just stared out at her yard, wondering how it could still be light out. So much had happened since she'd come home from work. The doctor's news. Facing up to a possible return of her cancer. The argument with Luke. Had the sun become so engrossed in watching the stage play of her life that it had forgotten to move?

"Thanks for the repair job," Luke said, indicating his injured hand.

"That's okay. When I was a little girl, I dreamed of being Florence Nightingale."

"I imagine you could've been whatever you wanted to be."

Gabbi shrugged. The silence closed in on them again, and she fought not to shiver. He sighed, and she could feel him letting go of some sort of control.

"I'm sorry about everything," he said quietly.

"That's okay." She didn't think it was, but brutal honesty hadn't brought her anything but pain. "I shouldn't have butted in."

"I'm sorry." He rubbed his face with both hands. "Things just seem to be in a pit right now."

They wouldn't be if he were reaching out to people instead of pushing them away.

"I have to—" He paused a long moment. "I have a lot of things to think through."

Gabbi didn't know what to say. It seemed obvious to her what needed to be done. But maybe it was a guy thing to follow your mind instead of your heart.

"Anyway," he said. "I just wanted to say that I appreciated your coming over."

"Your wounds weren't all that bad."

"I know that." He rubbed his face again. "What I most appreciated was your advice."

What advice? She couldn't remember saying anything that could have been interpreted as advice, unless it was to imply he shouldn't punch doors. And surely he didn't need her to tell him that.

She looked at him and suddenly saw much more than just a neighbor and friend, more than a lover, even. She saw deep into his soul and knew that she had been wrong. It wasn't that Luke had remained untouched by others, but that he had been touched too much.

He'd cared too deeply for others, so their pain had become his.

She'd thought he avoided responsibility because he hated for anyone to lean on him, but it wasn't that simple. He wasn't trying to get out of work or commitments; he didn't want to cause more pain. He didn't want to let anyone down and have to live with the pain of being responsible.

He kept people at arm's length because it hurt too much to let them get closer. She couldn't let her pain become his. She couldn't add to the strains already on him.

She'd been so worried about how his reaction to her past would affect her that she'd never stopped to think how his reaction would affect him. She needed to set him free, to concentrate just on Adam.

"Things have been so crazy lately," Luke was saying. "But I didn't want that craziness to spill out over on us." He took her hand in his, staring down at it as if it were something so precious. "I can't tell you how empty I felt when you left before. It seemed like everyone I cared about was leaving me."

Gabbi took a deep breath and slowly pulled her hand away. "I'm not exactly leaving you," she said. "But I'd like to cool things down a bit."

He looked puzzled, lost. "Okay."

She flirted briefly with a lie. She could make up some story about an old boyfriend or needing more space or some other stupid line that people used all the time in these situations. Or maybe she should come up with a way to make him angry, to make him fly out of here in a rage, believing that he was better off without her.

But she loved him so much, she could only tell him the truth.

"You remember those scars on my left breast?"

Luke nodded. The look of puzzled confusion was still there.

"Well." Gabbi paused to swallow hard. "They didn't come from any accident. They're from an operation."

He didn't say a word. Didn't even blink.

"Seven years ago, I had a lumpectomy. Cancer."

Luke seemed to crumble before her eyes, as though someone had hit a statue with a giant sledgehammer. "Why didn't you tell me?" His words came out in a whisper.

She shrugged.

"You should have told me. It wasn't fair to keep something like that from me."

"No, what wasn't fair was keeping up this relationship, knowing that I wasn't going to tell you about the cancer."

He stared at her as if he didn't see the difference. "But you are."

She wished that she could speed dusk along, make it suddenly dark so she would have a place to hide. "I'm not keeping up the relationship," she said gently.

When he said nothing, she went on. "I've known all along that this is a burden I have to carry myself," she said. "That hasn't changed. But I shouldn't have gotten involved with you. It was selfish and inconsiderate. And I'm sorry."

He just shook his head. "I must be stupid, but I don't understand. Why are you saying we're through? What does this have to do with the cancer and with me?"

"Because it's my burden and mine alone. I'm not sharing it."

Something changed in his eyes. "Because you figure I'll let you down."

"Because it's not fair to put a burden like that on anybody else. Doug taught me that."

Luke stood up. "But I care about you. I love you."

She got to her feet also. Her heart should be turning cartwheels, but it was too busy weeping. The real heartbreak was admitting she had been wrong all along.

"Love's not enough," she said slowly, amazed that saying the words didn't cause her heart to stop right then and there. "Doug taught me that, too. I always thought it should be. Love should be able to work miracles, should be able to knock down any obstacle, but it can't. Sometimes love is best served by saying goodbye."

She couldn't bear the look in his eyes, that tortured, haunted look, but she couldn't let herself look away, either. "Goodbye, Luke," she said softly and planted a quick kiss on his cheek.

Before he could answer, she had fled inside. She and her breaking heart.

Chapter Thirteen

"Are you all right?" Trisha's face was wrinkled with concern.

"I'm fine," Gabbi insisted. "I'm just fine."

Her words did nothing to ease the worry lines in her daughter's face. Gabbi paused a moment to stare out across the vast expanse of the park. Another game had started on the field where Trisha's soccer game had finished. Young boys who looked to be about ten dashed around and chased after the ball like a swarm of bumblebees after a bear.

"So," Trisha said. "What did you want to talk about?"

Gabbi smiled. She couldn't sneak anything past that kid. "What makes you think we have to talk about something?"

"Hey, I didn't just get off the turnip truck, you know." Trisha climbed up and sat on the split-rail fence lining the edge of the park. "You usually have a whole list of stuff for us to do on Saturdays after my games, but today you just want to hang around the park."

Gabbi cleared her throat and concentrated on the little munchkins dashing around the field. "I like it here. It's peaceful."

"Yeah? 'Cause you want to talk, right?"

Leaning forward, her elbows on the top rail, Gabbi stared out at the park and let the scene before her blur. How did one start?

"It ain't about me, is it?"

"What?" Gabbi turned to stare at her daughter. The concern mirrored there tugged at her heart.

"Things have been going good for me lately," Trisha said. "My grades are okay. Nobody from Harvard is gonna come chasing me, but I'm passing everything."

"That's good," Gabbi said.

"And things are cool with the other kids. I ain't been in any real fights since we moved."

Gabbi's smile froze in place. "Real fights? What's the difference—"

"We were talking about you," Trisha said. "You and Luke are having some problems, right?"

Gabbi let the little con artist change the subject. It wasn't the time to talk about Trisha and school, anyway. "I do want to talk to you," Gabbi admitted. "But it has nothing to do with Luke."

"He hasn't been around much in the last few days."

Had it only been a few days? It seemed as if Gabbi'd been missing him for years now.

"I went in for a mammogram last Tuesday," Gabbi said.

Trisha's brow wrinkled. "That's the thing where they pinch your breast and then take a picture?"

Gabbi nodded.

Suddenly Trisha's face turned hard, almost adultlike. "There's something wrong."

"Maybe," Gabbi replied. "They found a lump."

"Ain't that a problem?"

"Only if it's malignant," Gabbi replied.

Uncertainty tugged at the corners of Trisha's eyes.

"Malignant means it's cancerous. That's what it was the last time when they had to operate."

"You can have a lump and not have cancer?" Trisha asked.

"Yes," Gabbi replied, nodding. "In that case, they wouldn't have to operate or do anything about it."

Trisha nodded and looked down at the ground.

"I'm going to have a biopsy Friday," Gabbi said. "That's where they look at a piece of the tissue."

"Yeah, that's what I thought it was." A dawning horror filled Trisha's eyes. "How do they get a piece to look at it?"

"They do a needle biopsy." Gabbi turned away. The poor kid's face was twisted in pain. She'd put things together very quickly. "They give you a local anesthetic, stick a needle into the lump and take out a sample of the cells to look at."

Trisha rubbed her breast. "How big is the needle?"

Gabbi forced a laugh. "It's done very quickly. I don't even have to stay overnight. It's all done on an outpatient basis."

Trisha turned around slightly, and they both stared out at the field. The little boys were laughing and having a wonderful time. The sun was bright and warm, the birds were singing the praises of spring, and the smell of newly cut grass lingered in the air. Life was good, and she had no intentions of giving it up. Especially not now. She had a daughter to raise.

"How about a burger, kid?"

Trisha nodded and slowly slid off the fence. They walked to the car.

"Does Luke know yet?" Trisha asked.

"No."

She could feel Trisha's eyes on her, like twin laser beams trying to bore a hole in her head, trying to see what secrets she held.

"Luke and I are just friends," Gabbi said. "And you don't just drop a load like that on casual friends. Some things you just have to face alone."

Suddenly Trisha seized her in her arms. "You ain't alone," she whispered harshly in Gabbi's ear. "You ain't never ever gonna be alone anymore. You got me."

Gabbi was unable to speak. She just held Trisha tightly.

"And we're gonna beat this thing, Mom. We're gonna kick ass. And we don't need no guys around to do it."

She leaned her head on Trisha's shoulder and fought back the urge for tears, thinking how dumb this all was. Trisha was the daughter and yet Gabbi was so much shorter than her. Life was strange. After a moment, they parted and continued on their way to the car.

"You feel all right?" Trisha asked.

"I'm fine."

"You're not tired or anything?"

"Not really." They reached the car, and Gabbi unlocked the passenger door for Trisha.

"You know—" Trisha leaned casually on the car "—if you're really tired, I could drive."

Gabbi gave Trisha what she hoped was one of her better "get real" looks.

"I mean, if you're tired."

"Thanks." Gabbi smiled. "I didn't think you had a license. Did I miss something? Like a couple of your birthdays?"

Trisha shook her head, silently opening her door and taking her seat. "You're really a rules kind of a person," she said as Gabbi settled in her seat. "Aren't you?"

"Sorry," Gabbi replied as she inserted the key in the ignition.

"Luke said you were," Trisha mumbled.

She looked at Trisha and saw a potpourri of emotions in her face. Pain, embarrassment, anger and more. They both wanted him here with them, but both knew something stood in the way. Trisha didn't know what it was, and Gabbi had to admit she didn't, either.

"So what does that palooka know, anyway?" Trisha demanded. "Probably been catching too many fast balls with his head."

"Yeah," Gabbi replied. "Let's get some lunch."

"Come on, guys," Luke called out, trying to make his voice more cheerful than he really felt. "We can still do it."

Their baseball season was about to end, thanks to the LaPorte Slicers, unless they could hold the Slicers for one more out and come up with three runs of their own, but Luke had a hard time caring. Adam still was barely talking to him and Gabbi had held true to her promise to ignore his existence. With his life falling apart, a baseball game was the last thing on his mind.

A Slicer sent a pop fly out to the right outfield, and a St. Joe player ran under it. The ball hung a moment in the air and then fell right into the outfielder's mitt. A smattering of applause came from the stands. Third out. Bottom of the ninth. Crunch time.

As the teams changed positions on the field, Luke turned to scan the stands. He didn't expect to find Gabbi and Trisha there, but he couldn't keep himself from looking. Even so, his heart sank even further when he didn't find their faces amid the crowd.

It had been two days since Gabbi had called it quits, and he still didn't have a clue in hell what it was all about. All he knew was that a cloud was hanging over his head. She had come tiptoeing into his heart, then had ripped it out from the inside. How could his love have meant nothing?

He forced his attention back to the game. Adam was going up to bat. "All righty, Adam," he called out, hoping that no one would notice the falseness of his bravado. "Let's have a run."

Adam ignored him. Could be just his game face. Could be he was still pissed off. What happened to loyalty and promises? Didn't they count for anything anymore?

The first pitch was low and outside. Ball one. The second one was a curve ball that just nicked the edge of the strike zone. Strike one.

Luke's vision blurred. He saw Ron standing there, back in their youth. He had that same determination, that same hunger to excel. He owed Ron so much. How could he take away his son?

His vision blurred some more, and he saw Adam with Gabbi on Mother's Day. She had given him peace that day, peace that Luke hadn't even known he'd needed. Hell, she'd given something to all of them that day. A sense of belonging, a sense of continuity.

The third pitch came low and hard. Adam swung at it and connected. The ball arced slightly, so that it went long rather than high. Longer and longer it flew until it landed just outside the fence. Adam's home run!

Amid the cheers of his teammates and the crowd, Adam ran the bases. Luke called his own congratulations as the boy rounded third; then he was swallowed up by his team as he crossed home plate. Luke waited for Adam to look his way, to share his excitement with him, but he never did. After the back-patting was over, Adam trotted over to the dugout so the next batter could take his turn. His eyes never came near Luke.

Well, so what? Luke turned back to his position as third-base coach and awaited the next pitch. The kid was a teenager, and teenagers were notoriously unwilling to share emotions with adults. Adam hadn't been that way before, but maybe he was getting into that stage.

Maybe he was shutting Luke out. Maybe he would always shut him out. In that case, the next three years or so would be silent and long. They would talk only when necessary and then in stilted, clipped sentences. Luke stared into the sun, letting it blind him since the future held nothing worth seeing.

A year ago, things had been so simple. So uninvolved.

The pitch was a slider, and the batter fell for it. He tipped it, but only barely. The catcher sent it down to first base before the runner was halfway there. One out.

The next batter got a good hit, but an outfielder made a great catch. Two outs.

The last batter swung at everything. And missed everything. Three strikes and then the third out. Game over. Season over. The boys shook hands with the other team, then collected the equipment before trudging to their cars.

"Nice hit," Luke said as Adam walked morosely at his side.

"Thanks." His voice was anything but pleased.

"You don't sound like someone who just reached his dream," Luke pointed out.

Adam gave him a look. "Dreams change."

Luke shrugged. "Hey, it was only a game, and we're only losing one senior. We'll be really strong next year."

Adam's look doubled its negative quotient, and he picked up his pace. Luke picked up his.

"Too bad Gabbi and Trisha weren't here to see your home run," Luke said. "I thought maybe they'd show up."

"Trisha had a soccer game."

"Oh."

Adam tossed his equipment into the back of the truck and climbed into the passenger side. He waited in silence as Luke got in, staring out the front window as if he were hypnotized by the parking lot and its fascinating yellow stripes.

"You'll have to tell them about it," Luke went on. It hurt to talk about them, but then it hurt not to. "They'll be thrilled for you."

"Yeah." He slouched down in the seat. Every part of his body said to leave him alone.

Luke ignored his body language. "Your dad would be really proud of you."

Adam moved, but only to stare out the side window. "My dad's dead," he said.

"But he's still your dad."

"And he's still dead. He ain't coming to any of my games or seeing any of my home runs."

"But you can't just forget about him."

Adam turned to look at Luke as though he was some sort of idiot. "I'm not some birdbrain, you know. I'm not going to forget about him." He turned back to the window as if searching for someone to talk to who had some sense. "Jeez, as if I could forget about him just 'cause he's not here anymore. I ain't that lousy a son."

"I never meant that," Luke said, but the conversation was dead, and there was no reviving it.

They drove home in silence, and Adam disappeared into his room once they got there. Luke just wandered into the kitchen to stare out at the backyard and the house beyond. A robin hopping around the lawn, looking for worms, was the only movement.

And even the bird would probably leave if it knew I was watching, Luke thought, turning away. His heart was cold, and the prospects for warmth were dim.

Why the hell wasn't his love enough for anyone?

"Don't you have a softball meeting today?" Gabbi asked. She'd been sure the meeting had been scheduled for Monday evening.

"I'm not going," Trisha replied.

Gabbi put the bucket and sponge down and leaned against the doorway to Trisha's room. The kid had been close to driving her nuts ever since she'd told her about her upcoming biopsy. Gabbi couldn't go anywhere without Trisha following.

"Why not?" Gabbi folded her arms across her chest, noticing that Trisha stole a surreptitious glance at her breasts. "No, it hasn't fallen off and it isn't swelling up."

Trisha glared at her. "'Cause."

"That's not a reason," Gabbi said.

Her daughter looked away.

"Trisha, I asked you a question."

"I do a lot of things," she replied. "You know?"

"So," Gabbi said, shrugging. "I thought you liked to keep busy."

Trisha made a face and refused to look at her. "Yeah, but not too busy."

"So you want to relax?"

"Not really." The frown indicated that her daughter didn't like this conversation. "I just don't want to play softball."

Gabbi went over and sat on the edge of Trisha's bed. "I'm fine, really I am."

Trisha picked at a tuft on her bedspread.

"I don't need someone watching over me all the time." Gabbi put an arm around Trisha's shoulders. "In fact, you're close to driving me up the wall."

"I'm sorry," Trisha mumbled.

Poor kid. She was so worried, and she wanted desperately to help. But if Gabbi got any more help from her, she would die of suffocation. She put her other arm around Trisha and hugged her tight.

"I just want to help," Trisha said.

"I know you do, honey." She gave her daughter another squeeze. "And the best way you can help is just to carry on with your life the exact same way you did before."

Trisha looked at her a moment and then ducked her head.

"Go to your softball meeting."

"There's just the two of us," Trisha said. "I don't want anything to happen to you."

A little trickle of fear showed around the edges of Trisha's facade of strength. And it certainly wasn't surprising. Still, there wasn't anything Gabbi could do at the moment except tough it out. And she knew that when push came to shove, the kid would be there, ready to fight tooth and nail. But right now her daughter needed a little boost, and fortunately Gabbi was in shape to give it.

"Honey, nothing is an absolute sure thing in this life. Sometimes that's good and sometimes it isn't. Right now, that's good."

Trisha blinked, confusion on her face.

"Just because my mammogram showed a spot, doesn't mean I have cancer. We won't know until the biopsy."

Her daughter stared at the floor.

"So go to your softball meeting."

"I want to stay here and help."

"Help?" Gabbi asked. "With what? Cleaning the bathroom? I don't need any help."

"Yeah, you do," Trisha protested. "You're running around like some freaky character in a cartoon, washing, cleaning stuff, everything."

Gabbi let go of Trisha and stood up. "I'm a little nervous."

Trisha looked at her.

"What do you do if you're nervous about something?"

"Stuff," Trisha replied with a shrug.

"Sports stuff?" Gabbi said. "Like running and chasing and batting and kicking. Working up a sweat, right?"

Trisha nodded.

"Well, I'm not good at sports, but I'm a whiz at cleaning house. So that's how I keep active."

Her daughter went back to staring at the floor.

"It helps me release my tensions," Gabbi said.

"Having sex would help, too."

"What?" Gabbi stopped and stared at her, certain she'd heard wrong. "Where in the world—"

"Hey, chill out." Trisha was standing up, hands in front of her. "I'm not talking like it's something I really know anything about."

Gabbi continued glaring.

"I read in a magazine that you older women get like that."

"What kind of magazines are you reading?" Gabbi asked.

"It was in health class," Trisha explained. "It said a woman's sexual desires peak in their thirties, while a man peaks in his teens."

A million questions whirled around in her mind, but Gabbi knew that now was not the time to discuss Trisha's health class with her. She needed to be calm and relaxed.

"Trisha, go to your softball meeting."

"I guess I can," Trisha said. "It's just a short meeting, and it's at Mary Anne Kosnecki's house. I can bike over."

"Good," Gabbi replied through clenched teeth. She really needed to scrub the walls, the floor, the ceiling, everything. Work her muscles until the sweat was pouring out of her body. "Do you need to take your mitt?"

"Nope." Trisha dropped down on the floor, feeling under her bed. She pulled out a shoe, then stopped to look back up at Gabbi. "Maybe that's what's wrong with Luke."

"Maybe what's wrong with Luke?" Gabbi asked, realizing that she should have just gone into the bathroom and started washing.

"You know." Trisha slipped her shoes on. "Old Luke's on the downhill side. Maybe he's reached bottom faster than most guys."

"Trisha."

"Yeah?" Her daughter's face was full of innocence, like an angel's.

"Go to your softball meeting before I murder you."

Luke stopped, the garbage bag in one hand, the other on the gate into the alley. "Hi," he said softly.

Gabbi looked up from where she was dumping her trash. She looked so beautiful, her eyes alight with softness, her hair catching the long, last rays of the evening's sun.

"Hello," she said.

Her voice told him nothing had changed, but he was dying of thirst and eager for a drop of water. No matter how small the drop.

"How've you been?" he asked.

"Fine. Just fine." She closed her trash can carefully, avoiding his eyes.

"How's Trisha?"

"Fine. Just fine." She locked the cover on, pulling the handles up over the edge of the lid.

"We're all fine, too," he said. Look at me, he wanted to shout. Look at me and tell me why my love's not enough. But he didn't say it.

"That's good." She glanced his way then. Her smile was curved properly but no brighter than a night-light. "Say hi to Adam for us."

Smile still in place, she hurried into her yard, closing the gate quite definitely between them. Luke didn't move. He just watched the top of her head as she crossed her yard and went in the back door. Then it, too, was shut and she was gone.

The scent of her lingered, though, or was it just his memory of her? He closed his eyes and took it in, but it didn't satisfy him. It was like a picture of a lake, not the real thing. He needed to be able to dive into her waters, to let her wash over him and swallow him up. He wanted her to own him, to consume him and keep him locked in her depths forever.

But his love wasn't enough for her. He'd failed her without ever being tested.

He smashed the garbage onto the can, slammed the lid back on and strode back into the house. The damn place was as silent as a tomb. Adam was off at a friend's, studying. Matt was at home or out with Irma. Luke was alone, as he always used to be and as he would be in the future. Funny, how easily he'd gotten used to having someone around.

He walked through the house, without turning on lights even though the evening was progressing and it was getting dark. Damn. Damn. Damn! Seeing her hurt was like ripping open wounds that had barely had time to heal. Ripping them open, then poking around in them to see if he could bleed anymore. He couldn't. He was dry. Nothing was left.

He stared into the coming dusk. God, he was thirsty. He closed his eyes and felt the calm comfort that only a drink could bring. It called to him, luring him like a Greek siren, promising him peace and tranquility.

His eyes flew open and he hurried over to the TV, turning it on and flipping through the channels. He'd find something. Anything to occupy his mind. He had to.

Gabbi breathed a sigh of relief as she washed out the paintbrush. Her clothes were soaked with sweat, and her arms ached. It was great. She was sure that she'd sleep well tonight. Nothing drove the worry devils into their hole like working yourself into sheer physical exhaustion.

She brought her left hand up to wipe her brow when a knock at the back door stopped her. Oh, no. There was only one person who used the back door and she looked like super grunge. For just a moment, she was tempted to run in the bathroom and spruce up.

"Oh, the hell with it."

With the shape she was in she'd need at least dynamite to look presentable, and it just wasn't worth it. She sauntered over to the door, where her eyes opened wide with surprise.

"Adam?" She wasn't disappointed. Not really. "Is anything wrong?"

He looked so downcast that Gabbi was sure he'd had another argument with Luke. "No," he replied. "Everything's cool."

"That's good."

They stood for a long moment and stared at each other through the screen door.

"Ah, can I come in?"

"Oh, certainly." Gabbi's hands groped for the door handle. Boy, she was a real zero as a neighbor and hostess. "Come in."

Adam stepped into the kitchen, where he stood in the center and looked all around him. "Is Trisha around?" he asked.

"No, she's biking with Angie."

Adam nodded. "Cool."

Gabbi looked at the package he was holding in his hand. It was gift-wrapped, probably by the store where he bought it. She wondered what was going on. It wasn't Trisha's birthday or anything.

"Would you like to wait for her? She should be back soon."

"Oh, no."

She fought to control her smile. The poor guy actually looked terrified. He'd probably just like to leave the gift and run.

"You can leave the gift with me if you like," Gabbi said. "I can give it to her."

"Huh?"

Gabbi wondered if she'd ever get the hang of communicating with a teenager. "I'm sorry," she said, pointing at the box in his hand. "I thought the gift was for Trisha."

Adam stared at the object in his hand as if he were seeing it for the first time and wondering how it got there. "It ain't for Trisha," he said. "It's for you." He shoved it into her hands.

"Oh." Now it was Gabbi's turn to stare stupidly at the small box. Why would Adam bring her a gift? "Thank you."

"You can open it," Adam said as she continued looking at it, turning the box over in her hands. "I mean, if you want to."

"Okay."

She slipped off the ribbon without breaking it and carefully tore the wrapping off. Then she opened the box and took out the gift. It was a transparent globe on a round black pedestal with a single red rose inside.

"It's very pretty, Adam."

"Yeah, I thought it was kind of nice."

Gabbi stared at it, wondering what else she should say.

"They had them on sale at this store at the mall, you know," Adam said. "So it didn't cost much."

She looked up. The poor guy seemed to be struggling with a legion of emotions, the key one being embarrassment. For the life of her, Gabbi didn't know why Adam found it necessary to get her a gift.

"You really didn't have to buy me anything."

He shrugged and looked away. "Me and some of the guys went to the mall a couple of weeks ago." He looked at her and forced a smile to his lips. The effort appeared to be excruciatingly hard. "You know, they like had to get something for their mothers."

She nodded slowly, seeing the teenage bravado at her dinner the day she moved, the day before Mother's Day. She remembered Adam's moodiness. Poor guy probably hadn't known what to do. He missed his own mother, and like all teens, he didn't want to be different. So when he was at the store with his friends, he bought a gift just like everybody else.

"Thank you, Adam. It's lovely." Her throat was tight and her words barely came out.

"That's okay." His words were a tad on the loud side. "And it ain't a Mother's Day gift."

"Right," Gabbi said. "Mother's Day is past."

Adam nodded vigorously. "Yeah, it's like a gift you give when someone moves into a new house."

"A housewarming gift?"

"Yeah, right. That's what Matt said it was."

She nodded her agreement and watched Adam's shoulders straighten, as if a weight were removed.

Suddenly a frown of concern filled his face. "Ah, you gonna tell Trisha I bought it?"

"Oh, sure."

His frown grew deeper.

"I'll put it on the shelf in the living room," Gabbi said. "Then I'll wait until she asks me where it came from."

Relief flooded in and smoothed the wrinkles in his face. "Cool."

Gabbi found herself nodding and wondering what to do next. What she really wanted to do was hug Adam, but she was afraid that if she broke through his thin shield of macho, she'd crush him.

"Well, I gotta get going." He started backing away from her.

"How are things between you and Luke?" Gabbi asked. "Everything straightened out?"

"Oh, yeah," Adam said loudly. "Everything's cool. Super."

Adam strained, as if his smile weighed ten tons. God damn Luke and his stiff-necked pride or whatever the hell his problem was. Nothing had been resolved. He probably hadn't talked to Adam about adoption again. And the boy was afraid to bring it up.

She followed Adam as he walked to the door, where he stopped and looked all around before stepping out. Probably hoping no one was there to see him.

"Adam," she said softly. He turned, and she swept him into a quick hug. "Thank you. It's the nicest housewarming gift I've ever gotten."

His face was a bright red, but his smile was genuine. "'Bye."

Once he was gone, out of the yard and out of sight, the tears she'd been holding back finally forced their way out. Damn everything.

Why couldn't life be simple? Why did people have to lose that which meant the most to them? She clutched the globe and shut the door carefully.

"Luke," Adam said. "I'm going to Joey's house for a while, okay?"

"All done with your homework?"

"We don't have any homework. Finals are next week."

Luke knew he should ask Adam if he'd studied for his finals, but the hard look in the kid's eye didn't issue any kind of an invitation.

"We're gonna study together for English and maybe history."

"Good idea," Luke said, nodding slowly.

Adam gave him a curt nod, then walked toward the front of the house. Luke pushed the newspaper aside and turned to stare out his backyard. His fence was solid wood, so he couldn't see into Gabbi's yard, but he didn't have to. He could see her elfin grin in the shadows and her chatty hands flitting about like mockingbirds.

Jovial voices from his foyer drew his attention inward. He really should quit looking across the alley. There wasn't anything there for him anymore. He gritted his teeth at the loud laughter that echoed through the house and buried his face in his hands. Hell. Why did he always have to be the bad guy?

"Hey, Luke."

He took only a moment to look at his father's cheerful expression. He couldn't take much more than that, so he pulled the newspaper back toward him.

"Nice to see you're talking to me again," Luke grumbled.

"You're my son. I gotta love you."

"Thanks." Luke squinted and tried to put the letters swimming before him in some kind of a readable order.

"You know, that's all Adam wants."

He didn't want to get into this again, but Luke raised his head and looked at his father.

"He just wants to feel that you'll love him no matter what he does. Kids need that kind of security."

Luke shook his head. "Damn it, he's got that! He has a home here as long as he needs it."

Matt just blinked.

"Hellfire!" Luke exclaimed. "I signed a whole bunch of legal papers saying that I'd take care of him, without qualification."

"That's nothing," Matt snapped. "Just a bunch of papers drawn up by a lawyer. And whatever a lawyer has put together, another lawyer can take apart."

Shaking his head, Luke turned and looked away. But looking out over his backyard gave him some more pain. Damn. No matter which way he turned there was a load of hurt waiting for him.

"He doesn't want papers, Luke. The kid wants it from your heart. He wants you to be his father."

Adam wants him to be a father. The guys at school want him to coach the football team. Matt wants him to get married. Gabbi wants him to— Oh, hell! Why couldn't they all just leave him alone?

He wanted nothing more than to run and hide, but Matt was there looking at him. Life, and everybody in it, was there looking at him. There wasn't anyplace he could go. He could run, but he couldn't hide.

"How are you and Gabbi coming along?"

He wasn't going to look at Matt. He didn't want to. It was said that the eyes were the windows to a man's soul, and his weren't in any shape to show anyone.

"Fine. We're friends."

"You're not getting along with her, either, huh?"

Luke wanted to scream and holler, but he continued looking at the newspaper. Damn it. Why didn't Matt talk to her about all this? She could tell him she'd looked into Luke's soul and saw nothing there. Saw that the foundation wasn't solid. Saw that if she'd put any load on him, he'd just crumble. He had before and he would again. She was smart to leave. Love wasn't enough.

"Don't let her fly away, Luke. She's the best thing that's ever come into your life."

Luke looked up at his father. The man who had been mother and father to him for most of his life. The man who knew him better than he knew himself. At least he should.

"Dad," he said softly. "You can't keep something you never had."

Chapter Fourteen

"Give me a call when you're ready to come home," Luke said as he pulled to a stop in front of the public library.

"I know my way home." Adam's tone was short.

"I don't mind coming out," Luke said. "Besides, I'd prefer you didn't walk home alone. Downtown is pretty deserted this late at night."

"There're other people doing work here tonight," Adam said. "I can probably get a ride with someone."

Luke sighed. "Well, I'll be home. So call me if you need a ride. I can drop others off, too."

Adam just strode off toward the door. Luke watched him go into the library; then he pulled slowly away from the curb. He concentrated on the traffic until he reached St. Joseph Street and slipped into the flow toward home.

He crossed the river and took a left at Riverside. The mansion on the river still had a For Sale sign out, causing Luke to remember the outing to look at homes for Gabbi. The four of them had had fun that day. It wasn't even two months ago, yet it seemed as if those events had happened decades ago. Back when they were all carefree and young.

Back before he had failed Gabbi in some unknown way.

He went to pick up some groceries, then turned toward home. By the time he got there, he had a slight headache and an onset of the grumps. He closed his eyes and massaged the back of his neck before he slowly got out of the car.

It wasn't dark yet, but getting there, so the *thumpity-thump* of a basketball being dribbled in the alley caught him by surprise. His heart did a double step and his breath quickened. Was Gabbi out in the alley?

Reality came back like a kick in the ass. What difference would it make? He went into his house, carrying his groceries into the kitchen. The window had been left open. The sound of the basketball floated in. Whoever was out there was a dedicated player.

He put the milk away, then the onions, but the sound kept calling to him. Finally he went outside, slipping open the gate and poking his head out into the alley.

"Yeah?"

His heart fell with a thud. It wasn't Gabbi.

"Hi, Trisha."

"What do you want?"

"I heard someone playing out here and I wondered who it was."

"So now you know."

She took a shot and missed, not surprising since the light wasn't all that great anymore. The kid appeared to be in one of her foul moods.

"You're in a great mood tonight," Luke said.

"What's it to you?" she replied as she dribbled away from the basket.

"Nothing. I was just wondering what was the matter."

"Why does anything have to be the matter?" She shot and missed again.

"It doesn't have to be." Luke was trying to be reasonable but finding it hard. He should probably get back into his house before he got into an argument with the kid. "It's just that you always get grumpy when you're worried or scared about something."

Trisha was throwing the ball more than shooting it. It hit the rim and came flying out toward Luke. He caught it.

"I'm not scared of anything," she snapped. "And give me my ball. Now!"

Clenching his jaw for a moment, Luke took a deep breath and lightly bounced the ball to Trisha. "That's good," he said. "But it's no disgrace to be afraid. Sometimes fear is smart."

"That's dumb." She threw the ball against the backboard again. This time it came straight to her. "Gabbi and I aren't afraid of nothin'."

Gabbi? Luke frowned. He didn't remember Gabbi as having the same macho attitude as Trisha. "What's there for you and Gabbi to be afraid of?"

"What's it to ya?"

Luke sighed. He really should go in. There was nothing for him here.

"We're gonna kick butt." Trisha was glaring at him and pointing her finger. "You can take that to the bank."

"Well, good luck." He turned to go into his yard.

"We don't need luck," Trisha snapped.

Luke paused. "I guess that makes you lucky, then."

"Only chickens need luck."

Why wasn't his love enough? What else did she want from him? The questions haunted him, and Luke couldn't sleep. He'd never felt so alone, so hurting. Finally he got up. Adam was sound asleep, and so was most of the world if the neighborhood was any indication.

Luke wandered outside, but all he did was disturb the birds sleeping in his bushes. "Great," he muttered as he returned to the house. "Another failure to notch on my belt."

He got his car keys. A little drive would relax him, get his mind off the present and let him get some sleep. Get his mind off the thirst creeping back into his life. His lips felt so dry he thought they would crack.

As a member of AA, he'd been assigned a buddy; someone to call whenever he felt the urge for a drink. Luke couldn't even remember who his buddy had been. He'd always had Ron. Ron had been there when he needed him. He didn't need a stranger.

Unfortunately, there was this little problem with Ron. He was, as Gabbi had so succinctly put it, dead. Gone.

His mouth got even dryer. His tongue went out to wet his lips. "Damn it, Ron!" he said out loud. "I love her. I even told her I love her, and she said it wasn't enough. What more is there?"

He stopped for a red light and wiped his dry lips with a downward motion of his right hand. He needed a drink so bad, his stomach hurt.

The light turned green and he slowly went through the intersection. Suddenly a flashing sign up ahead caught his eye. A package liquor store. Hot damn. That was just what the doctor ordered. Something for home. Something to wet his tongue and warm his soul. Something to help him sleep. Then when he woke up tomorrow everything would be fine. He'd be over Gabbi and all the hurt that wrapped around his heart. Luke pulled into the parking lot.

He opened the door slightly and slid into the store. There was no reason for him to be ashamed. Hell, he was an adult, he wasn't doing anything illegal. It's just that he hadn't been in a liquor store for ages. The clerk behind the counter scowled at him.

Luke looked away and scanned the shelves. Something cheap. A little bottle of Thunderbird. That was what he needed.

"Luke? Luke Bennett?" the clerk said.

Damn. Luke nodded.

"I'm Al Cornish. Doug Cornish's father."

Oh, hell. The joys of living all his life in this little old town. "Yeah, Al. Good to see you." Luke walked up to the man and shook his hand. "How is Doug doing? He went to Wabash College, right?"

"He's doing super," the man replied. "Made all conference last fall. Hoping to quarterback the team to a title this year."

"That's good." Luke nodded. "Tell him I said hi."

"He'll be home in a couple of weeks. I'll have him drop over and see you."

"Good." Luke's eyes scanned the shelves.

"I can't begin to thank you for what you did for him," Al said. "It it wasn't for you, I'm sure he would have been in jail or dead by now."

"Ah, forget it." Maybe he should just walk out. Find himself another liquor store. There had to be one with a clerk that didn't know him. "He was basically a good kid."

"So what can I do for you, coach?" Al gave Luke a sharp glance. "Haven't seen you for a good while."

On the other hand, it would look weird to just walk out. What would he say? I thought this was a drugstore. "The men's group at our church is holding a smoker and my dad is supposed to get the drinks."

"What kind? Beer, wine?"

"No," Luke replied. "Other guys are getting that. He's just supposed to get the hard stuff."

"Scotch? Blended whiskey?"

The only problem was that now he'd have to buy a number of bottles. Al would get suspicious if he only bought one bottle.

"Yeah. Give me a fifth of Scotch, a fifth of Bourbon, two fifths of whiskey. Something in a medium-price range." Luke cleared his throat. "I've forgotten what's what. Don't drink the stuff anymore."

Al studied him for a moment, then slowly moved out from behind the counter. He picked four bottles from his shelves and brought them back with him.

"Make it fifty-eight dollars even," he said, after totaling the prices on his register. "That's with a discount for the church."

Luke counted out the money. "Thanks, Al. My father and his friends will appreciate it."

Al took the money, then bagged the bottles for Luke. "There you go, coach. I'll tell Doug to give you a call. He'll want you to know how good things are going for him."

Luke forced a smile as he nodded and hurried toward the door. His hands were shaking on the wheel by the time he pulled out of the parking lot. He didn't want to be in love, he'd never meant for it to happen. For years, he'd been really careful to stay free, not to take on more than he could handle. Then *bam!* a little lady walks into his life and walks off with his heart before he even knew what was going on.

He'd never felt so happy in his whole life. Or so helpless. What else did she want from a man besides love?

He took a direct route home, his stomach quivering by the time he pulled into his drive. His mouth was dry. Needed a drink. A little drink to cut through all the crud in his life. Just one.

He unlocked his door and stepped inside, sweat pouring down his face. The house was still and quiet. Just one drink. A little one. Then he'd be in control again and all the problems with Gabbi and Adam would be nothing.

He pulled one bottle out of the bag and split the seal on the cap. Grabbing a glass from the sink, he poured out a good, stiff measure, then stopped to stare at it.

It was the color of Gabbi's eyes in the sunlight.

Why wasn't his love enough? It was all he had to offer, and yet it wasn't enough for her. Did she want somebody wealthy? Somebody younger? Somebody more handsome?

Maybe she wanted a head coach. Or an adoptive father. Maybe a better basketball player, or somebody who knew how to open up about their feelings. He picked up the glass.

He put it down. What the hell was he doing? He wet his lips.

He'd failed Adam. He'd failed Gabbi. Why not complete the trio and fail himself?

He picked up the glass again.

What were Gabbi and Trisha afraid of? Everything was going their way. They had their house. The adoption was finalized. Suddenly the shakes hit him and he put the glass down, spilling some of the liquor onto his hand and the counter.

They had nothing to be afraid of.

The phone started ringing just as he saw the truth. It looked him straight in the eye and dared him to ignore it. Suddenly everything fell into place. Love. Belonging. Sticking together in good times and bad. Being there. His hand started toward the phone but then stopped. The answering machine would get it. This wasn't the time to talk.

"Luke? Luke, this is me. Pick up the phone."

What the hell did his father want?

"Luke." Matt's voice was loud and commanding. "Pick up the phone. I know you're there."

With a sigh, Luke reached out and grabbed the receiver. "Yeah, Dad."

"I, uh—" Matt cleared his throat. "I thought maybe you were correcting papers and needed a break."

Correcting papers? What kind of cockamamy excuse was—

A picture of Al's sharp eyes floated in front of Luke. The clerk had called his father. He hadn't bought his lie for one minute.

"I don't have any papers," Luke said. "Finals are next week."

"Oh."

"I was just planning our baseball schedule for next year. You know, we've got to get those games set up a year in advance."

"Yeah, right," Matt said.

There was a long silence, and then Matt cleared his throat again. "I was just wondering if you and Adam would have some free time Saturday."

"I suppose," Luke replied. "Why?"

"A friend called me a few minutes ago. He's got a cottage on Eagle Lake and he wants me to look at rewiring it."

"Oh, yeah?" This friend called at midnight? Luke leaned against the wall.

"Yeah," Matt said. "And I was wondering if you guys would have some time to run up with me. Guy said his boat was out and we could do a little fishing. What do you think?"

"I'll have to check with Adam when he gets up in the morning, but I don't think he has anything planned."

"We could have dinner at The Dock. Make it an outing."

He could read the hopeful, almost pleading tone in his father's voice. Luke couldn't speak for a long moment. That was what love did to you, tied you up and turned you inside out. Yet life without it was as empty as a bird's nest in the fall.

"Sounds good, Dad."

"Yeah, I thought it would be nice."

They sat in their silence, savoring it. Then his father cleared his throat a couple of times before he spoke again. "Well, I guess you'll call me, then."

"Sure thing."

"You can call anytime, you know," Matt said. "I'll be up. There's a John Wayne movie on cable."

"Adam won't be up until morning."

"That's okay. Just wanted to let you know I'd be up."

He felt a lump rise in his throat. "There's no need for that, Dad."

"Hey, no problem. Us old guys don't need all that much sleep."

"I'm fine, Dad." Luke bit his lower lip and tried to swallow the lump in his throat.

"You want to talk, just call."

"I'm okay, Dad. Everything's under control."

Matt cleared his throat. "That's good. I know you've taken a few bumps lately, but things will work out."

His father certainly knew about his problems with Adam. He wondered how much he knew about him and Gabbi. "Yeah, I know," Luke said. "Peaks and valleys. Ups and downs."

"Yeah, that's life."

"Everything's cool, Dad."

"I'm glad to hear that, Luke."

"Don't stay up all night."

"See you tomorrow, kid."

Luke hung up and walked slowly to the sink. He took a knife out of the drawer and cut the label around the other caps. Then he opened each bottle and turned on the water. He looked at the first bottle, shaking his head. A lot of money was going to go down the drain. He tipped the bottle and watched the liquid disappear.

He didn't need this stuff. He had some answers to get, and crap like this would only get in the way. And he wasn't going to take any cock and bull story. He was only settling for the truth.

Luke smiled as the last of the liquor swirled away. He could feel Ron watching him. "Things are going to change, old buddy," he said. "I don't know if it's for the better or not, but they are about to change."

He picked up the bottles, caps and the bag, carrying it all out to the garbage in the alley. He had a bit of work to do.

Gabbi was almost asleep. It had been hard, trying to will the demons away each night and force sleep to come, but she was almost getting good at it. Or almost good at convincing herself that this still recumbency in bed was sleep. Especially tonight when her biopsy awaited her in the morning.

"Take me out to the ball game!"

She sat up in the darkness. Someone was singing. Or had she actually been asleep and dreamed it? She glanced at the clock. It was one in the morning. She must have been dreaming.

"Take me out with the crowd!"

She wasn't dreaming. She flew out of bed and sped to the window. What was going on? But she could see nothing outside. Her window looked out on the front yard and the street. The houses were all dark and silent. The streetlight in front illuminated the emptiness.

"Buy me some peanuts and Cracker Jack!"

Good lord, what was going on? She ran into the hallway only to collide with Trisha.

"Mom, Luke's got the backyard all lit up."

"He what?" Gabbi asked, then sped into the kitchen without waiting for an answer.

"What's he doing here at this hour?"

"I have no idea." Though her heart had an idea, and it struck fear down to her bones. Had he been drinking?

"I don't care if I never get back!"

The kitchen floor felt ice cold to Gabbi's bare feet, but she just raced over to pull open the back door. Luke, indeed, had the backyard all lit up. He had some sort of lights perched on the fence at various places, and the outside garage lights were on. All were shining into the middle of the yard where some sort of baseball field had been marked out.

He was standing just down the steps, fiddling with a radio-tape player, and turned to face her.

"Let me root, root, root for the home team!"

He frowned at her. "'Bout time."

"What is going on?" She came out on the step, though the wooden porch was even colder to her feet. There was a chalkboard resting against the garage, with some sort of markings on it. Was it supposed to be a scoreboard?

"Yeah, what's going on?" Trisha said from right behind her.

"What does it look like?" Luke asked, waving his hand at the yard. "It's a baseball game. Tenth inning."

"Cool," Trisha said. "Score's tied, huh?"

So much for staying in Gabbi's corner. She paused to send a glare the girl's way before turning back to Luke. "What is the purpose of all this? It's late. We should all be asleep."

"You're right," he said easily. "It is late. That's why I made it the tenth inning."

"If they don't win it's a shame!"

"Hey, what's all the racket out there?" someone from the house to the west of Gabbi's shouted.

"Nothing," Gabbi called back. "Sorry it woke you."

"You okay, honey?" someone called from the other side.

"I'm fine."

"What's happening?" a sleepy voice asked from behind Luke. It was Adam, and he looked as if he'd rolled out of bed. He was wearing an old T-shirt and baggy old sweat-pants. "I heard somebody singing out here."

Luke frowned at them all and bent over to turn down the volume. "It's like this," he said as he straightened up. "It's the tenth, the score is tied."

He nodded toward the chalkboard, and Gabbi could see that she was listed as one team, Luke as the other.

"It's sudden death," he went on. "Whichever team scores first, wins."

"They don't have sudden death in baseball," Trisha pointed out.

"It hardly matters," Gabbi said. "I am not playing some stupid game in the middle of the night." She was tired, not just physically, but emotionally. She wasn't up to some sort of skirmish with Luke. She wiggled her bare toes. "I don't have any shoes on."

"That's the beauty of this baseball game," Luke said. "You don't need any bats or balls or mitts, even. Just questions and answers."

"That's a dumb way to play," Trisha announced. "I'm not sure I wanna be on her team."

"You aren't on anybody's team," Luke said. "You and Adam can be the umpires."

Adam rubbed his eyes. "I don't know about—"

"Nobody asked, you were drafted." Luke gently shoved him over next to Trisha. The two kids sat on the steps. "Okay," Luke said to Gabbi. "You're up first. Ask me a question."

Gabbi frowned at him. She wanted him to leave, just go away and leave her alone, but she saw that it wasn't going to be that easy. Maybe playing along would be the best solution.

"What kind of question?" she asked.

"That should be a strike, it's such a bad one," Luke said. "But I'll take pity on you. Ask me anything. Anything at all."

Her eyes narrowed as she frowned at him. "Okay. Have you been drinking?"

"Nope." He turned to the kids. "Well, strike, pop fly or caught for an out?"

"It's a good question," Adam said. "Our kitchen smells like a bar."

"The sink is soused," Luke said. "I'm not. Trisha, what's your call?"

"Out," she said. "Good question, better answer."

Luke bowed slightly. "My turn at bat. My turn to ask." He turned to face Gabbi, all laughter going out of his eyes. "Why did you dump me?"

Gabbi took a step back. The directness of his question took her by surprise. "I didn't dump you," she said, floundering for words. "I just wanted to cool things off. I just..."

Luke looked to the kids.

"Base hit," Trisha said.

"Ball one," Adam argued.

"Ball one?" Trisha repeated a bit louder. "You want to be out here all night?"

Adam just shrugged and pulled his T-shirt down further on his arms. "Base hit," he said quietly.

Gabbi gave him a look that she hoped reflected her disgust at his wishy-washiness. "So you got on base," she said to Luke. "I can still get you out. Next question."

"What else do you want if love's not enough?"

Gabbi held her ground, though her heart quivered slightly. "It's not something you can put into words," she tried to explain. She wished he'd turn off those silly lights that were getting in her eyes as she tried to think. "It's just something that I know."

"Boo!" Trisha said loudly.

"Double," Adam said. "Man on second and third."

"Hey," Gabbi protested. "Whose side are you two on?"

"Truth, justice and the American way," Trisha snickered. "Come on, batter up."

Gabbi faced Luke once more. So what if she lost his stupid little game? It meant nothing that she could see. She had more important things on her mind. Like getting back to bed and away from that intensity in his eyes.

Luke looked at her long and hard for an eon before he spoke again. "What were the results of your mammogram?"

She stopped breathing, stopped feeling, stopped existing. "What?" she croaked.

"Home run!" Trisha shouted and pulled Adam to his feet as she got to hers. "Come on, Stretch. Want some cold pizza?" She dragged the confused Adam into the house with her.

Gabbi saw them leave, saw them desert her, but her mouth couldn't find the words to beg them to stay. To protect her.

Luke said nothing, just went around and turned off his lights. The night returned and so did her heartbeat, though it seemed almost deafening in the silence. Then Luke was at her side, taking first her hands and then pulling all of her into his embrace.

"I won, you know," he said. "You have to answer. How bad is it?"

"It may not be bad at all," she whispered into the soft flannel of his shirt. "It's just a small lump. I have a needle biopsy in the morning."

"And you didn't tell me?"

"I couldn't," she said, trying to make him understand. "I couldn't risk being rejected all over again."

"You know," he said on a sigh, "you are the biggest chicken I ever met."

"No, I'm not." His embrace was giving her strength. Confidence. Hope.

He laughed quietly, and the sound warmed her heart.

"You take on a bratty, know-it-all kid. You buy a house on your own, talk to thousands each day without flinching, but when it comes to trust, you are definitely a chicken."

"Maybe." Her voice was quiet.

He pulled away from her slightly, so he could look down into her eyes. "Do you have any idea how much I love you? And how much it hurt when you turned me away?"

It hurt her, too, but she didn't want to think about it. "Where'd the liquor come from?"

"I bought it."

"But you didn't drink it," she said. "Why not?"

"Because you needed me. You weren't willing to admit it, but you did. You do. You need somebody you can lean on, even if he isn't a head coach."

"Or Adam's father."

"That might change," he said slowly. "I'm beginning to see that maybe really taking him on as my son is the best way I can repay Ron. I was just so worried about trying to take Ron's place in his life."

She was starting to feel stronger, starting to believe. "You wouldn't do that."

"I know that now." He smiled down at her. "Good thing you didn't ask me about it, though, or I might have lost."

"I doubt that. I suspect the umps were in your pocket all along."

"So what time's the biopsy?" he asked.

"Eight-thirty."

"What time do we have to be there?"

"You don't have to come," she said. "You have a class."

"My first-period class can live without me. So can my second-period one, or all of them, for that matter. I'm going to be where I ought to be, where I intend to be for the rest of our lives. At your side. My love is enough. It's more than enough. It's all you're ever going to need."

She closed her eyes and just let his love surround her.

"I'm coming, too," Trisha announced. "I already wrote a note for my teachers telling them I was going to be sick."

Gabbi just sighed. How long had Trisha been out here?

"Hey, I'm not going to school if nobody else is," Adam declared.

She pushed away from Luke. "You know, my biopsy is not the social event of the season."

Luke pulled her back into his arms. "No, but it's where your family intends to be tomorrow morning, so get used to it." He looked up over at Trisha. "Hope you don't object too much to getting a dad and a brother, 'cause it looks like you're getting both."

"Cool," Trisha said, then reached over to punch Adam on the arm. "Hey, bro'. What d'ya say to that?"

Epilogue

"Happy lunchtime, Michiana," Gabbi said into the microphone. "We have a really special show for you today. We have three survivors of breast cancer here— Barb Orion, a vice president at First Source Bank. Molly Timmons, activities director at the Y. And yours truly. It's been seven years since my lump was found, and outside of a false alarm last week, I've been leading a perfectly ordinary life since."

"Oh, I don't know about that," Barb said with a laugh. "I wouldn't consider that diamond flashing on your left hand as ordinary. I'd say your life was pretty extra-specially good."

Gabbi just smiled. The radiance in her heart shone through. "And that's just what we want to tell you. That cancer doesn't mean an end to life. That you can still go on to find love and happiness and everything else a person could want from life." She paused, then turned to the third woman there. "Molly, tell us a bit of your story."

As Molly talked, Gabbi's mind went to Trisha, who was still too loud and too prone to fighting, but occasionally showed them glimpses of the strong and capable woman she would be someday. Of Adam, who had taken the acquisition of a mother, father and sister with quiet nonchalance, though she could see the relief and excitement in his eyes at times. And most of all, of Luke and his acceptance and support of her, of the way he held her when they had heard the news that the lump was nothing to worry about. Barb was right. There was nothing ordinary about her life. She had everything.

Love was more than enough; it was everything.

* * * * *

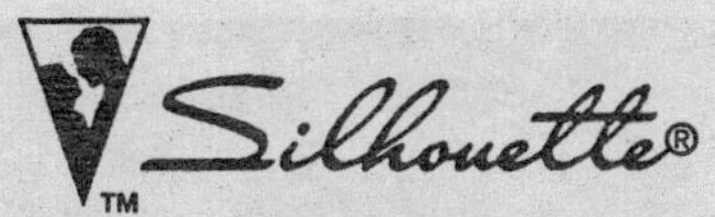

by

Laurie Paige

Maddening men...winsome women...and the untamed land they live in—all add up to love! Meet them in these books from Silhouette Special Edition and Silhouette Romance:

WILD IS THE WIND (Silhouette Special Edition #887, May)
Rafe Barrett retreated to his mountain resort to escape his dangerous feelings for Genny McBride...but when she returned, ready to pick up where they left off, would Rafe throw caution to the wind?

A ROGUE'S HEART (Silhouette Romance #1013, June)
Returning to his boyhood home brought Gabe Deveraux face-to-face with ghosts of the past—and directly into the arms of sweet and loving Whitney Campbell....

A RIVER TO CROSS (Silhouette Special Edition #910, September)
Sheriff Shane Macklin knew there was more to "town outsider" Tina Henderson than met the eye. He saw a generous and selfless woman whose true colors held the promise of love....

Don't miss these latest Wild River tales from Silhouette Special Edition and Silhouette Romance!

SEWR-4

INDULGE A LITTLE 6947 SWEEPSTAKES
NO PURCHASE NECESSARY

HERE'S HOW THE SWEEPSTAKES WORKS:
The Harlequin Reader Service shipments for January, February and March 1994 will contain, respectively, coupons for entry into three prize drawings: a trip for two to San Francisco, an Alaskan cruise for two and a trip for two to Hawaii. To be eligible for any drawing using an Entry Coupon, simply complete and mail according to directions.

There is no obligation to continue as a Reader Service subscriber to enter and be eligible for any prize drawing. You may also enter any drawing by hand printing your name and address on a 3" x 5" card and the destination of the prize you wish that entry to be considered for (i.e., San Francisco trip, Alaskan cruise or Hawaiian trip). Send your 3" x 5" entries to: Indulge a Little 6947 Sweepstakes, c/o Prize Destination you wish that entry to be considered for, P.O. Box 1315, Buffalo, NY 14269-1315, U.S.A. or Indulge a Little 6947 Sweepstakes, P.O. Box 610, Fort Erie, Ontario L2A 5X3, Canada.

To be eligible for the San Francisco trip, entries must be received by 4/30/94; for the Alaskan cruise, 5/31/94; and the Hawaiian trip, 6/30/94. No responsibility is assumed for lost, late or misdirected mail. Sweepstakes open to residents of the U.S. (except Puerto Rico) and Canada, 18 years of age or older. All applicable laws and regulations apply. Sweepstakes void wherever prohibited.

For a copy of the Official Rules, send a self-addressed, stamped envelope (WA residents need not affix return postage) to: Indulge a Little 6947 Rules, P.O. Box 4631, Blair, NE 68009, U.S.A.

INDR93

INDULGE A LITTLE 6947 SWEEPSTAKES
NO PURCHASE NECESSARY

HERE'S HOW THE SWEEPSTAKES WORKS:
The Harlequin Reader Service shipments for January, February and March 1994 will contain, respectively, coupons for entry into three prize drawings: a trip for two to San Francisco, an Alaskan cruise for two and a trip for two to Hawaii. To be eligible for any drawing using an Entry Coupon, simply complete and mail according to directions.

There is no obligation to continue as a Reader Service subscriber to enter and be eligible for any prize drawing. You may also enter any drawing by hand printing your name and address on a 3" x 5" card and the destination of the prize you wish that entry to be considered for (i.e., San Francisco trip, Alaskan cruise or Hawaiian trip). Send your 3" x 5" entries to: Indulge a Little 6947 Sweepstakes, c/o Prize Destination you wish that entry to be considered for, P.O. Box 1315, Buffalo, NY 14269-1315, U.S.A. or Indulge a Little 6947 Sweepstakes, P.O. Box 610, Fort Erie, Ontario L2A 5X3, Canada.

To be eligible for the San Francisco trip, entries must be received by 4/30/94; for the Alaskan cruise, 5/31/94; and the Hawaiian trip, 6/30/94. No responsibility is assumed for lost, late or misdirected mail. Sweepstakes open to residents of the U.S. (except Puerto Rico) and Canada, 18 years of age or older. All applicable laws and regulations apply. Sweepstakes void wherever prohibited.

For a copy of the Official Rules, send a self-addressed, stamped envelope (WA residents need not affix return postage) to: Indulge a Little 6947 Rules, P.O. Box 4631, Blair, NE 68009, U.S.A.

INDR93

INDULGE A LITTLE
SWEEPSTAKES

OFFICIAL ENTRY COUPON

This entry must be received by: MAY 31, 1994
This month's winner will be notified by: JUNE 15, 1994
Trip must be taken between: JULY 31, 1994-JULY 31, 1995

YES, I want to win the Alaskan Cruise vacation for two. I understand that the prize includes round-trip airfare, one-week cruise including private cabin, all meals and pocket money as revealed on the "wallet" scratch-off card.

Name_______________

Address_______________ Apt._______________

City_______________

State/Prov._______________ Zip/Postal Code_______________

Daytime phone number_______________
(Area Code)

Account #_______________

Return entries with invoice in envelope provided. Each book in this shipment has two entry coupons—and the more coupons you enter, the better your chances of winning!

 MONTH2

INDULGE A LITTLE
SWEEPSTAKES

OFFICIAL ENTRY COUPON

This entry must be received by: MAY 31, 1994
This month's winner will be notified by: JUNE 15, 1994
Trip must be taken between: JULY 31, 1994-JULY 31, 1995

YES, I want to win the Alaskan Cruise vacation for two. I understand that the prize includes round-trip airfare, one-week cruise including private cabin, all meals and pocket money as revealed on the "wallet" scratch-off card.

Name_______________

Address_______________ Apt._______________

City_______________

State/Prov._______________ Zip/Postal Code_______________

Daytime phone number_______________
(Area Code)

Account #_______________

Return entries with invoice in envelope provided. Each book in this shipment has two entry coupons—and the more coupons you enter, the better your chances of winning!

© 1993 HARLEQUIN ENTERPRISES LTD. MONTH2